ARMOIRE

OF

ADVENTURES

Dear Sarah,
Hope these stories keep
you cozy in the
Summer !

ALSO BY CAMILLA TRACY

Of Threads and Oceans

Of Flowers and Cyclones

Of Blood and Tides

Soxkendi: A Family of Dragons

Of Spools and Billows

Of Gates and Typhoons

Armoire of Adventures

Join my animal loving community and learn about my newest book releases by clicking below or scanning the QR code:

https://geni.us/CamillaTracynewsletter

CAMILLA TRACY

ARMOIRE
OF
ADVENTURES

THREADS OF MAGIC
STORIES

Camilla Tracy

Published by Pudel Threads Publishing

First Printing 2025

Tracy, Camilla, author

Armoire of Adventures/ Threads of Magic Stories

ISBN (paperback) 978-1-998506-01-9

eISBN 978-1-998506-00-2

B&N ISNBN 978-1-998506-02-6

Under a Federal Liberal government, Library and Archives Canada no longer provides Cataloguing in Publication (CIP) data for independently published books.

Technical Credits:

Cover Image: MiblArt

Editor: Bobbi Beatty of Silver Scroll Services, Calgary, Alberta

Proofreader: Lorna Stuber - Editor, Proofreader, Writer, Okotoks, Alberta

Created with Atticus

To Thali,

What an adventure you started us on!

CONTENTS

A Day for Storytelling

I T HAD BEEN A long day, one where Thali and Elric hadn't had a moment to themselves since the previous night. Thali had leapt out of her dress and gone training before bed, so now she pulled off her boots and tossed them unceremoniously on the floor. Because she'd been training outside, the thump of her boot scattered a ring of mud across the beautiful, pristine wood. She groaned, but she was so tired she didn't care enough to clean it up. She did, however, gently place her other boot on the ground.

"I have a question," Elric said. He was already tucked into bed, papers scattered over and around his lap, a tiger across his feet, and a poodle belly bared between his legs.

Thali didn't have the energy for words. She just looked at him and raised an eyebrow.

"That armoire was moved in here after we were married. I assume it's yours?" He pointed to a cabinet directly across from her; she had forgotten it was there. She smiled. That cabinet had been a constant in her life. She had picked it out long ago from a flea market she and her family had visited when she was six. Even though it was simple, she'd added different touches on and in it over the years. She laughed as she looked at it now. Within the rooms of a royal palace, it was a bit of an eyesore. It was chipped, scratched, and a little crooked. The outside looked as though a few panels of wood had been varnished by a child—which it had. Against the plush blues and purples of the room, it looked like it belonged in the trash.

"What's so funny?" Elric asked.

"It's just ... it's so out of place, but not," Thali said.

She thought of the items within. Feeling a sudden burst of energy, she bounded over to the doors and reached underneath with her right hand and above with her left. She danced her fingers along the tumblers, setting them to levels she'd created so long ago. She reached behind the armoire with her left hand next, fiddling with the mechanism that she'd made. The doors cracked open with a *pop!* She opened them and turned to see Elric leaning over the bed, watching with interest.

"It's where I keep my most precious things," Thali said. It was much more than that though. She opened the doors of the armoire wide. Necklaces of all kinds hung on the inside of the doors. She had organized them by length and chain color. The more delicate chains hung closer to the hinges, so they didn't have to swing around so much with each door opening. She brushed her hands along the jewels, pearls, and delicate filigreed silver. She pushed the memories that each brought aside; she didn't have the energy to reminisce right now.

The main compartment was filled with tiny drawers. Thali pulled one out and tipped it in Elric's direction. It was filled with gems in small boxes. The back row of boxes was filled so full of loose gems sorted by color that Thali couldn't tip the drawer much. The next row had pendants with various-sized gems, again organized by color. And the closest row was filled with tiny charms and earrings.

"But your ears aren't pierced."

"They're all from Tariq. He said I should have earrings in case I ever do get my ears pierced." Thali explained.

"No wonder you're so hard to impress," Elric said. "I don't think I've ever seen that many gems in one place that wasn't in the royal vaults."

Thali smiled and put the drawer back. She pulled out the next one, bringing it to the bed. Again, it was bursting with tiny boxes. Elric peered into the boxes. Five contained pearls, some strung together, some loose, and one had a strand of tiny pearls.

"My brother gave me these when we were little. He'd seen me eyeing my mother's jewelry and had collected oysters for a month while we were at sea to find the pearls and string them together."

She picked up the thin strand of pearls; all were uneven and different. But one was a little darker than the others, a little bigger too. She remembered that Rommy had told her he'd refused help from the crew when they had offered, wanting the present to be solely from him.

Elric pointed to another strand filled with pearls the size of walnuts, all a soft gray.

Thali laughed. "My uncle gave me that one. We always get weapons from my uncle. But one time, I think when he realized I was nearing marriageable age, I opened the usual oilcloth to find this strand of enormous gray pearls." Thali smiled, remembering how upset she'd been. "I think I was thirteen. Rommy got a dagger that had this wicked curved blade. I was so upset. But I'd learned long before to be appreciative of gifts, so I'd smiled and put it on. It must have looked ridiculous. My uncle leaned in and whispered in my ear that as a woman, when I married, jewelry would always be mine. It was a way for me to have my own funds should I need them. Then he winked at me and said he'd get me a sword next time."

"And did he?"

"He did. That one there actually." Thali said. She pointed to the sword leaning against the nightstand. "The scabbard came the year after."

"He's right you know," Elric said.

"What do you mean?"

"The jewelry. It's a common way for ladies of the court to accumulate wealth. They use jewels from previous suitors to pay for things they might want or need," Elric said.

Thali shrugged. "I've never really wanted for anything."

"What about that one?" Elric asked. He pointed to an old, beat-up leather cuff with a huge red gem in it.

Thali smiled. "I don't know if you'll believe me if I tell you."

"Try me," Elric said. He had stacked his papers on the bedside table and sprawled between the tiger and dog, resting his elbows on the bed, his head cupped in his hands.

Thali reached for the cuff, but as she pulled it out, a pearl-and-diamond collar clattered to the floor.

"Is that a necklace?" Elric asked.

Thali snatched it off the floor, carefully checking that each pearl and diamond were still safely secured. She smiled, thinking about the day she'd received it. "Yes, but I like using it this way instead." Thali slid the stiff collar behind her ears and then up along her forehead to sit in her hair.

"It's beautiful," Elric said.

"My friend, Daena, gave it to me." Thali sat down as she pulled the jewelry off her head and ran her fingers over the pearls.

"Tell me about her," Elric urged.

Thali smiled nostalgically and thought back to her childhood, her exhaustion fading at the memory.

DAENA

"IT'S TIME." LADY JINHUA glanced at eight-year-old Thali, who was tilting her chin up as high as possible. Her hope was that if she stayed very still, she'd be able to see more of the land they were about to visit. Shiny brass roofs on the shore reflected the sun, making the collection of buildings look like one long, continuous brick structure. Rommy had told her that this place didn't have a fortress wall but that the entire city was made to look like one long building. A massive courtyard filled the center, where adults trained for combat. There, he'd seen more people practicing their weapons skills in one place than ever before.

Lady Jinhua coughed and raised her eyebrows at Thali, who pushed herself off the barrel. Her brother patted her arm as she passed, and Crab followed her as she went down to her family's quarters.

Crab grunted a bit as he pushed the bed away from the wall, then opened the trap door underneath it. "Got a good book?" he asked.

Thali lifted a small sketchbook and dug in her pockets for charcoal. Crab nodded and Thali climbed into her hidey hole. She adjusted the pillow and blankets to her liking.

"See you at supper," Crab said.

Thali nodded. He closed the door and Thali heard the creak of the bed as he moved it back over the trap door. Then she heard the metal latch that secured the bed to the wall. They were common on ships so the beds and other furnishings didn't slide around with the ship's movement. Silence fell momentarily before she heard metal clang on metal as he wrenched the bolt tight. She knew the brief silence came because Crab had finger-tightened the bolt first. She was an old hand at this hiding thing now.

Thali's little hand went to the tiny latch behind the pillow she was leaning on. Her other hand went to the small satchel that she now strapped around her body.

"If you ever hear this knock," her mother had said before knocking quickly twice, then pausing and knocking once more, "You open this hatch. Do you remember how we practiced it?"

A tiny Thali had nodded.

"Then you jump out the window and into the water. Swim to land. Do you remember your swimming lessons in the ocean?"

Thali had nodded again, thinking about the map she'd had to memorize. Once she was old enough, she'd learned that there was a safehouse in every port and had been given a password. Those at the safehouse would bring her to Tariq's family in Bulstan if anything were to happen.

Thali heard shouts from the dock now, and they brought her thoughts back to her dark hole. Her eyes took their time adjusting, but she could see a tiny bit as she opened her sketchbook and started to draw a bird she'd seen the other day. It had taken a ride on their ship and then left as soon as they had seen land.

She swallowed, hoping, as she did every time, that she wouldn't have to open the latch, wouldn't have to use the daggers hidden on her, wouldn't have to call on the dolphins and ask them to help her get to the safehouse. Her father had told her that at this port, the safehouse was red brick with a green roof, and ivy covered it so much that it obscured windows. The inhabitant would be Cerisan. She would have herbs drying inside the windows and high over the hearth and an orange tabby cat.

Thali took a deep breath and then slowly let it out. She listened to the sounds of her family gathering their goods and the shouts of the crew as they unloaded their wares and prepared to set up at the market.

Thali took three more breaths, but then she heard scratching behind her.

She blinked, wondering if she'd heard wrong. More scratching. Thali blinked again. What was she hearing?

More scratching came then, and this time, Thali used the trick that helped her win hide-and-seek. She closed her eyes and focused on a specific part of her mind. It always told her when someone, especially animals, were close by. People were harder to sense. In that corner of her mind, she could feel the consciousness of living things; they felt like threads to her. She felt some fading threads first as fishermen handled their morning catch. It made Thali cringe. Then she felt a couple of dolphins nearby and a whale that seemed closer to shore than he should be. But there were no animals near her let alone on the other side of the hatch she was leaning up against.

Three taps sounded on the hatch at her back. Then it stopped. Then came three more taps before it stopped for longer. Thali froze. Was there a person on the other side of the hatch?

She listened above again. It all sounded normal. There was nothing out of the ordinary. She could hear Crab hollering as he directed the unloading, feet shuffling on the deck, and the squeak of pulleys as merchandise was hauled out of storage.

Then Thali heard the crinkle of paper. But it was much closer. She scooted over and moved the pillow. Then her hand found the latch, and she opened it a little. Thali hissed when she felt the edge slice through the pad of her finger as the paper slid through the crack. She grabbed the paper with her other hand as she brought her tiny cut to her lips.

Hi, I'm Daena. Your parents and my parents are meeting, but I wondered if you wanted to come out and play. Your brother is very boring.

Thali didn't know what to do. Her mother had told her what to do in case of an emergency and that she wasn't to reveal herself. But Daena already knew she existed. Thali was already discovered. She wondered if Rommy had sent Daena. If so, it would be rude not to go out and play with her.

Three more knocks sounded on the little door, and another paper slipped through. Thali took it more carefully this time, thinking of her paper cut.

It must be very boring in there. There's way more to do out here. I promise you'll have a good time.

Thali was half scared but half excited. She wanted so badly to be out and amongst the people at the port. She could do it. She could handle herself. The callouses on her hands from the hours of training her mother put her through should be evidence enough. The fact she could disarm every member of their crew was proof of that too. Besides, her parents had let her come out at a couple of the smaller, safer ports; they just hadn't been sure about this one.

Another three little knocks on the wood told her Daena was still on the other side.

Thali patted the daggers in her boots, the one across her midsection, and the tiny one along her upper arm her brother had made her hide.

She reached for the latch, pushed the pillow and blankets further aside, and palmed another dagger just in case as she opened the tiny door.

"Finally." A small girl shape filled the hole.

Thali blinked. The sun was blinding after being in the dark hole for so long.

"Hi, I'm Daena." A tiny hand thrust itself into the hole and grabbed her hand. Thali had to stuff the dagger up her sleeve quickly so as to not stab the girl.

"What's your name? I only know that you're Lord Ranulf and Lady Jinhua's younger daughter, Romulus's sister."

"How ... how did you know?" Thali asked. Some of the girl's features were finally coming into focus, and she saw dark hair mostly tied back, dark-brown eyes, and a smile with missing teeth. She was probably about the same age as Thali herself was.

"Your brother obviously has a sister. When I met him, he wasn't like the other boys who don't. He ruffled my hair before remembering his gentlemanly manners. I knew he had a sister."

Thali saved that piece of information to poke her perfect brother with later. "How did you know where to find me then?"

"I guessed. I was pretty sure parents might hide their daughter in their own quarters and under the bed." She crawled halfway out the hatch. "You coming? We'll go out this way, swim over to my secret pond, then surprise your parents. And then they'll have to let you stay, and we can play," Daena said.

Suddenly she was gone, and Thali crawled out of the hole just in time to see a splash in the water. They were the last ship at the docks, just as her father liked, and there wasn't anyone on this side to see them. She kept her things strapped on her, squeezed out of the hole, and dropped into the ocean.

A few years later ...

Thali ran ahead and leapt into the arms of the girl bouncing up and down on the dock and waiting for her. "It's so good to see you!" she said.

"Eeeee! I can't believe you're finally here!" Daena said.

Thali looked back and saw her mother and father nod. She let Daena take her hand, and they ran up the dock past all manners of ships and workers and ran into the city, where they leapt into a little wagon.

Daena grabbed the reins and shouted, "Go!" The two horses attached to the wagon took off along the gentle slope to the palatial building on the top of the hill. Instead of stopping at the front of the building like normal guests, Daena steered them around back and practically leapt out of the wagon as the horses stopped at the barn. "Let's go!" Daena said as Thali jumped down to follow her. They ran gleefully to a smaller white stone building beyond the main building.

"Hi, Mother! Hi, Father! They've arrived!" Daena yelled as they ran past her grand home.

"Hello! It's nice to see you!" Thali shouted, trying to remember her manners as she ran sideways.

Daena grabbed her hand and pulled her along as they ran to the smaller building. Once there, Thali stood at the entrance, staring at all the things that surrounded them. This was Daena's room, even though it was its own separate building. The first thing that always caught her eye was a plethora of sculptures lining the walls, all at different heights. It was like watching Daena grow up in front of her eyes as she slowly dragged her gaze around the room. Daena had a statue done of herself every year, and some looked better than others, but the statues started as busts and eventually became full body sculptures in the nude.

"Don't you get cold, posing like that?" Thali asked. She could feel heat rise to her cheeks as she turned her eyes away. Around Daena, she was braver, bolder, but not quite as much as Daena.

Her friend, however, was in another room digging for clothes, probably for Thali. Daena always told Thali she had to dress like her if she wanted to fit in when she visited.

"Come in here so I can hear you better!" Daena shouted from the other room.

Thali moved carefully through the first room, fearing if she breathed too hard, she might knock over a sculpture.

"We like showing off our bodies here remember," Daena said without missing a beat. "You're sleeping there, by the way." She threw a hand out behind her and to the left.

Thali had been in Daena's so-called room many times, but was always amazed at how spacious it was. Daena's voice was a little muffled because she was buried in her room—not a closet but a room—of clothes, which were really just swathes of cloth she draped over herself in different ways. But Thali followed the direction of Daena's hand and turned to see a giant pillow-covered bed of white linen. The windows on the other two walls were open to allow the breeze through.

"Ah, there it is." Daena dragged a trunk out and threw it open. "I kept these for you, though we might have to get creative. You've grown some since I saw you last." Daena wiggled her eyebrows and made an hourglass shape with her hands.

Thali's face felt even warmer as heat rose to her cheeks again.

"Put these on. We're going out to play in the water," Daena said.

Thali went and picked up a swathe of cream cloth. "You're going to have to help me. I don't remember—"

"Get undressed," Daena said.

Thali slowly started to peel off her vest, then her trousers, suddenly feeling very self-conscious. Daena was looking at her wall of jewelry though, studying each piece before she picked up a collar of pearls. Thali loved it; it had some of the largest pearls she'd ever seen, and along both edges was a row of diamonds. There was no mistaking that Daena was from the wealthiest family on the island. Thali couldn't guess even with her merchanting experience what that collar cost.

"Thali, hurry up. I've seen you naked many times before. So strip or I'll do it for you." Daena said. She placed the collar around her own neck before turning back to Thali with her hands on her hips.

Thali grinned; her friend was still the same Daena. Thali quickly shed her clothes, and Daena draped the cloth over one shoulder, grabbing a belt and tying it at her waist as she crossed the cloth at her sides. It was a little shorter than it should have been; the cloth only reached midthigh.

"Hmm ... that's a little short," Daena said. She ran into her room of clothes and came back out with another, blush-pink, swathe of cloth.

She pulled off the cream one and put the pink one on Thali. Pink was not Thali's favorite color, but she wasn't about to complain about something that was a little longer. Daena brought the fabric over her chest and tied it once there, then snaked it down. She grabbed a layer of fabric under the longer swathes that reached her ankles and wrapped them under and around each leg. Thali was glad she didn't have to walk around in a sheet.

"There. Now let's go," Daena said. She took Thali's hand and pulled her out the door.

Thali nodded at the guard standing there and let Daena pull her along. They ran toward the busiest part of the city—the central training grounds.

Shouts and grunts rang through the air as they ran toward the tall structures. Poles, ropes, pulleys, rings, and spinning objects were all raised high above the ground as people tried to make their way through the obstacle course from one end to the other. Thali and Daena headed for the end of the looming obstacles. Thali only got to look at their starting point once Daena finally stopped in front of it.

"This one's new as of last week. I've only had a chance to practice twice. Lawt made it especially with you in mind," Daena said.

Thali looked up. Between two giant pillars of wood as tall as masts was a wheel with five thick spokes, and on each spoke were tiny platforms at various angles.

"Why did Lawt think of me when he made this?" Thali asked. She felt her heart rate start to speed up as she grinned at the challenge.

"He said the shorter you are, the more difficult it is." Daena grinned.

Thali let her eyes roam for a moment across the other obstacles. Daena's people had created a training ground that was an impossibly large field with three rows of pillars stretching down its length. Different obstacles stood between the pillars: wheels, bars, platforms, pendulums. This was how Daena's people trained as warriors. Thali had arrived early enough today to catch the individual practice time. The three rows were easy, medium, and hard. After the midday meal, people would take turns running through the entire length.

"You ready?" Daena asked as she tied her flowing hair back with a piece of leather.

Thali nodded and they ran up to the new obstacle. The point was always the same: get from one pillar to the other without falling to the ground or touching it. For this particular obstacle, Thali would have to navigate the different platforms, which she guessed required agility given they sat at different angles, as the wheel spun.

"Let me go first because it's not quite what you think." Daena said.

Thali nodded and Daena leapt to the first, only the ball of her foot fitting on the first tiny platform. But instead of it falling with gravity, the platform started to rise as the wheel spun in the opposite direction. And it took off faster than Thali would have expected it to, almost as if something else controlled the speed. Daena crouched and grabbed hold of the tiny platform with her hands as the wheel spun. The wheel spun fast enough that it would have thrown her from the top of it if she hadn't. Then Daena spun around on the ball of her foot and leapt to the next platform.

Thali's eyes were wide as she blinked.

"Come on, Thali!" Daena said.

Thali swallowed; she was suddenly very glad Daena had gone first.

Thali leapt. She landed on a tiny platform with the ball of her foot and crouched down immediately. She gripped it with her hands as it spun quickly upward. It seemed to go faster even than when Daena had crouched on it. Then, before she could think about it too hard, she turned and jumped because she knew she would miss the platform if she didn't jump right away.

Thali turned around to watch the next person navigate the obstacle. They did similarly but hesitated. The wheel went even faster at that moment, and Thali saw the contender's knuckles turn white as they gripped the tiny piece tightly.

"Ready for the next one?" Daena asked.

Thali nodded.

"One sec. Put these on," Daena said as she dug into her fabric swathe and pulled out a couple of pieces of leather with finger holes on top. "For your palms."

Thali swallowed. If Daena was giving her these, it meant she was really going to need them. Thali slid her fingers through the holes and wrapped the bottom strap around her wrists.

"Do you want to go first?" Daena asked.

Thali nodded and glanced at the obstacles ahead. She had tackled these before and was excited to test her skills now that she was older and hopefully more physically capable.

Leaning around the pillar's platform, she looked up and saw the buckets of water and the handholds she'd have to swing across. It reminded her of the monkeys she'd seen in the jungle.

Daena put a hand on her shoulder. "You'll be great," she said with a smile.

Thali felt like Daena was a true friend in that moment. She knew she had to get moving though, or more and more people would join them on this platform, and it would back everyone up. Thali took a deep breath and launched herself upward, grabbing hold of the vertical stick and squeezing tightly as she started to slide.

The next obstacle was horizontal, but it also had a bucket on top of it. Water had been feeding into the buckets for some time since she'd waited so long, so she knew they'd be full. She swung to the horizontal bar, which pulled the bucket and dumped the water on her, but she let it. She had braced herself for it. The bucket of water was there to try and rush people so they would be sloppy. But the next hold was a vertical stick again, which was more difficult to hold, especially when you were wet.

Thali swung again and at each horizontal hold, she was drenched with a bucket of cold water. But she held on with both hands and closed her eyes as the water fell on her head. When she grabbed the vertical sticks, she swung faster. She got wetter and wetter and started slipping regardless of how hard she squeezed.

She had three more sticks to go before she could swing to the platform. Thali started to shiver in the cold water and almost missed the last vertical stick. But as soon as she caught it, she felt herself slide. She tried to grab it with her other hand, but she was too soaked and tired to keep her hold. Instead, she slid and fell, throwing her legs out from under her as she landed in a sitting position in the net below.

"All right there, T?" Daena shouted from above. She swung to the next platform easily. She was right behind Thali, so she didn't get nearly as wet.

Thali waved at her friend before she crawled to the edge of the net and swung herself over it. The ground was only a couple feet from there, and she landed softly.

Rommy had joined them by then, and Thali felt her cheeks heat as she realized her family had watched her fail.

"That was a tough one. Get back to it though," Rommy said.

Thali took a deep breath and nodded. She squeezed some of her cloth to ring it out, went to the next pole, and climbed up. Daena had started on it already, so Thali joined in. She was sore, embarrassed, and still cold from the water, but this time, she had to hop or leap from one platform to the next, all of varying sizes and angles. She only had to crouch for better balance once before she made it to the other side where Daena was waiting for her.

"Welcome back. Two more and then cookies!" Daena said. She started on the next obstacle.

Thali followed. She was quiet as she stayed focused, watching what Daena did so she knew better what to expect.

The next obstacle was a climb. There were three phases, and Thali set herself next to Daena, who was gripping the bar. Thali let Daena go first, then followed, moving the bar up one side and then jumping it to the next rung on the other side. She had to be careful how much momentum she used because she could end up sliding right off the hooks, all of which were uneven, so it was extra hard to move to each rung.

Daena waited on the highest platform. Thali joined her shortly, but her whole body sagged and drooped.

Thali took a ladle from a bucket and dropped water into her mouth before she took a deep breath. Daena offered her a staff, and Thali took it as they both stepped onto the bridge. It was just a row of planks held together by rope. It would sway terribly if they moved wrong.

They walked calmly out to the middle of the bridge before facing each other. Daena turned to Thali and waited for her to nod before they both took their positions. If there was one thing Thali thought she might be better at than Daena, it was staff fighting, and Daena knew it too. The wind picked up, and Thali's hair blew into her face, distracting her for a moment. Daena stomped her foot and the bridge started to tip, which threw Thali off guard before she shifted, moving her staff at the same time. She swept her hair off her face and then used her staff to sweep at Daena's feet, but Daena backed away quickly. The tension they created by separating helped reduce the severity of the swinging. Daena took the stiff pearl necklace at her throat and tossed it at Thali.

Thali caught it and glanced at Daena.

"For your hair. Wear it like a headband," Daena said.

"Aren't you supposed to be trying to win?"

"It's no fun to win if you're not at your best," Daena said.

Thali shoved the band into her hair, and Daena came at her quickly. Thali took a few steps toward Daena, who jumped as Thali rolled underneath her. Thali rolled herself flat along the bridge as Daena landed, sending a shockwave through the planks. The impromptu headband kept Thali's hair at bay as they faced each other.

Daena came back toward her with her staff raised, but Thali was ready and redirected Daena's downward movement, tossing her own staff away and grabbing Daena's as she pulled her friend toward her, twisting just so. Deana gripped Thali's hands on the staff, and they both went tumbling off the bridge, flying through the air to the net. They threw Daena's staff away and prepared to land in the net. As they did, they broke out in laughter and held up the line while they calmed down enough to breathe before climbing to the ground.

Thali followed Daena back to her rooms, where tea and a plate of cookies awaited them.

"Here," Thali said as she took the headband off and gave it back.

"You keep it. It looks better on you than it ever did on me," Deana said.

Thali paused as she looked at the beautiful necklace. "Are you sure?" She couldn't fathom the cost of this piece, never mind how flippantly Daena wore it.

"I've got others. Take it for all the birthdays I've missed." Daena took it from Thali and slid it carefully on Thali's head.

"Thank you," Thali said.

Reminiscing

"**N**O WONDER I COULDN'T woo you with jewelry," Elric said, interrupting Thali's thoughts.

Thali carefully placed the collar back into the armoire. While she had been reminiscing, Bardo had made his way over to the armoire. He slid up the leg into the space, then slithered through the little arm hole of a tiny vest that he lifted with his head.

"What's Bardo got?" Elric asked as he followed Thali's gaze.

A spear shot through her heart as she remembered one of her first animal friends, Tika. Before Ana, before Arabelle, there was Tika. Tika was a rat she'd found on board their ship when she was seven. She'd hidden Tika in her clothing trunk for a month before her mother had found her by accident. Mouse had heard the scream that had pierced the air as they had sailed in the middle of the ocean all the way up in the crow's nest.

Thali extended her arm to Bardo, who brought the vest to her. Only Bardo had known Tika, and Tika had been quick to teach Bardo not to try to eat her.

Indi rubbed up against Thali's leg as if she wanted to join in the reminiscing. Indi had been a baby and not allowed near the house or small animals when Tika was around. Thali took the little vest with both hands. It was a little ragged, but it was beaded with the rat's name on the back and lined with bright blue, purple, and white beads along its edges. Gold thread swirled along the surface of it too.

"That's a pretty tiny, flashy vest," Elric said.

"It belonged to my pet rat, Tika," Thali said. The pain wasn't as strong now; it'd been so many years ago. Now, she found her heart filled with more fondness than pain as she thought of her first steadfast friend.

"I assume the vest is a gift from a friend?"

Thali nodded as she remembered the last letter she'd received from Pevvie. She spun on her heel and grabbed a piece of parchment to scrawl a few words down before heading to the door and handing it to the runner in the hall with instructions to deliver the message.

She was back in moments, and Elric had sat up in bed. He slid Indi and Ana over a bit and adjusted his position. "Well, let's hear about the tiny vest," he said.

PEVLU

W HEN THALI WAS NINE, she found herself in yet another foreign market, where people dressed in unfamiliar outfits had danced down the aisles, catching everyone's attention. That night, Thali and her family had packed up their stall early enough to go and see the performers.

It had been a good market day; they were almost sold out of the goods they'd brought, so Thali's father had decided to take everyone to the show advertised for that night. Only Crab had declined, choosing to stay with the ship. He'd even guilted Mouse into staying with him.

Thali's family followed the crowd as they were funneled toward a well-lit square. Thali looked around in wonder at how more silver dishes than she'd ever seen even in a palace had been strung high up into the air, large thick candles upon them reflecting light on the wide area. Once in the square, the crowd split apart to view all the different performers. Thali's father reached down to hold her hand even though she was starting to feel too old to hold her parents' hands.

Her brother took her other hand. "Stay close, Rou, and tell me before you stop to watch something, all right?" Rommy said.

She nodded.

Each performer had their own little stage. Thali's eyes bugged out of her head as she watched people playing with fire, swallowing swords, and juggling knives. She wasn't keen to admit it, but more than once, she stepped behind her father so she wouldn't have to watch. As her family continued walking from performer to performer, she saw tumblers somersaulting through the crowd and people walking on ropes tied high up in the sky. "What if they fall?" Thali whispered to Rommy.

"They've practiced a lot. I imagine it's just like what we do onboard our ship," Rommy said.

"But we get on those ropes because there's something to do."

"They're doing something. They're entertaining everyone."

"Does it count as entertaining if we're scared for them?" Thali squeaked the last part.

Rommy patted her hand comfortingly. He stared up at the performers as they swung each leg before taking the next step. Thali didn't want to watch anymore. She looked beyond the rope walkers to a little stall with few people. Rommy was busy, so she pulled on her papa's hand until he looked down. She pointed to where she wanted to go and he nodded, letting go of her hand. Rommy leaned over, placing a hand on her back. His fingertips brushed the dagger tucked under her vest along her spine. He nodded before he let go of Thali's hand and she wove through the crowd.

"Stay there until we come get you," her father said.

Thali nodded. She ducked under some people's joined hands and made her way to the lone performer placed in the quietest spot, hidden behind the rope walkers and tumblers.

Thali felt a little self-conscious as she walked up; she was the only person near the performer now. This area wasn't as fancy as some of the others. The performer didn't have any draped silk behind him, only a sheet hanging between two poles and ropes outlining his imaginary stage. What had caught Thali's attention was the dog he had with him. As she approached, she realized the performer was younger than she'd originally thought. Maybe that was why she suddenly felt bolder and braver. He was older than Rommy but younger than her parents, nearer in age to the young men they recruited to work on her family's ships.

With him was a brown dog with black streaks along its back, almost like a tiger. The performer caught Thali's eye and stood waiting with his dog until Thali was right in front of the ropes of his stage. He flicked his hand up, and the dog rose on two legs, walking like a human across their little space. Then the man made a clacking noise with something in his hands, and the dog returned to four legs.

Next, the man twirled his finger in the air, and the dog did something Thali had never seen before: the dog started to spin, slowly rising up again on their hind legs as they spun as if it had been caught by a slow tornado. Again, the *clack* sounded, and the dog returned to the normal standing position.

"That's amazing," Thali said. She wondered whether she'd found someone else like her, someone who could suggest things to animals.

"Thank you, miss." The young man bowed deeply, flourishing his arms backward. Thali didn't move, so he continued. He brought out a ball about the same size as the dog, and she—Thali had determined it was a she when she'd spun around—hopped up on it as soon as it was in the middle of the space. And she did it without direction. The dog looked at the young man, and he waved his hand to the side as he backed up to the rope. The dog rolled atop the ball toward to him. Then he shooed her back with his hand, and she moved backward. Suddenly, he held a palm up, and she froze on the ball. He brought out a set of rails. They inclined in the beginning, became flat like a bridge, then descended. The dog's tail wagged more enthusiastically.

The performer moved aside and swept his arm toward the rails. The dog rolled the ball forward and up onto the rails, continuing to roll it up until it reached the bridge, where she stopped. She looked at the man and he smiled, taking something out of his pocket to feed her. Then the dog continued down the rails until she reached the ground. The clacking noise sounded again, and the dog jumped off the ball, running to him to collect her morsel of food.

Thali clapped enthusiastically. She'd never seen someone communicate with an animal like that before. Even without peeking into her mind, she could tell the dog and young man were happy to perform with each other. "How did you teach her all that?" Thali asked. She was careful about how she worded her questions, though she hoped against hope that he was like her, that he could see animals thoughts and feelings like she could. But her parents had warned her to keep her ability hidden, so she wanted to be careful.

He put a hand out, palm down, and the dog laid down as he put the rails away. Then he came over and sat on the ball his dog had been walking on. He ushered his furry companion forward, and Thali could see her up close. She didn't have the scars or marks of other animals she'd seen before, those that had been forced to perform. The dog curled up by his feet, content to take a snooze while he spoke.

The young man smiled down at the dog. Then he reached into his pocket and produced two wooden seashells. "See these? They mean 'Yes, the food is coming.' My sister is a dancer. She uses them all the time. Oni here loves my sister. As soon as she'd hear the clacking while my sister was dancing, her tail would wag. So I started to use them before I fed her. Then one day, they fell out of my pocket and clacked as Oni was leaping up onto a bucket. She froze on the bucket and looked at me like she was asking, 'Do I get food?' So I gave her a piece of my lunch. And then she tried it again, jumping to the next bucket. Then I made the noise again and again, and the same thing happened. Now I use it to tell her what I want her to do."

"That's incredible." But Thali had noticed that he hadn't let her look closely at the wooden shells. He tucked them back into his pocket.

"Do you like animals?" he asked.

Thali nodded.

"Do you have any pets at home?" She noticed that his eyes scanned her, likely gauging her worth.

Thali nodded. She reached for the pocket of her dress and opened it; her rat climbed out of her pocket and up her dress to her arm. Thali raised her arm so her elbow and wrist were aligned with the floor. "This is my rat, Tika."

The man looked surprised, then angled his head in curiosity as she asked Tika to stand on her back legs and walk from her elbow to her wrist. She then took her finger and spun it in a circle, and Tika spun in a circle on her arm.

"That's remarkable, just like Oni." He gave her a huge grin. "How did you teach a rat that?"

Thali shrugged. "We just play all the time." She'd forgotten to sever the connection in her mind, so the rat shrugged as she had. She quickly put Tika back into her pocket, hoping the man hadn't seen it.

He had a strange look on his face, and his eyes narrowed. But then he shook his head. "My name is Pevlu, and it is indeed an honor to meet you." He bowed his head.

"Thali." She stuck out her hand, and Pevlu took it and kissed the top as a gentleman might. "It is a true pleasure to meet a fellow friend to the animals."

Thali smiled. She'd never been treated like an adult before.

"What do rats like to eat?" Pevlu asked.

"Anything. Meat for sure, but Tika likes a nibble of bread too."

"Ah. Is it okay if I write this down?" he asked. He pulled out a small piece of parchment from his pocket and a stick of charcoal.

"I suppose so," Thali said. She felt important. She was flattered that an adult would be so intrigued by what she had to say. Usually they dismissed her.

"Where did you get your rat? She or he? Did you raise them from a baby? Is it a common rat?" he asked.

Thali giggled. "She's an ordinary rat. I found her among our supplies on the ship one day, and we started to play. I kept her hidden from my parents for a long time before they discovered her."

Pevlu smiled widely again. It made Thali feel special, like she was the only one he smiled for.

"Pevvie, are you boring the child?" A woman who had been dancing in one of the other spaces sashayed over. She was beautiful with voluminous, long, dark curly hair. She wore colorful clothing that showed off her curves.

"Ah, Bella. You're back." Pevlu rose and embraced the woman, kissing her on each cheek. Oni ran over and leapt up into Bella's arms; she gave the dog a big kiss right on her nose before the dog flipped over and the woman held the dog like a baby, scratching her belly. Thali didn't feel quite as special anymore.

"Come meet my new friend, Thali," Pevlu said.

"Pevvie, you're always making new friends." Bella rolled her eyes at him but glided over to Thali nonetheless.

"I hope he hasn't bored you with this silly dog," Bella said. The dog wagged her tail faster.

Thali shook her head, feeling a little defensive about her new friend and his beautiful dog. "Not at all. I really liked their show."

"Thali, show her Tika. Sister, wait until you see her rat. They're just like Oni and me."

Thali took the rat out, but this time she was much more careful. She only asked the rat to stand up on two legs and then scurry back into her pocket.

"Ah. Hopefully she's not as crazy as you are with animals." Bella winked at her. "Be careful, brother. If she wants to steal your show, she could. She's much prettier than you are."

"That's why I have you around," Pevlu said, grinning.

Bella laughed at that and picked up four little gold disks after putting Oni back on the ground. "You stay where you are, little one. The tumblers are done. You'll have the best spot now," Bella said. She started yipping then and clapping her little gold disks together, swirling and twirling her skirts in waves of color.

"What are you watching?" Rommy came up behind Thali, startling her. Her family had come to watch this performance with the rest of the crowd that had gathered. Thali grinned from ear to ear as she watched Pevlu and Oni dance and perform different tricks, while Bella twirled and music played to attract the crowd's attention.

"And now, we would like to request the help of a volunteer. Maybe a smaller friend?" Bella said. She scanned the crowd as if she were truly looking, and Thali thrust her hand up, hoping to get even closer to Oni and Pevlu.

Bella came up to her, smiling, and she winked. "You, young lady, come, step over the rope and join us." She put her hand out and Thali took it. Bella guided her to the center of the space.

"Now, can you make a big 'O' with your arms? High above your head," she said. Thali did as she was told. Pevlu winked at her and then made a huge sweeping motion with his arm as Oni followed him. They stopped at the edge of the space behind Thali.

Pevlu went to stand in front of Thali. Winking at her once again, he raised both arms, and Oni barked. She jumped right over Thali's head and through her arms. Thali wasn't very tall, but it was still quite high for a dog to jump. Thali could feel the fur of the dog's tail brush against her fingertips just before Oni landed in front of her. The crowd applauded enthusiastically. Then Pevlu asked Oni to lay down on the raised platform in the middle of the space and took Thali's hand to guide her back to the crowd. He bowed low over her hand like he had before and grinned at her before turning back around to continue the performance.

Rommy put a hand on her shoulder as soon as she was back. "That was neat! You should teach Tika that."

As the show ended, Thali watched as Pevlu and Bella went around the audience. Pevlu kissed the hand of every lady. Bella seemed to smile for every gentleman and flutter her eyelashes at them. Finally, they reached Thali's family.

"You must be the most beautiful woman I've ever seen," Pevlu said to her mother.

"That's very kind of you. Thank you for your kindness to our daughter." Lady Jin said as Ranulf put an arm around her waist.

"Of course. She is very special. I had the privilege of meeting Tika. They are an even more amazing duo than Oni and I." He bowed with big sweeping arm motions.

"You brought Tika?" her mother turned an inquiring eyebrow to Thali.

Thali felt her cheeks warm; she opened the top of her pocket and Tika poked her head out for a moment before ducking back in. "I know you told me to leave her, but she wanted to come to the show too!"

Lady Jinhua smiled as she turned back to Pevlu. "Well thank you. It was a lovely performance."

Pevlu swept another bow and kissed the back of Lady Jinhua's hand again. "It was our honor," he said.

Bella kissed Rommy's cheeks, and he turned pink.

Pevlu came over to Thali again. "Us animal friends need to stick together. This is a list of the cities we'll be performing in and when. We'd love to see you again. Maybe I'll be able to show you some new things with a rat of my own." He winked at her and bowed low over her hand, pressing a piece of parchment into it. He kissed the top of her hand, and she closed her hand over the piece of parchment.

Six years later ...

The paper Pevlu had secretly placed in her hand had included an address, a way to find him should she ever be looking for him. It turned out she didn't really need it, for they would often end up in the same cities and villages. The same markets popular with merchants were also profitable for performers, so even though she wouldn't always get to visit him, Thali would see the dancers enticing the people and smile knowing Pevlu was there.

"Please, can I bring Indi and Ana to show Pevvie?" Thali asked. They had seen the dancers at the market that day when she and Rommy had helped Crab unload goods. Thali and Rommy no longer minded the booths, but in the busiest months, they still helped set up.

"She'll do it whether or not you let her, you know," Rommy said as he passed their parents carrying a bolt of heavy fabric.

"Go around the back," her mother finally said. She watched her crew as they too walked by and checked the items they carried off her inventory list. "Hey, don't forget to move the rest of your pile first."

Thali nodded. She made packs for Ana and Indi so they could help carry household objects to the stall. It was still early in the morning; most of the inhabitants hadn't woken up yet, and that was the only reason she was allowed to take Indi and Ana off the ship. Now, they helped her haul her pile of inventory to the stall. She finished and untied Ana's pack. She told Crab where she was going, then disappeared around the back of their stall.

They had seen Pevlu and his sister, Isabella, the day before, so Thali knew where to find them. Fifteen now, Thali was excited to introduce Pevvie to Indi and Ana. Ana had only recently joined them, and Indi still wasn't quite full-sized, but her fur still stuck out in random places just like a teenager's hair might. Despite having a tiger companion, Thali had still made sure to take her staff with her and had her knives strapped to her back and tucked into her boot.

This city's sheriff was familiar to her from yesterday, so he nodded at her, though he narrowed his eyes as he took in the tiger. He didn't stop her though, likely since they were headed for the performers' area.

Instead of walking to the edge of the area where Pevlu had been stationed when they'd first met, Thali now strode to the biggest stage, right in the middle of the space. She smiled when she saw him in the middle, working with the rats that were now part of his show. Bella was nowhere in sight, but she was probably organizing the performers. Pevvie had twelve rats, and Thali watched as they all ran along a rail, then stopped and turned. When he raised his hands, they all jumped at the same time to the opposite rail, then turned back and ran down the rail to their basket and snuggled in on top of each other.

Thali felt Indi lick her lips. "No, Indi, definitely don't eat those rats." Her heartstrings pulled at her as she remembered her dear Tika's passing a few years ago.

Pevlu turned around, and his smile brightened like the sun coming out from behind the clouds as he saw Thali. "My beautiful, lovely girl." He grabbed her hand and bent low in a huge bow, kissing the top.

Thali grinned in response. She'd seen Pevlu become a true entertainer and heartbreaker over their many visits and knew his lavish responses were normal. "Do you remember Indi?"

"Of course. No one forgets a tiger. My, she has grown quite a lot, though she was just a ball of fluff when I saw her last. You are the most beautiful tiger in all the world, Miss Indi." He bowed low in front of the tiger. Indi sat and licked her paw.

"And this is our newest addition, Ana."

Pevlu went over and Ana wagged her tail, always happy to meet pretty much anyone.

"Look at your fur. How curly it is! You remind me so much of my Oni." Pevlu said. Tears sprang to his eyes, and he wiped them away hastily.

"I know. I thought the same thing when Ana sprang at me as a pup. I couldn't give her up," Thali said.

"Well, I know you'll carry on her legacy with great pride." Pevlu puffed out his chest and offered his hands to Ana. She leapt into them and knocked him over, but he laughed as he scratched her under her fur.

Thali took the opportunity to look around. Pevlu had come a long way from his tiny little show off to the side. He was now the lead performer, recruiting performers as he went, and his animal show was world famous. To her, he was the same Pevvie as when she had been a child, just with fancier clothes. She was so proud of his work with animals. He didn't have the same ability she had, but he worked methodically and cared thoughtfully for the animals.

"All right, now that we're acquainted, I was hoping to get your mama to help me out." Pevlu stood and tried to brush the dirt off himself, but it was a halfhearted attempt.

"The rats looked great," Thali said.

"I named my star rat Tiko in Tika's honor," he said.

"Thank you," Thali said, swallowing her tears before they could fall.

"Now, let's go see my newest friend." Pevlu offered the crook of his arm, and Thali took it gladly as Indi and Ana followed. She was surprised that Indi hadn't tried to jam herself in between them as she often did whenever she was around a male.

They moved to the quieter back area where the performers had set up camp. Pevvie nodded at the guards he now posted near his animals and troupe so they would feel safe.

"Before this part of our annual cycle, we usually tour the area by the sea. My newest friend here was tied to a rock near our camp. One of our patrols found him. I have to warn you though, he's in bad shape. I've done what I can and he looks better than the first day, but he's still nothing like your Indi there." Pevlu nodded to Indi.

Indi had left Thali's side and sauntered closer to a covered box. She sniffed, then looked at Thali as if to ask, "Would you please take the sheet off?"

Pevlu removed the sheet. There was indeed another tiger inside the cage, but it was half Indi's size. Emaciated and sad looking, it saw Indi right away and the air went tense and quiet. It tensed all its muscles and pulled its lips up, growling, as its whiskers flared upward to show Indi all its teeth. Indi jumped back. Thali felt how startled she was. Indi huffed and raised her own lips to growl back, offended. Indi turned away and sat, focusing her attention on grooming herself instead. Ana moved to sit with Indi, comforting her friend.

"Well, that's no way to make friends," Thali said. She turned her attention to the other tiger now sitting in the back of the cage, shrinking as far away as possible from Pevlu and Thali.

"I'm the only one to feed him. Isabella can get a little closer than I can, but she's terrified of our newest friend. I haven't been able to use the clackers either since all he does is shrink away," Pevvie said.

Thali looked around. She spotted no one, so she looked at Pevlu. She was pretty sure by now that he knew more about her gift than he let on.

"I trust you completely. I'm going to go get a present for Indi and Ana since my new friend here was so rude. Consider it a peace offering." Pevlu turned and left Thali alone with her animals and the new tiger.

Thali closed her eyes. She could feel Indi and Ana behind her and gently stroked Indi's thread in her mind. Standing alone behind the door inside her mind, she saw a single teal thread. It belonged to the new tiger. She sent him images of comfort and ease and safety. The new tiger's mind was full of images of abuse the tiger had suffered, especially at the hands of a man of similar height and hair color as Pevlu. The other man was much more muscular though and had apparently felt the need to prove his strength to himself by using it on animals. It made Thali sick to her stomach, but she wanted to understand what this creature had gone through. While this tiger did like Pevlu, he didn't trust him. So Thali pushed through thoughts and feelings of goodness and kindness attached to Pevlu's image, then showed him that the clackers meant food would follow. Finally, Thali showed him one of

Pevlu's sessions, of how certain signals indicated the actions he would ask of him.

After a deep breath, Thali opened her eyes and approached the cage. The tiger was now stretched out on the ground, peacefully watching her with interest.

Pevlu returned with a bucket of meat, and Indi and Ana noisily slopped it up. "So, what do you think?" he asked.

"I think this tiger was badly abused by a man with your hair color. It'll take time, but he's trying." Thali grabbed a piece of meat with flat, wide chopsticks and placed the meat in the cage. Then she backed away to let the new tiger eat.

She turned back to Pevvie, sad that she couldn't help more.

His eyes were shiny with tears. "That's the first time she hasn't launched herself at someone when they approached."

Thali smiled. "You are a wonderful, patient person, Pevvie."

He turned his charm back on and took Thali's hands as he sat on a nearby rock. "Come with us," Pevlu said.

"Sorry?" Thali said.

"Come work with us. Help me teach the animals. Perform with us. You would be so perfect for all of this," Pevlu said.

"But ... my family. I can't just—"

"Why not?"

"Because, we have things to do."

"But here, Indi and Ana wouldn't have to hide. You wouldn't have to hide. You'd have your own tent, and they could be with you all the time. You could collect more animal friends."

Thali thought about what that would be like, traveling by land, performing, gathering more animals. Then she thought about the ocean, about the markets, about her family. About her animals at home. "I'm sorry, Pevlu. I can't leave my family."

Pevlu swallowed. "Are you sure?"

Thali didn't trust her words, so she just nodded.

"If you ever change your mind, you always have an invitation to join us. We could be so great together, Thali. We'd create the most incredible show the world has ever seen. We'd be invited to palaces! Just think of all the things we could do together." Pevlu smiled, slipping into a dream he had obviously thought of before.

Thali smiled too. "Tell me about what you're working on now."

"With pleasure." Pevlu grinned. He slid the rest of the meat to the tiger without looking at her and then covered the cage up again. He led Thali to the basket of rats. He opened it and the rats all piled out, climbing the rail in front of them and stopping at little circles drawn onto it. Pevlu twirled his finger in a circle, and they all spun in a circle. Then he pointed at each rat, and as he flicked his finger upward, each rat jumped upward, the rat in the middle jumping an impressive couple of feet and landing in the exact same spot.

"I'm working on getting them to cross their paws. Tiko and Tappy have it down, but the others are taking a little longer. Oh, hold on, I'm going to go and grab some grains of rice. They love rice," Pevlu said, leaving Thali there with the rats. Thali closed her eyes and saw the familiar orange strands of rats. She pictured Tiko's memories of crossing his paws and sent them to the others. Then she suggested they watch the others to learn. When she opened her eyes, she saw Pevlu in her peripheral vision, leaning up against a beam. As soon as she took a deep breath, he walked back onto the stage.

"Give it a try," Thali said.

Pevlu grinned and crossed his index and middle finger in front of each other. All the rats followed suit. "I wish you could show me how to do it," he whispered.

"I wish it always felt this good to do it," Thali said. She glanced behind her, sure that her mother would be looking disapprovingly at her use of her ability, but she had only been paranoid. No one was behind her.

"Where is everyone, anyway?" Thali asked. A place like this, especially with Pevlu in the center of it all, should be buzzing with people all the time.

"Isabella is holding a mandatory meeting for everyone," Pevlu said.

"So no one sees what I do?" Thali asked.

Pevlu nodded.

"Thank you," she said.

"My offer still stands. If you want to join us, we would love to have you," Pevlu said. "You'd be my star."

"Thank you," Thali said, but the thought of being the center of attention made her uneasy. "I don't think I've ever wanted to have that many eyes on me."

"Don't tell me you haven't seen the boys clamoring for you to notice them. You're a beautiful girl, Thali."

Thali could feel her cheeks turn hot. "Um, no."

Pevlu smiled. "I don't mean to embarrass you. You're one of the only people I can truly be myself with. Isabella knows how I really am, and I think she thinks I'm going to go nutty sometimes. But you're like me."

Thali shook off her embarrassment and smiled again. "There aren't many of us, but there are some." She thought of Deshi and the other people she'd met who loved animals, though Pevlu was the only one to use a clacker and whose animals loved him as much as he did them.

"Thali, just ... just make sure you fall in love with someone who's worth it. Someone who will let you be you."

"All right, Pevvie, I will." Thali said. She had a hard time imagining marriage. Boys were her friends, but there wasn't one she could imagine looking at like her mother looked at her father.

Pevlu jumped up then and grinned at her. "Ready to see more animals?"

At her vigorous nod, they went to visit all his various animals. Pevlu described what he was having difficulty teaching each of them, and Thali closed her eyes and showed the animals what he wanted with the new signal. Sometimes it took a little adjustment between the three of them, but the animals got it eventually.

Thali stumbled as they walked back to the main stage.

Pevlu caught her and tucked her securely under his shoulder as they walked. "Oh dear, I've exhausted you." He brought her to one of the benches set up in front of the stage.

"I've enjoyed every minute of it," Thali said. She did feel lightheaded after draining herself connecting with all the animals, so she reclined on the bench. "Pevvie, do you love anyone?"

"You mean someone besides you?" Pevvie grinned.

Thali rolled her eyes. Pevvie was like her brother. "And Isabella, but I mean like marriage type of love."

Pevvie looked down before answering. "I did, a long time ago. But she didn't want me."

"I'm sorry, Pevvie."

"Don't be sorry. I have my animals, and Isabella, and you. And all the ladies that love my animals too." He gave her what was supposed to be a smirk, but Thali could see right through it. She knew he never took anyone to bed like many other sailors or performers would. He was a charming entertainer but not nearly as promiscuous as other performers and sailors.

"It seems I've arrived just in time." Rommy strode up, and Thali turned to him.

"Ah, Rommy, my you've grown up," Pevvie said.

"It's good to see you too, Pevlu," Rommy replied.

Thali tried to sit up, but lying on the bench was just too comfortable.

"You ready to go, Rou?" Rommy asked.

Thali tried to nod, but the bench was so warm and comfy.

"I'm afraid I may have exhausted her a little," Pevlu said.

"I'd say more than a little," Rommy added.

Thali felt a warm jacket wrap around her before her brother scooped her up in his strong arms.

"We'll see you tomorrow," Pevlu said.

"I wouldn't miss it for the world," Thali tried to say. But sleep called her more strongly than the words did.

"I'm glad you get to use your gift here, Rou, but you need to practice more. I know our parents say you shouldn't, but why do you even have it if you can't use it?" Rommy said.

"Wait, Indi and Ana," Thali said.

"They're here with us," Rommy said.

Thali went into her head and saw the familiar threads that were Indi and Ana. She smiled and let sleep take her.

An Unexpected Visitor
Elric

THE MORNING AFTER THALI had revealed some of the secrets in her armoire, Elric found himself with a few minutes before his next meeting, not enough to track Thali down, but enough to go outside and breathe in some fresh air. He stepped out of the shadow of the stone archway and closed his eyes as he turned his face upward, the warmth of the sun soaking into his soul like a flower drinking in the sun's rays. He took a deep breath in and out.

"Please, let me through!" a man shouted. Elric tried to ignore the protestations and sounds of struggle but after a squeal that sounded like a pig's, he snapped his eyes open and turned in the direction of the kerfuffle.

Two of his guards were restraining a man in an exquisite green coat with flamboyant embroidery. The man flailed his arms as he tried to escape their grip.

"What seems to be the problem here?" Elric asked as he strode toward the guards. His own personal guards, he noticed, formed a tighter circle around him.

"Ah! You must be her husband. Good afternoon, Your Royal Majesty." The man stopped fighting, straightened his coat, and offered Elric a low, full-armed, sweeping bow.

Elric raised an eyebrow. Now that he was closer to the man, he saw streaks of white cream or make-up on his neck; a long, dark mustache curled into a spiral on each cheek; and sharp green eyes. The man was younger than Elric had initially thought, maybe only fifteen years his senior.

"Your Majesty, I'm a very dear friend of Thali and her family. If you could only tell her I'm here—I'm early, you see. We made good time on the journey here. Please, tell her Pevlu is looking for her." Again the man bowed low, sweeping his arms to the sides and flipping his tailcoats as if performing.

Elric looked at the messenger posted at the gate, who jumped, apparently startled by the king's attention. Then he ran up the stairs into the palace. Elric turned his attention back to the man. "May I ask why you'd like to see my wife?" He swallowed. Even to his own ears, he had sounded jealous.

"I've known Thali for many years—actually, that's not all. I've pursued her talents for many years as well, trying in earnest to get her to join our family of performers. You see, Your Majesty, I have a troupe of performers. We're like storytellers, except our family consists of animals, jugglers, tightrope walkers, and acrobats."

"Ahh," Elric said, understanding dawning. He'd known that name sounded familiar. But as he opened his mouth again to reply, he heard a squeal behind him. Everyone's heads turned. Thali was running full tilt toward them, the messenger lagging behind the guards chasing Thali down the stairs. Elric was glad that at least Isaia and Nasir were keeping pace with Thali as she ran right past Elric and launched herself at the man in front of them.

The messenger nodded to Elric before resuming his post, his breathing still ragged.

The guards who had initially blocked Pevlu turned back to the gate and busied themselves with the next visitor as Thali finally released Pevlu. He took her hand and bowed low over it, kissing the back of it. *Thankfully*, Elric thought, *at least one of them remembered who she was*. He wondered if he ought to remind Thali about the proprieties needed around watching eyes.

"Elric, this is my dearest friend, Pevlu." Thali finally turned back to him.

"We've met," Elric said. Avery floated into sight, a signal that he was late for his next meeting.

"I didn't know you were early. I hadn't let the guards know you were coming yet. I'm sorry you were held up at the gate, Pevvie," Thali said.

"You, my dear, have grown into the most beautiful woman in the world," Pevlu said.

Thali rolled her eyes. "And what would you say to my mother if she were here?"

"I'd be unable to speak. I'd be the luckiest man in the world to be in the company of the two most beautiful women in the entire world. Trust me, I have traveled the world, *and* I could never lie to you." Pevlu stopped as he raised his hand as if swearing an oath.

"Where is everyone?" Thali asked, turning to look behind Pevlu and around him.

"They're waiting in a field aways from here. My excitement to see you made my boots grow wings to fly here and cast myself at your beautiful feet," Pevlu said, throwing himself to the ground. Thali giggled and took his arm to pull him up. He somersaulted into a standing position and smoothly tucked her hand into the crook of his elbow.

No wonder my charming tricks didn't work on her, Elric thought. *This man oozes with excessive charm at every word.*

"We'll send the next messenger we see to go invite them all here. Oh, come. I'll show you the guest building. Elric—" Thali paused and smiled brilliantly at Elric. "—gifted me an animal sanctuary for my birthday."

"Hmm ... while my evaluation is still pending, this will definitely earn him an extra point in my books." Pevlu turned his attention on Elric for a moment as if inspecting a prized horse.

Avery was now hovering close to his elbow, clearing her throat to get his attention. While he didn't feel like Pevlu was dangerous or the type to seduce Thali, he was intrigued by this man who had earned so much of Thali's affection. It would never cease to amaze him how Thali had complained about the difficulty in befriending her classmates and the court of nobles when she had kindled so many affectionate relationships with people of all kinds from all around the world.

Avery coughed again, and Elric sighed as he waved at Thali's retreating back. He turned to let Avery usher him to his next meeting.

Thali

Thali and Pevlu rounded the rear of the palace and headed for the looming side wall of the massive building Elric had commissioned for Thali's animals. Two long, finished buildings were attached perpendicular to the main building still under construction. Paddocks of various sizes filled the building nearest the castle, while the opposite building was the healing center. Elric had even been insightful enough to hire Jito, a friend of Thali's from home, to help him build it as Thali would have wanted.

"Oh my, this is the biggest building dedicated to animals I've seen in the whole world." Pevlu stopped and stared at the buildings.

Thali smiled and stood a little taller. "We even have a space big enough for Eleanor." Elric had given her, Deshi, and Jito no limits with the building's construction and layout. She knew animals best, he'd said, and he knew she'd give careful thought to how every space would be best used.

"I can see that." Pevlu started walking again, a little faster. Thali picked up her pace to match. They ended up runnning toward the building. They were out of breath and giggling like children as they arrived at the doors.

On the way there, Thali had encountered a messenger and instructed him to bring Isabella and the rest of Pevvie's family to the animal sanctuary. She was hoping Eleanor wouldn't cause too much of a disturbance as she walked through town, but an elephant walking the streets was probably going to cause a disturbance no matter how careful she was.

As Thali started showing Pevlu around, they ran into Jito. Together, they sorted out where each of Pevlu's animals could stay.

"I'm sorry I couldn't make it here in time for your nuptials," Pevlu said when Jito left.

"You were overseas somewhere. I'm sure that was stressful enough with all the animals. So don't worry. It's all right," Thali said.

"I wanted you to ride Eleanor down the aisle. I think that would have been beautiful."

"It definitely would have been memorable. But Indi and Ana held the train of my dress, and even that was all the audience could handle."

"Ha! I bet."

After the tour, Thali led him to the reception room she used for meetings and receiving animals. Tea and baked treats were waiting for them. "How have you been, Pevvie?"

"I'm all right. It's the end of our season, so I'll catch up on sleep now."

"You can stay here over the winter if you like. I wouldn't mind the company, and I'm sure Jito wouldn't either. He might even enjoy watching you work."

Pevvie nodded. "You know, I worry about you."

"You don't need to worry about me," Thali said as she looked at her hands.

"Really? I remember a teenage you telling me the thought of being the center of attention would be terrifying. And now, you're queen."

Thali smiled at the thought; it was still so foreign and strange to her. "Well, things change."

"Don't get me wrong. If I could handpick a royal that would do the most good, it'd be you."

"Then what's really bothering you?" Thali asked.

"How can a king put his queen before his kingdom? Elric seems like the good kind of royalty, but you deserve to be the supported, not the supporter."

"I don't know if I understand what you're trying to say, Pevvie."

"Elric has a kingdom to take care of. Now, so do you. But you're not like other people. You see the world differently. So is Elric doing what he was raised to do, or is he listening to your perspective?"

Thali was a little shocked. She'd just had this same conversation with Elric earlier that morning.

"I'm right, aren't I?" Pevvie asked.

Thali looked down at her hands again, unable to meet her old friend's eyes.

The sound of many approaching people caught their attention, so Thali—relieved at the interruption—and Pevlu left their refreshments to meet them. Thali smiled at Pevlu, raising an eyebrow. She reached into her mind and found all the animals' threads easily. She showed them each their new homes and beds as they came in the door. Eleanor the elephant led the parade, then went straight to her quarters, as did the streams of animals that followed.

"You've been practicing," Pevvie said as Isabella entered last with baskets of rats and smaller animals.

Thali and Pevvie rushed over to help Isabella, and Thali embraced her after they had let the small critters loose in their zone. Thali had asked Jito to find them little beds, so now there were rows and rows of them like bunks in the guards' barracks. All the rats and assorted tiny animals ventured out of the baskets and organized themselves into the little box beds.

It didn't take long before Thali, Pevlu, and Isabella had the animals settled, and they headed up to the palace for supper. The three friends and Elric enjoyed a relaxed, conversation-filled dinner. Thali showed Pevlu and Isabella to their guest rooms, purposely in the wing closest to the animals. After she'd bid them goodnight, she returned to her own rooms and found Elric sprawled out in bed, paperwork once again strewn around him.

"They're settled in all right?" Elric asked.

"They are. Though I wouldn't be surprised if we found them staying in the barn in a day or two," Thali replied.

"Maybe we should build a couple of guest rooms attached to the barn," Elric suggested. He narrowed his eyes. "Maybe on the forest side. We'd have to take down some trees—"

"You are wonderful."

"Wonderful enough for another story from the armoire?" Elric asked.

Thali laughed. She pointed to the bed, and Indi and Ana jumped up as Elric scrambled to collect his documents before pawprints stamped them. Then she placed her hand on the top of the armoire, and Bardo slid out of her sleeve and coiled himself on the cushion she'd placed there. He'd really come to enjoy the luxuries living in a palace afforded too.

She opened the armoire doors, and candlelight caught the facets of the gem on her finger. She blinked the discomfort from her eyes as she thought of another ring she'd received long ago. Thali reached for the drawer on the left and opened the door of the tiny compartment.

After opening the tiny door, she dipped her fingers inside to pull out a delicate silver ring. It was a beautiful, intricate twisting of thistle leaves that held a little gem in the shape of a thistle.

All her friends were dear to her, but this ring ignited so many more emotions: pride at winning his friendship and respect, accomplishment in their work together, even fondness. He was the way-too-smart little brother she'd never had.

ANDERS

"**L**ET THE CHILDREN PLAY, Lady Jin. They'll be safe in the court-yard. I need to show you some of my finest wines." The beautiful lady with golden hair took Lady Jinhua's arm in her own. She expertly maneuvered around her own wide purple skirts to accommodate Lady Jinhua's skirts. As they approached the edge of the courtyard, she called out to her son, "You make Lady Routhalia feel welcome, Anders. We'll be back in a little while."

Lady Jinhua nodded to Thali, then turned back to her host.

Anders, a little boy of about six, stood next to a dead rose bush, hacking it with a stick he'd found nearby. A replica of his mother, he had blond hair and dark-brown eyes, but they were dulled by his father's pale skin and hooked nose. Thali, two years older than Anders, had brought a book and hoped to catch up on her reading in the courtyard. Seeing Anders was busy, she took a seat on a bench under a tree across the courtyard and opened her book.

"What are you doing?" Anders's mop of blond hair peeked over her book.

"Reading," Thali answered.

"We have the biggest library in the whole of Drevendi," Anders boasted.

"That's nice." Thali tried to ignore the little boy and get back to her book.

"Can you climb a tree?" Anders asked as he clambered up the tree behind Thali. "I bet you can't. My cousin isn't even allowed to try. Girls aren't as strong as boys." He stuck his tongue out at Thali.

"I can too!" Thali shouted and leapt up. She put her book back in her pocket and climbed up the tree with ease, sending a silent thank you to Jaon for teaching her how just a few months ago.

"Oh yeah? Well, I bet you can't climb that wall over there." He pointed to the wall that separated the courtyard from a small stable.

"Can you?" Thali answered.

"Of course I can." The little boy scrambled down the tree and started to scale the wall.

Just as he was struggling to find another foothold, Thali scrambled up the wall and sat atop it, offering her hand to the younger boy floundering about halfway up the wall.

"I can do it by myself!" Anders clawed desperately at the wall as Thali carefully climbed back down. She reached the ground just as he yelled out and fell on top of her.

Several guards rushed over and pulled Anders off Thali as Lady Jinhua and Lady Andell rounded the corner. Thali picked herself up off the ground while Anders cried and held his wrist.

"They were climbing the wall, m'lady, and Master Anders fell and landed on top of Miss Routhalia," one of the guards offered.

"Anders, I asked you to be a good host, not crush ladies with your falling body. You should be grateful Lady Routhalia tried her best to catch you. You could have broken a lot more than your wrist. Now come. Let's get you to the infirmary and get that wrist wrapped up." She turned to Lady Jinhua, who was checking Routhalia over. "Ladies, I'm so sorry for my son's behavior. If you'll excuse me for a few minutes, I'll be right back."

"Of course, An, take your time." Lady Jinhua nodded.

Lady Andell left with Anders and all the guards returned to their posts but one. He asked, "Lady Jinhua, is there any way I can be of service to you or your daughter? Is there anything I can fetch for you?"

"No, thank you. I think we'll just wait in the courtyard here." Lady Jinhua took her daughter's hand and led her to a stone bench. She sat down and placed Thali in front of her. Thali's eyes had filled with tears. "Are you all right?" she asked her daughter.

Thali could only nod. Her shoulder was sore and one of her fingers had bent the wrong way, but she hadn't felt anything snap or crack.

"Where does it hurt?" Lady Jin asked.

Thali could only point to her shoulder and hold up the two last fingers on her left hand.

"Having Anders fall on your shoulder is not what I had in mind when I left you with him," she said. When Thali began to sob, she added, "There, there, you'll be all right." Lady Jin pulled her daughter into her lap and whispered a story as they sat together.

By the time her favorite story about a trickster monkey was done, Thali had relaxed and forgotten all about her injuries.

Lady Jin sat Thali next to her. "What happened on the wall?" she asked gently.

"Anders said girls were stupid and we couldn't do what boys could. He thought I wouldn't be able to climb the tree over there, but I did. And then he bet I couldn't climb the wall. But I did and he was only halfway up and I was scrambling back down to help him and then he yelled and fell on me."

"Ahh. I see." Her mother held her hand. "While it wasn't very nice of Anders to call you names, you have to know that you can't fight all the battles that will be presented to you. There's just not enough time in a day! In all the lands we visit, with all the people we meet, we're bound to find people who have very different beliefs than we do. We can't fight them all or prove them all wrong." Thali nodded as her mother continued. "Sometimes, we have to bow out or let them believe what they want, let them win, so we can have peace."

Thali nodded. She wasn't quite sure she understood all that her mother was telling her, but it felt nice to sit with her mother and have this quiet moment as Jinhua stroked Thali's hair.

"Ah, there you are. Apologies again, ladies." Lady An hurried over. "Miss Routhalia, I am so sorry that Anders found it acceptable to land atop you. Are you all right? Is your dress all right? I'll have him pay for a new one in your favorite color as an apology. Would you like that?"

Thali looked to her mother, who simply nodded at her. "That is very kind, Lady Andell, but it is unnecessary. I'm fine, and I'm glad Master Anders will be all right."

"Yes, he'll be just fine, thanks to you! You'll be our guest of honor tonight!" Lady Andell sat and chatted with Lady Jinhua as Thali fell asleep on the bench, her head in her mother's lap.

That night, Rommy ribbed Thali with his elbow as she sat at the head of the table. "Heard you got crushed by little Anders earlier."

Thali nodded.

"Glad you're all right, sis. Or else I'd have to go challenge his brother, Anser, for you." Rommy grinned.

He and Anser loved challenging each other in combat, so Thali just rolled her eyes. "You've probably already challenged him as many times as he's challenged you."

Rommy grinned again, shifting his weight to show Thali the wooden sword he sat on.

As supper was winding down—and Thali had only received two pointed looks from her mother for bringing a too-large piece of chicken to her mouth and not breaking her bread into small enough pieces—Anders slunk over to her chair.

"Are you all right, Master Anders?" Thali asked to be polite.

He lifted his wrapped wrist to show her. "Yes. Thank you, Miss Routhalia, for trying to catch me as I fell." He looked at his mother, who was watching them intently. "I'm sorry for the words I said this afternoon and for challenging you. It was not gentlemanly, nor was it being a good host." He looked down, likely thinking of whatever punishment he was going to have to face later.

"I like climbing trees," Thali replied. Smiling, she leaned closer to Anders. "Tomorrow, I can show you how to climb a tree with one hand."

He grinned from ear to ear at that, but when he glanced at his mother still watching them, he looked down solemnly again. "I'd like that very much," he said softly. He turned to go, but when his mother gave him a pointed look, Anders quickly turned back. "Miss Routhalia, would you do me the honor of the first dance this evening?" He stumbled through the words as his ears turned pink.

"It would be my honor," Thali said. Her mother had warned her this might happen.

The dance was awkward since Anders had one wrist wrapped; it sat awkwardly at her waist as they both stumbled through the steps.

As the adults conversed, "See you tomorrow," Anders said before scampering off with his nursemaid. Thali sat in a chair off to the side, taking her book out of her pocket at first but eventually falling asleep, curled up in the chair. She barely registered her father scooping her up and tucking her into bed, where she dreamt of battling giants and climbing bean stalks.

A year later ...

"I bet you didn't know there are only two kinds of mammals that lay eggs," Anders said as he climbed the turret stairs backward.

"Actually, there are three," Thali countered as she followed him, waiting on his slow pace. Being stuck on a ship most of the time made her always want to take stairs two at a time.

"No! There's only two. The platypus and the echidna." He stuck his tongue out before turning back around.

"No. There's three. The platypus, the echidna from the southern island, and the echidna from the eastern island."

"They're the same *thi-ing*," Anders said. He turned backward again and stuck his tongue out again. Once he reached the landing, he walked down the hallway to a set of double doors. A guard opened one, and the little boy looked pointedly at the other guard, who scrambled to open the other door as Anders turned back to Thali.

"The echidna from the southern island has a short beak, and the one from the eastern island has a long beak. One's this long, and one's this long. They're completely different!" Thali held up her thumb on one hand and her index finger on the other.

"How do you even know that?" Anders threw himself into a plushy chair in the library.

"I've seen it with my own two eyes," Thali said, standing tall. She was trying really hard not to admire the library they had just walked into. But she couldn't help herself and started looking around at the towering walls covered in rows of books from floor to ceiling all the way around the room—and then at all the shelves in the middle!

"You've *seen them?!*" Anders's eyes bugged out of his head. He turned around in the plush chair and hung off the seat as he watched her upside down.

Now it was Thali's chance to be smug. "Yes. The ones with the shorter beaks are usually black. The longer-beaked ones are brown."

"What are they like?" Anders said. Sitting up and leaping over the back of the chair, he ran to a shelf on the far wall and grabbed a book. He ran back to Thali with it. But before she could answer his previous question, he opened the book to a specific page and pointed at the drawing. "This is what they look like, right?"

Thali looked down at the little echidna staring back at her. She cocked her head. "Actually ..." She scurried over to a nearby desk to fetch a quill and dip it in the ink. Then she grabbed a piece of parchment and sketched an echidna with longer spines than the one in the book had.

"They look more like this," she said when Anders came to see what she was doing.

"What about the other one?" he asked.

Thali quickly sketched out the one with a longer beak.

His hand reached out before freezing midway. "May I?" he asked, still looking carefully at Thali's drawing.

She wished she could have made a better drawing, but it'd have to do. "Of course." Thali handed it to him, remembering she was a guest here and her mother's reminder to be a respectful, polite guest. However, Thali was surprised by Anders's sudden politeness. He blew on the ink gently and took out the powder to absorb the extra liquid. Carefully, he laid the piece of parchment flat on the table and brushed off the extra powder before delicately placing the drawing in the book.

"Thank you," he said. "Wait, what are they like? Do they move quickly or slowly? Are they curious?" He waited, holding his breath as he stared expectantly at her.

"They move quickly, like rodents. I didn't want to get too close in case those spines were venomous. But they definitely look sharp. They get startled and run back to their homes at loud noises." Thali thought back to when she'd last seen an echidna.

"Have you ever seen an ostrich? Or the iguanas that swim?" Anders was like a different little boy now. He had been so stuck up when they met, perhaps expecting Thali to fawn over him.

"I have an ostrich at home. And I've seen the swimming iguanas. I was swimming in the ocean and was ... startled when a giant black lizard swam under me," Thali said. She modified her words so she didn't have to admit how scared she'd been in that moment.

"You have an ostrich at home?!" His eyes bugged out again. "Can you draw one for me?"

Thali shrugged; she didn't have anything else to do, so she sat at the desk, pulled another parchment out, and thought of the grouchy old ostrich at home. She sketched it out carefully and then showed him.

"Are their legs really as long as we are tall?" Anders asked.

"Yes, almost. Maybe up to here?" She brought her hand to his chin.

"Amazing," Anders said. He spent the afternoon running around the library, pulling out familiar books and asking Thali questions about different animals.

That night, he insisted Thali sit next to him and continued to bombard her with questions until her brother was kind enough to take over answering so she could eat the dinner that had gotten cold.

A few years later ...

Lord Ranulf and his wife and daughter had arrived at Ranulf's family home in time to head north for the annual ball hosted by that town's lord and lady – Ander's parents.

"I'm not even officially invited. Why do I have to go?" Thali complained.

"You're going with Rommy," her mother said.

Thali was desperate for any excuse to avoid it. Anders would be there. When they were alone together, he still took to bombarding her with questions. But if there were other children or adults around, he pretended she didn't exist or worse, mocked her for her boys' clothes and common blood. He must be so stuck up now, she couldn't imagine the humiliation he'd make her suffer.

Her family always packed one set of beautiful formalwear in case an occasion called for it, but Thali found lady's dresses constricting and uncomfortable. "Mama, can't you just tell them I'm sick?" She pulled her arms around her stomach, feigning belly pain.

"I know you had your cycle last week, so you can't pull that one on me," Lady Jinhua said. "It's only one night. Besides, it's good practice. This life means you'll have to get along with all kinds of people. Consider it a learning opportunity."

Crab knocked on the door, and Lady Jinhua ushered him in. Despite being a fierce warrior, Crab also had many sisters and was therefore a master with hair. His giant hands, roughened with callouses, were incredibly gentle as he brushed Thali's hair and swept it up to twist it into a knot, as was the fashion.

In too little time, Thali found herself on her brother's arm as he led her down the hall to the festivities.

"You're walking like a duck," Rommy whispered from the side of his mouth.

"I feel like one." Thali tried to smooth her gait in the awkward shoes her mother had made her wear.

"Can't you just put one foot in front of the other?" Rommy said.

"What do you think I'm trying to do? Put both feet next to each other?" Thali hissed back.

Lady Jinhua shot them a sharp look as she turned to glance at them, then at the closed doors of the banquet hall.

A raised eyebrow was all it took to hush both her children.

They were announced and Rommy kept a tight grip on Thali's arm as they walked into the banquet. They were always noticed in any court they walked into, for her mother's darker skin and sleek black hair and her father's pale skin and auburn hair and beard were a stark contrast. Rommy and Thali both had their mother's dark hair and their father's gray eyes. Rommy was the charming one, and Thali was getting used to more and more girls lingering around them, ogling him.

Rommy guided her over to a wall, where Thali planned to hide and lean up against something to help herself balance in her shoes. "See ya later, Rou," he said as he abandoned her and started across the floor to where the other young ladies were, smiling the whole way.

Thali hadn't seen Anders in a few years and wondered if the arrogant teenager was the same as the arrogant boy. The only time they'd ever gotten along was when they were in the library, talking about animals.

Thali gladly melted into the shadows of the ballroom, happily watching fancy men and women whisper and dance. No matter what ball she was at, it was always the same. Men and women exchanged sickening glances; women whispered behind fans, hands, or in quiet corners; and men let their eyes roam up and down ladies as if imagining what might be underneath the stiff, voluminous fabric.

Suddenly, Anders appeared between two people. He was barely recognizable. His arrogance had bloomed him into a full-scale awkward pompous dandy. His blond hair, greasy and half pinned up, twisted in curls to his shoulder. His face had sharpened into features too angular to resemble anything proportional. His nose was still huge, so it was as if all his features pointed toward his nose. His brown eyes were now surrounded by lush, long lashes, and his lips were thin lines. He looked terrible as a teenager. Worse, he was dressed in the finest of gaudy clothes, bringing all the more attention to him.

Thali pressed her lips together to try and not laugh. The laughter died in her throat as she saw the crowd turning their backs to him.

Ladies moved further away, almost disappearing as the crowd parted. Anders started to walk through the lane of turned backs, his head held high. Thali only saw the waver of his mouth as he kept his head up because he made the same face when he was unsure of a piece of knowledge.

Her brother floated over, and Thali gripped his arm. "How do I help him?" Her heart was breaking with how people were treating Anders. He wasn't her favorite person, but he didn't deserve to be ostracized. It was like when she was ostracized, but worse.

Rommy leaned in and whispered in her ear. Thali swallowed and nodded. He nudged her forward, and she repeated the words he'd whispered to her as she approached Anders.

The path was clear, so she met him halfway. She curtsied deeply and with flourish as her brother had instructed and stayed there until Anders took her hand and pulled her to standing.

He bowed to her, his lips a thin line. Anders tucked her hand into his arm just as she was about to topple, and they walked about the room. She smiled and sneakily glanced at him, giggling behind her other hand as her brother had instructed.

"Have you been well?" Anders asked. His voice was tight as he scanned the room. She could tell he was thinking several steps ahead.

"Yes, thank you." Thali continued with her show as they continued to weave throughout the room. Thali's foot slipped and Anders tightened his grip on her arm.

"Thank you for the drawings," Anders said.

"I didn't know if you'd still want them," Thali said.

"Always. Knowledge is power, and you have direct access to interesting knowledge," he whispered in her ear.

"And you, are you well?" Thali asked. It was late for her to ask, but she had to direct her focus.

"Better now," Anders said.

"So what role am I playing right now?" Thali asked. She hadn't fully understood what her brother was doing when he had instructed her. She just wanted to help her friend.

"You mean you didn't orchestrate this yourself?" Anders faked surprise.

Thali used it as an opportunity to look away again and giggle. This was getting old. "I don't think it's fair they treat you poorly. I asked Rommy for help," Thali admitted. She had leaned in to his ear so they looked like they were whispering to each other.

"Thank you, Thali," Anders said. "That was thoughtful of you, but let me explain what's going on. You are an exotic beauty, so people are now seeing that I have connections to beautiful people and things beyond these lands. And you approaching me gave me a lot of credit. Your famously protective brother not stepping in is him giving approval. Both our statuses will rise now."

"I suppose you want me to thank you?" Thali tried not to snort as her mother glanced over.

"It would be a start," Anders said. He stood taller, and despite him being insufferable most of the time, Thali was glad Anders was more himself. Then he added, "You really need to learn how to walk in those shoes. I'm going to have bruises from how hard you're gripping my arm."

"Sorry," Thali mumbled.

"Stop walking on your flat feet. Roll from heel to toe. And kick your leg out in front of you to move your dress when you take a step." Anders leaned in again and whispered near her neck.

Thali couldn't help but giggle when his breath tickled her neck. "I know what you're doing," she whispered back. But taking his advice, she found she had more balance in her shoes and didn't trip over her skirts.

Mock shock filled his face. "What, no thank you again?" He grinned.

"Your mind games are exhausting."

"And you need to be more mindful of yours." Anders said. He smiled brightly then, and Thali tried really hard not to roll her eyes as he turned his body further away so he could be better seen. "Can you dance?" Anders asked, smiling a shining, unfaltering smile.

"Yes," Thali said.

Anders led her to the middle of the ballroom and led her through a dance, staring intently at her. "It can be fun too, you know."

"Oh? What can be fun? Mind games or dancing?"

"Mind games, silly. Just wait. You'll see."

When the dance finished, Anders bowed with a flourish of coattails and kissed Thali's hand before leading her back to the side of the room. As he turned and bowed, a few other ladies started to put themselves in his path.

Thali wondered what game he meant when another young noble appeared in front of her, bowing and introducing himself. Thali was glad she'd been able to help her friend but hadn't thought through what it meant for her. It seemed she was now on the market. At least she would be entertained this evening instead of standing scowling in the corner all night. Rommy tipped his head at her. She was on her own. After a few dances though, she was having more fun than she'd thought she would. She made a mental note to draw Anders a spectacular new animal to send to him as a thank you.

The following year ...

It was the first year Thali was officially going to the ball. She had her own invitation. Her mother had specifically packed this particular dress that she and Thali's friend Mia had made for exactly this occasion. Yet Thali had spent all day dragging her feet as she'd scrubbed herself clean, brushed her hair out, and let her mother paint her face and braid her hair. She was jealous of Rommy, who only had to wash and dress. She wished it was that easy.

"Here." Her father opened a box for her. In it lay a string of beautiful creamy pearls. Her mother clipped it around her neck.

"Don't make that face. It'll freeze that way," her mother said, "Can you pretend to have a good time tonight? Anders will be there. I'm sure you'll get to catch up."

"At least there's that," Thali grumbled.

"And I'll dance with you," Rommy said. He was fully dressed and ready to go.

"Because I don't see enough of you every day," Thali said.

Her mother's eyebrows started to rise, her first warning to be more considerate and thoughtful.

"You'll be the belle of the ball," her father said.

Her mother finally stood after adjusting Thali's dress and took her husband's arm. She too was already dressed and done up for the evening.

Thali navigated her way carefully up the small steps of their ship to the deck, where the crew was lined up waiting for them. They each held a candle and were smiling widely as her parents walked by them. Then they turned to her. Crab had tears in his eyes.

Thali opened her mouth to make a smart comment but tripped as her dress dragged her back. Rommy was there, hooking his arm through hers and keeping her from falling. He kept his hold on her arm as they walked across the deck and down to the dock. Thali smiled all the way but tried not to look any more of their crew in the eye. It was her first big ball; she didn't want to embarrass herself again. She knew she'd be teased about losing her balance for days to come. She could only imagine what Anders would say. He was still the most arrogant person she'd ever met.

They traveled by carriage to the ball, and Thali could only see lights going by as she sat next to Rommy and looked out the window.

"Let me know if you leave early for the ship, understood?" Thali's mother told them.

Rommy and Thali nodded.

When the carriage pulled up to the castle entrance, Thali's father was the first to exit. Then he helped her mother, then Thali. Rommy helped move her dress around so she wouldn't fall on the floor.

Once they were standing in front of the grand staircase, Rommy took her hand in the crook of his arm, and they ascended the steps to the great ballroom. Thali looked up, admiring the stone walls she and Anders had climbed up for fun. The gates were open wide tonight for the ball, and she smiled at the guards that knew her; even the ones Anders considered his own personal guards were working tonight. As they entered the building, her gaze moved to a small hallway as she passed it. She smiled. That was how she and Anders used to sneak into the ball unseen.

"Oh, Jinhua, you look so beautiful!" Anders's mother squealed as she and her husband welcomed Thali's parents.

Thali pasted on her fake smiling face. Her mother and father embraced the lady and lord. Her father nudged her mother out of the way as Thali and Rommy presented themselves, bowing and curtsying in greeting.

"Oh my, Thali, you've grown into a beautiful woman since we saw you last."

Thali smiled. "Thank you for officially inviting me to the ball this year."

Anders's mother An embraced her and whispered, "Isn't it nice to have your own invitation instead of accompanying Rommy or peeking through the crack in the door this time?"

Thali grinned for real this time.

As the lady of the house stepped back, Thali noticed a tall, slim, blond man next to her wearing a navy velvet jacket with gold and silver threads. Panels of dark green along his coat had swirls of gold. He was the definition of a dandy, and even though she recognized the hooked nose, all his grown-up features now somehow enhanced his face in a beautiful way. His shoulders looked a little broader, and she would swear he was taller. He was too beautiful for her, but she was impressed with how Anders had grown up. He was like a tall, slender peacock.

"Thali," he said. He grinned, gently taking her hand and bowing over it to brush his lips over her knuckles.

"Anders," Thali said. She grinned. She was happy to see him but a little shocked at his appearance.

"Mother, would you mind if I take my leave and show Thali around?" Anders asked.

Thali was pleasantly surprised to hear that his voice had gone from squeaky to a lovely melodic baritone. His mother nodded, and Anders took Thali's hand and tucked it into his elbow, pulling her away from Rommy. He walked with her into the crowd of people in the main ballroom.

"You look ridiculous," Thali said under her breath.

"You look quite beautiful," Anders replied.

Somehow it still felt like an insult. "Gold and silver embroidery? It's a little much, isn't it?" Thali asked.

"Maybe. But I'm making a statement."

"What did you think of the last drawings I sent you?" Thali asked. She had sent him drawings of some strange birds she'd seen when she was visiting a tropical island.

"They reminded me a lot of those you sent me from the island to the northeast of where you were then, though I'm not sure I have the right island. You'll have to show me on the map." He was whispering so only she could hear, though he had a smile pasted on his face.

"Why aren't you looking at me when you talk to me?" Thali asked.

"I'm paying you back for the drawings. If I give you my full attention, no one will touch you. But right now, I'm again elevating your status so you have fun tonight," Anders explained.

"What do you mean? We're walking around the room," Thali said. She noticed that everyone turned to stare as they walked through the room. It was a marked difference from the last time.

Anders tipped his head in her direction and raised the eyebrow closest to her so only she could see it.

Thali remained waiting for his reply. He turned his head a little more, still not looking at her, but smiling in her direction. "Do you remember any of the local dances?"

"I think I've watched enough in years past—and practiced them last year when I accompanied Rommy—that I can pick them up again quickly," Thali replied.

"I have no doubt." As the music started, Anders led her to the dance floor, his hands the only guide as they crossed the room, dancing. Even his dancing was better; not only were his steps smooth, but he also added a little flourish here and there that drew people's attention to him. At the end of the song, they were in the middle of the room, where he bent low over her hand and kissed it. Then he led her to the edge of the room. "I'll see you tomorrow morning, library," Anders whispered in her ear before leaving her standing there.

Anders would always puzzle her. Thali never understood his nuances, but she *was* thirsty, so she turned and made her way to the refreshment table. Before she reached the water though, a young man about Rommy's age planted himself in front of her. He had red hair, green eyes, and freckles across his cheeks and nose. He was thicker than Anders but slimmer than Rommy, though maybe about the same height as him.

"Excuse me, I wonder if I might have the honor of a dance?" he asked.

She didn't even know his name but didn't want to be rude, so she smiled and nodded, putting her hand in his outstretched one. She did admire his eyes for the simple fact that she'd never really seen eyes as green as the darkest jade. He was a good dancer, light on his feet and generous in guiding her around the dance floor. He seemed nervous though and didn't speak much during their dancing as concentration filled his face.

"I'm sorry, I'm very new at this," Thali said, hoping to take some pressure off him.

"You're also very beautiful, like the morning dew at the first rays of sunrise," he said in return.

Thali had no idea what that even meant. He wasn't even looking at her but rather out at the crowd as if checking to see that they were watching. Thali felt like she was on the receiving end of a bad market deal. When the music stopped, she excused herself politely and headed for the refreshment table. She hoped having a cup in her hands would prevent anyone else from asking her to dance.

Another young man blocked her path to the refreshments again, but he looked younger than her, and the moldy stench of a child just entering adulthood followed him. Thali swallowed, wondering if she'd have to dance around the room enveloped in that smell. Her mother had always taught her never to be rude because oftentimes they were guests in other lands. Thali swallowed; at least it would be better than cleaning the deck after the crew had been out on the town.

"Please pardon me. I am in need of my sister to settle a debate I am having." Rommy cut in and pulled Thali away before the young man had a chance to answer.

Relief flooded Thali like a tidal wave of cool water.

Rommy led her first to the refreshment table. Thali downed three glasses of light fragrant tea before she finally stood satiated, a fourth in her hand.

"Well, that's ladylike," Rommy said.

Thali rolled her eyes. But she was amazed that no one approached her while Rommy stood next to her. She drank the fourth glass as slowly as possible to annoy her brother before taking a fifth.

Rommy led her away from the refreshment table. "Do you understand what Anders did when he accompanied you around the room?" He leaned closer to her so only she could hear him.

"Yes. We walked around the room. He was annoying and cryptic, as usual," she said.

Rommy looked at her. "How do you understand all the intricacies of a market and yet none of a ballroom?"

Thali had no response, so she just shrugged and looked around.

"It's like ... like you're the highest-priced commodity, say a golden bowl. And Anders has the best stall at the market, the only one where everyone can see him. Him strolling around the room with you is like the vendor standing on their table telling an embellished story about the golden bowl."

"Did you just compare me, your sister, to a bowl?" Thali grinned. The implication made her feel uncomfortable.

"Focus."

"I'm trying," Thali said. "I just don't enjoy being compared to an object."

"Marriage is a transaction. And since you don't see that, I'm trying to make you see it," Rommy said. "But then, you're too annoying to be a bowl. Maybe a fork," he muttered.

Thali's eyes went wide, and she elbowed him.

"Ouch!" he said, though he didn't flinch.

"Well, I'm not going to be choosing a husband tonight," Thali said, a little horrified.

"They don't know that," Rommy said. He looked out at the crowd.

Thali rolled her eyes at him. She wanted to pretend he hadn't told her any of that and knew he was waiting for her to beg him to tell her what to do about it. But she was feeling very annoyed at her brother and how he always seemed to know more than she did.

"This bowl is going to wobble away now," Thali said. She finished her fifth drink and turned around to put the glass down on a table. As soon as she had put it down, she turned around only to see another young man there, blocking her path. She almost wished she had her staff so she could swat him away.

"Excuse me. I wonder if you would do me the honor of this dance?" He was thicker than most of the young men, a thickness she found pleasant. It wasn't from eating too much but from exercise.

"The honor would be mine," she said with a smile. When she placed her hand in his, she was excited to feel the calluses and recognize them as those of a swordsman. "You're a swordsman," she said as he led her to the dance floor.

He stepped lightly, though she saw the sweat beading his brow. He laughed sincerely as he took his place across from her. "I am." He smiled widely and she knew they could be friends.

"Your reputation precedes you, Miss Routhalia."

"Which one?" Thali asked. They started to move along the dance floor, but Thali was more interested in what he had to say next.

"The one of your warrior mother and how she trains her children on a ship's deck as you all travel the world. And the one of how you once took down three men by yourself when you were barely tall enough to see over a counter."

"You're not from around here," Thali said, her eyes narrowed.

"Correct again."

She enjoyed the crinkle of his eyes.

"How did you know though?"

"Anders would never have told anyone good stories about me." Thali didn't point out that he had a way of dropping his "R" sounds that most people here didn't.

He laughed again, and Thali enjoyed how he laughed with his whole body. His movements were crisp and light, though his timing was a little off the music. Thali was happy to be a little off with someone so jovial.

"I apologize for my terrible timing."

"No need," Thali said, "Though timing is as important as anything else as a swordsman."

"True. But we follow the timing of movement, not the timing of music," he replied. "I was speared in the ear when I was a child. My hearing isn't quite what it should be in this ear." He tapped his left ear with his fingertip.

"That's terrible."

"I don't remember much of it, so it's not so terrible for me. It's only that it makes me a terrible dancer." He bowed his head.

"I don't mind at all, for you have many attributes that make up for it."
Thali smiled at him.

He beamed back at her.

Thali realized that she might have just said too much.

"I wonder if it would be too forward ..." he started to say.

Thali's heart leapt into her throat as she started to panic. She didn't
know how to refuse a proposal. She was too young to deal with this.

"... if I could ask you to train with me tomorrow morning?" he finally
finished.

Thali felt heat rise to her cheeks. Relief washed over her like a wave
crashing against a cliff. "I already have plans tomorrow morning, but
perhaps after the noon bell?"

"You would honor me," he said. The music ended and he bowed low
over her hand, brushing his lips just barely over her knuckles. Then he
offered her his arm, and she took it as he walked to the side of the room
with her. "I'll send a blue carriage to the dock tomorrow afternoon to
collect you, if that's convenient?"

Thali nodded.

"I don't want to impose myself on you any longer. Have a wonderful
evening." He bowed again before smiling and walking away.

Thali didn't have to wait long until the next gentleman put himself
in her path. No one else was quite so memorable as the swordsman
though.

One thing Thali did love about visiting Anders was that he was even
more addicted to coffee than she was. And like many of the luxuries he

enjoyed, only the best would do. So she had risen early that morning to train with her mother before making her way to the library, hoping to enjoy a cup of coffee before Anders arrived.

She pushed open the doors and saw the coffee on a table in the middle of the room. She didn't even bother to look around before heading straight to the coffee and pouring herself a cup. Then, sitting in one of the plushy armchairs and tucking her feet under her, she closed her eyes and brought the cup to her lips. She savored the feeling of the hot liquid sliding down her throat, and she melted into the armchair. A prickle at the back of her neck made her eyes fly open the same moment she heard a cough.

Thali looked around the room and saw the same young man she'd offered to meet in the afternoon standing by a shelf with an open book in his hands, smiling. "Sorry!" she said, looking at the coffee on the table, then back at him.

"I dare not come between a coffee lover and their coffee." He grinned, shut his book, and threw his hands up mockingly in defense.

Thali felt her cheeks warm. She should have checked whether the library was empty. "Are you supposed to be here?" This was Anders's library—well, it was the castle's library, but it was one of the only places Anders really cared about. She knew he was protective of it and had never seen another soul in here before.

"Anders told me I was welcome to educate myself as long as I was out before nine in the morning." The bells started to chime, and he tucked the book under his arm and said, "And with that cue, I should get going. I'll see you this afternoon." He bowed his head at her.

She dipped her own head and raised her coffee cup at him. This time, she checked the room twice before melting back into the seat and closing her eyes as she enjoyed the next few sips of coffee. Sadly, she only relished a few sweet sips before she heard Anders coming. Thali could hear him before he even neared the doors. He was slender, but for some reason his footsteps were like her father's: loud and booming.

"Good morning, Anders," she said as he walked through the doors. She leaned over and poured him a cup of coffee, dropping three sugar cubes in and then topping up her own cup. Without looking, she held out his cup and waited for him to take it. He did so gently and sat down adjacent to her, still not speaking. He leaned his head back, eyes closed as she had, as they silently drank their coffee. She snuck a peek at him over her own cup. He had certainly grown handsome. His face had elongated, creating a strong jawline and high cheekbones that took the attention off his giant nose and eyes that were too close together, giving him a brooding intensity.

"You're staring," he said.

Thali felt her cheeks warm, but not as intensely as they had earlier. "You grew up."

"And you find me handsome now?" he asked, half his mouth twisting upward.

Thali shrugged. The last thing Anders needed was another ego boost. "You look grown up."

"Ouch."

Thali grinned. She continued to sip her coffee and waited patiently. This was always how they spent the first half of their morning. Anders filled his cup a second time—no extra sugar cubes this round. He topped Thali's cup up again too. They sat silently in each other's company, sipping their coffee until Anders was done his second cup. Thali closed her eyes, knowing Anders would start their conversation. She was content to sit still and enjoy being surrounded by the smell of coffee and books and paper, the taste of the bitter liquid on her tongue, and the warmth that filled her from the inside.

"You've really started growing into your beauty, you know," Anders finally said.

Thali almost choked on her last sip of the beautiful brown liquid gold.

"If you can stop sipping like an elephant that is," he added.

Thali rolled her eyes. "Elephants are silent. Even though they're large, they have great control over their bodies—and squishy feet that soften their footsteps, not like your stomping."

"Interesting," was all he said. He had ignored the correction but taken instead to the facts. In one swift movement, he was standing and at the other side of the room, fingers dancing along the spines of a row of books. He grabbed one and opened it, his fingers racing through the pages like they were their own entity.

They stopped abruptly, and he grabbed a pen from nearby. Thali was surprised he was so quick to write in a book. "So they walk quietly then?" he asked, looking up at her.

Thali nodded. "Their feet, they're like a cushion. When elephants step down, their feet expand, like dough. And then when they rise, they contract again. They're silent when walking. Running makes the ground tremble some, but it's not loud."

"And with which elephants did you witness this? How many?"

"A herd? In some jungles in Cerisa."

Anders pursed his lips, eyes narrowed as he scrawled the details down. "And their size? Are they truly as large as a house?"

"A house, yes. Your house, no," Thali said. She looked around the library. "Their heads would reach the first break in the shelves in here, where the ladder connects and rolls. But with their trunks, they could reach the top." Thali looked up at the ceiling.

Anders muttered to himself, calculating, she guessed. "And the children. How big are they?"

"About the size of a pony, but wider. Maybe more like the armchair." Thali jutted her chin at the chair Anders had vacated.

"Did you touch one?"

"Their skin feels like leather, but more wrinkled."

"Do they have hair?"

"Very sparse, and it's wiry, like your uncle's dog's hair," Thali said.

Anders nodded, adding more notes to the book. Thali craned her neck and saw that he'd scrawled all over the margins.

"They eat vegetation? Not meat?"

Thali nodded.

"And the great horns that come from their mouth—wait, have you seen their teeth?"

"I didn't get close enough to see teeth. But their horns are more like the giant tusks on a hog than the horn on a rhino or deer."

"Do they grow with the elephant?"

Thali nodded. She thought of the giant male elephant she'd seen at a distance. She'd sensed it was older than its companion, given its two massive tusks. Digging out the notebook she'd brought with her, she flipped through the pages and tore out the one she'd drawn the elephant on. She handed it to Anders.

He took it gently, placing it on the table and tracing the pen strokes with his finger. "Thank you."

"You're welcome." Thali knew gratitude was rare from Anders and appreciated it as much as she did the coffee.

She sat silently, tempted to refill her coffee, but knowing how long it had been since she'd had coffee, she restrained herself. She'd be shaking like a leaf the rest of the day if she had any more. So, she savored every little last sip of what was left in her cup.

"Did you enjoy yourself last night?" Anders asked.

"Yes, as much as I can when I can't breathe and I'm on display like a sculpture."

"You give yourself too much credit," Anders said, choking on a laugh.

Thali grinned, realizing the meaning he saw in her words. "Do you like your new role?"

"I like being able to wear exquisite things," he replied.

She was quiet for a time, then asked, "Where do you get it all?" She thought of the dreariness of his area. There wasn't exactly a large city nearby, filled with seamstress options.

He was quiet as he gently closed the book and took his time putting it back on the shelf. He didn't face her when he spoke next. "I make them myself."

"Oh! You're very talented."

"It's not only difficult to find the right fabrics, but I also can't bear to explain what I want to a seamstress. Though I doubt anyone around here has the same knack for detail that I do."

"You know, I'm a merchant, capable of getting all kinds of fabrics and buttons, feathers, and accoutrements," Thali said casually. She was curious why Anders had never asked.

"I don't have any means of paying you until I become lord. Father doesn't believe in fine clothes. You've seen him wearing the same ones for all the formal events since I was born."

Thali was quiet. She didn't particularly like Anders, but he had been a good friend. He was trustworthy, and despite his vanity, he had always been mostly kind and thoughtful. "It's only fabric for a single person. How about I start a tab for you? Pay me when you can."

Anders turned and looked at her, searching her face. "You'd do that for me?"

Thali only nodded.

"How does a merchant make money being so generous?" Anders asked.

Thali wasn't sure if that was meant to be answered, so she just waited to see if he did indeed want a response. When he said nothing, she asked, "Tomorrow morning, meet me here in the library? I'll show you a few fabrics you can pick from."

"Really? You have some with you?"

"For a single person's needs, yes. There isn't much selection, but we always have something."

"Thank you. I'm going to go see what I need then," Anders said. He started toward the door, then stopped before pushing the doors open. "The lord you danced with last night, do you know who he is?" he asked as he turned back around.

"The one who's allowed in here before nine? No. I don't actually think he introduced himself," Thali said. She was surprised to realize that.

"His name is Phoen. He's the second son of Lord Restoffor. The family is famed for their fighting skills here. Most of them are brutes, bashing each other with swords and battle-axes. Be careful with Phoen. He's always been quiet. I think he's intelligent, but I wouldn't put it past him to trick you into marriage. Second sons are always ambitious," Anders said.

"Thank you, Anders. I'll see you tomorrow morning," Thali said.

Anders nodded and turned back to the door. Again, before he pushed it open, he paused. "Should you need to use my name, I give you permission to do so."

Thali's jaw dropped a little. She was surprised he was associating with her publicly. But if she correctly understood what he meant, he was offering his name to anything she might need to state, including marriage, should she need it.

"Thank you, Anders, thank you very much." It wasn't lost on her that she was thanking him more than he was her, but still, she had never thought to see this much generosity from him.

The bells started to chime, and Thali realized she had to run to get back to her ship in time to meet the blue carriage. When she'd mentioned it to Rommy and her mother, Rommy had suggested he go with her and she'd been annoyed, but now, after talking with Anders, she hoped he was still available and willing. She dashed out of the library and met Rommy on the dock, talking with the driver of the blue carriage. Rommy held her staff, a bag over his shoulder that she guessed was filled with the weapons they were required to strap on when off the ship.

"After you, sister," Rommy said.

She smiled with relief and climbed into the closed carriage.

He climbed in after her and dropped the bag at her feet. "I'm pretty sure the library isn't on the ship."

"It's just Anders. I had a couple strapped on," she replied.

He opened the bag's top flap, pulling out and strapping on the other daggers and knives. "Change of heart about me coming along?"

"Anders warned me that Phoen's family has a reputation as warriors, but the bashing kind. Also that Phoen is intelligent, but possibly ambitious," Thali said. There were no secrets between her brother and her.

"I found the same in my own research," Rommy said. "Lord Restoffor's anger is well-known throughout town. He has a short temper and often acts first, only asking questions after."

"What did you tell Mother and Father?" Thali asked. She knew her mother wouldn't have let them go if they had known.

"Nothing about my research, only that we're going to train some local lords."

Thali nodded, satisfied.

The carriage had been bumbling along for some time when Thali took her staff and opened the curtain to look outside. They were on the edge of town and pulling around a row of low houses. The manor that appeared before them was almost as grand as Anders's castle but not quite, as if on purpose.

Instead of a courtyard filled with flowerbeds and gardens, there was a large open space of packed dirt. Weapons on a rack leaning against the wall by the front door told Thali that this was their training ring. It was the first time she'd seen a training ring in the front of any home. Twelve boys were whacking each other with wooden swords; the youngest, Thali noticed, was about six. The oldest was probably about Rommy's age. When the carriage came to a stop, the boys stopped and lined up in front of the house.

Phoen approached the carriage, but Rommy opened the door and stepped out before Phoen could reach for the handle He looked surprised when Rommy came out and held the door open for his sister. Thali leapt out, unafraid of a few steps and not wanting assistance. She knew everything Rommy did in public was on purpose, though she didn't always follow why or what it meant. She'd have to ask him later why he'd held the door open.

Phoen took Thali's hand and bowed low over it. "Thank you for coming to visit us." He looked over at Rommy, so Thali said, "This is my brother. I figured two of us would be even better than one." She smiled.

She saw Phoen force a smile as he greeted Rommy and welcomed them both. "How very lucky for us that you've both come," Phoen said. Then he introduced each of his brothers. "I'm in charge of their training, so when I heard that the famed merchant family had arrived, I hoped you would challenge our skills."

Thali nodded. Anders's words of warning were stuck in her head, and she wasn't sure how she should feel.

Phoen stood next to his brothers and turned to face her and Rommy. He put his hands behind his back and waited.

"May I ask how you normally train?" Rommy asked.

Thali felt relief as her brother took over. She was never good at teaching.

"Of course. We normally meet out here every morning and afternoon and split up into our pairs, then attempt to land a hit," Phoen explained. He shooed his brothers off to grab weapons, and they paired off and started attempting to whack each other. Some were quick on their feet; others were just hitting and blocking.

"Do you ever change partners?" Thali asked.

"No. I don't want the little ones getting hurt," Phoen said.

"The older ones should pull back on their strength when paired with the little ones. That's a lesson in and of itself," Rommy said.

Phoen nodded. He went around to the pairs and switched them up, instructing the older ones to take it easy on the smaller ones.

"I'm not sure what you'd like us to help you with. Our training styles are very different, though I imagine changing partners will greatly benefit each individual," Rommy continued.

Phoen looked thoughtful. He had placed himself so his good ear was toward Rommy and Thali as they watched the pairs whacking each other with wooden weapons. "How do you train?" he asked.

"We have patterns, or specific series of movements that all must learn. We practice them as a group or individually and then we pair up and practice against each other."

"How do you choose the pairs?"

"We change them each time," Rommy said. Thali opened her mouth, but Rommy continued. "Except for Thali here. She's been training specifically under our mother."

"Why is that?"

"Our mother wanted to be the only one to oversee her training. Thali spars with our second-best warrior from time to time though, and me," Rommy said.

"Would you walk with me and adjust my brothers' stances as you see fit?" Phoen asked. He gestured to his brothers, who were still essentially beating each other with sticks.

"Sure," Thali said. She hurried to the closest pair and Phoen stepped up next to her. Her brother stood on her other side. "Your stance is good," Thali began. "See how he can't knock you over even though he's bigger than you?"

The smaller brother, possibly the youngest, nodded.

Thali continued. "But you need to remember your elbows. Keep them up. You move only your forearms, but you lose the power of the rest of your body weight when you leave your elbows behind."

The little boy lifted his elbows and was able to twist his sword around and land a hit on his older brother. Rommy didn't offer anything to the older, much more brutish looking brother. But the older brother continued to stare at Rommy, so he finally said, "Hold your sword a little lower on the hilt. You'll get more momentum and won't have to work as hard for your hits."

They moved quickly to the next pair, and Thali was acutely aware that Phoen moved as smoothly with her as he did when they were dancing.

"You need to look up," Rommy said, ignoring Thali and Phoen as he addressed another small brother. "Not at his face though, his shoulders and hips. They'll give away his next move. You can move faster than he can, so you can duck and dodge out of the way. But if you're facing someone smaller or the same size as you, their eyes may give away their next move."

The little boy nodded, and the older, bigger brother looked at Thali.

"Be quicker with your feet?" Thali said. She wasn't sure what to tell him. She had only seen him spar briefly and didn't really want to offer advice to someone who clearly didn't want it.

They continued down the line; Phoen had thirteen siblings, and there were six pairs here. Rommy and Thali moved from one to the other, fixing postures, changing feet angles and stances, and adjusting grips.

"You have an older brother?" Rommy asked Phoen.

"He said he'd meet us here when he was available. He helps my father with the estate," Phoen replied. "Ah. There he is. Perfect timing."

Thali turned to see a young man as wide as the rest of his brothers, but taller and more refined than even Phoen.

"Miss Routhalia. Master Romulus. Thank you for coming to assist my brute brothers. They're grateful even if they choose not to show it."

Thali and Rommy nodded and smiled.

"You haven't introduced yourself yet, brother," Phoen said.

Thali glanced back at Phoen and saw the feathering of his jaw as he clenched his teeth.

"My apologies. You'll have to forgive my family for our lack of manners. I am Volucris."

"It's a pleasure to meet you," Rommy said after dipping his head.

Thali dipped into a curtsy as was the custom, though Phoen cut in before anything else could be said. "Vol, would you like to train today? Or are you just stopping in to greet our guests?"

"I would not miss the opportunity to better my skills amongst the talented," he replied. "Miss Routhalia, would you do me the honor?"

Rommy grinned. "Just so you know, she has a temper." He moved aside with Phoen, and Thali wanted to go with them. Rommy looked like he was up to something, and Thali wasn't sure she wanted to leave Phoen alone with him.

"Would you prefer to use your staff?" Volucris asked.

Thali turned her attention back to him. Of all the brothers, he looked the most refined, but she had long ago stopped judging people by their appearances.

She pulled her staff out and watched as Volucris removed his fancy jacket and took a staff from the rack of weapons. She noticed it had a blade on the end.

"There aren't any without, unfortunately," he explained. "Don't worry though, I won't hurt you." The way he'd said it made her skin crawl, so she smiled and nodded. She could tell Volucris was not as kind or gentle as he seemed to be.

They stalked each other, and Thali noticed some of the other brothers pause their training to turn and watch. She also saw Rommy and Phoen in her peripheral vision. They were facing each other and circling too, and she lost sight of them as she circled Volucris. Then she heard the familiar *clack clack clack* of two staffs in an unfamiliar rhythm.

Thali saw the shift in Volucris's movement and reacted without thinking. His staff—blade out—swung down toward her. She leapt out of the way of the slicing blade and stepped on it, swinging her own staff upward. He jerked back and pulled his end of the staff upward; the blade snapped off.

"Now you have a staff without a blade," Thali said.

"How thoughtful of you," Volucris said.

Thali shut her mouth. She shouldn't have goaded him.

He swung his staff upward, the shard of the blade probably sharper than the blade itself had been. But at least it wasn't an extra six inches long.

Volucris moved smoothly but suddenly. Lucky for Thali, his body announced his movements well before his weapon ever started to move. She danced out of the way and struck hard with the butt of her staff in the places that mattered. He would be bruised and hopefully think twice before beating on someone half his size.

"You're so quiet," Volucris said as he swung at her.

Thali saw it coming and ducked under the swing, thrusting her staff into his diaphragm. She saw the quick exhale it caused and leapt back, out of the way of his staff. She stayed focused on him, and he stopped talking. He started trying to feign one way before striking the other, but he was sloppy. His footwork an afterthought. It took little effort to make him stumble. She tested his stumbling movements to see where he was weakest.

It seemed he thought he had the advantage, making her dance around, because he started to grin. It was an ugly grin, the kind that announced him as the wolf he was, and he was arrogant enough to stick his tongue out between his teeth as he smirked. Thali widened her gaze to watch his entire body. His arm movements were getting sloppy, but she recognized it wasn't from fatigue. He was holding back as if waiting for the opportunity to really slash at her.

"Brother."

Thali heard Phoen's voice nearby. She wondered how he and Rommy had faired.

"Miss Thali has been gracious enough to fight me, so let us be," Volucris said.

Thali watched and parried what he threw at her, waiting for her opportunity to finish what she'd started. His breathing was shallower now thanks to her blow to his diaphragm.

She knew that his thigh, bicep, and ankle should be throbbing given the hits she'd landed. Now she waited for him to make his big move. She could tell he was gathering energy and winding tight, getting ready to spring.

Thali swallowed. She felt the adrenaline pumping through her body; she loved this feeling of absolute alertness, the quiet feeling of knowing every muscle in her body and being ready for any twitch in her opponent's body.

Then she thought to lay a trap, so with her next step, she skipped on one foot, as if she'd tripped over her own leg. Volucris sprang, but she was waiting for him. He was quicker than she'd thought he would be and thrust his broken blade toward her belly. Thali had only hopped, not stumbled though, so she smoothly stepped out of the way, grabbing his staff with one hand while thrusting with her own, increasing the force with which the staff would hit Volucris in the chest. She aimed slightly to the side to crack a rib. His face contorted with surprise when he missed, and he could not stop his momentum as he ran into her staff. If she'd intended a killing blow, she would have positioned the staff on the ground so he risked running himself through. But she held it and let it bounce back after striking him. Volucris went down—clutching his side, face first in the dirt.

Thali kicked his staff away and saw Phoen pick it up. She went to offer Volucris a hand up, but he only looked at her angrily.

He stumbled to his feet, his face as red as a tomato. "You are a vile girl who will never find herself a husband. Who could love a warrior?" He stumbled back into the manor house.

"I apologize for my brother," Phoen said. He stood right next to her. "He's always been a terrible loser."

Thali nodded, smiling. She'd been even more energized than she had intended. "It's nothing." she said. "I only hope he learned something."

"If he did not, we certainly did," Phoen replied. He opened his arms, and the brothers surrounding them clapped and nodded.

"I think it's time we returned to our ship," Rommy said.

"Of course. Though I hate for you to leave with such a bad impression of us. You sail in two days?"

Rommy nodded.

"Please allow me to bring you a gift tomorrow."

"That's not necessary," Thali said. She wasn't sure she wanted anything they might offer.

Phoen nodded. He stood aside as the carriage pulled up and Thali and Rommy stepped inside.

After they had bid Phoen goodbye and the carriage had pulled out of the drive, Rommy said, "You did well."

"When did you know?" Thali asked.

"That Volucris is a miscreant? Or that Phoen intends to ask you to marry him?"

"Rommy!" Thali said. "I'm only fourteen!"

"That's marriageable age in many places." Rommy grinned.

Thali's cheeks felt hot, but she blamed it on the physical exertion.

"I'd heard rumors. But when he came out and didn't even greet his own brothers, I knew."

Thali nodded. "How did your bout with Phoen go?"

"It went well. He was polite, asking for advice on how to do this or that," Rommy said.

"I'd rather have had that."

"If you'd partnered with Phoen, you would've had to back out of a marriage proposal."

"So you left me to fight off a brute instead?"

"Its not the first time, and it won't be the last," Rommy said. "Like it or not, you're a target because you're small and female, because of our mother, and because of how different you look from everyone else."

"What do you mean, 'because of how different I look'?"

"You're half our mother and half our father. We—" He pointed to himself, then her. "—don't look like anyone in any kingdom or country."

"So what? You think people will pick fights just because of our skin and hair color?" Thali asked, bewildered. She had always known she looked different from everyone else in Densria because of her mother, but she'd never really given it that much thought.

"Yes," Rommy said as a blush spread across his cheeks.

"So you've had to fight people because you looked different," Thali said.

"Yes," Rommy said again. "I won. Easily. But they picked a fight with me because I look different, because *we* are different."

"How do you know it was because of that and not something else?"

"Because they called me a mongrel first."

Thali was stunned. She sat back for a moment as the carriage rolled on. "I'm sorry, Rommy."

"There's nothing to be sorry about. It wasn't your fault. I'm just telling you because I think women can be worse than men."

"What do you mean?" Thali said. Her heart had just plunged into her stomach.

"Men tend to beat each other physically. Women are much more subtle. They wound with words, with rumors and politics. Our parents have done a disservice to you by not having you grow up and make friends at court. If you ever do go to court, they'll shred you to pieces because you're new and strange."

"I won't go to court. Why would I? I want to be a merchant like Father and Mother."

Rommy shrugged. He was clearly done talking. He sat back in his seat and left Thali to her thoughts, to wander through the possibilities of how she might end up in a court full of nobles instead of at sea and city markets. The whole scenario sounded inconceivable, but the thought left her feeling uneasy, so when they arrived back at their ship, Thali went to grab a book, then climbed into the netting of the ship's mast so she didn't have to talk to anyone as she distracted herself. She saw Rommy do the same, settling himself in another netting.

Thali had been so unsettled, she hadn't even bothered to unstrap her many weapons, and she regretted it as she continued reading; some of the weapons were digging into her legs and sides.

The next morning, she went to the library on time instead of early like she had the day before. She didn't really want to run the risk of running into Phoen. She found Anders there waiting for her already.

"I hear you beat Volucris to a pulp," he said.

"He was asking for it," Thali replied.

"Well, as someone who has suffered at Volucris's hands, I thank you."

Thali raised her eyebrows, but when Anders didn't say anything else, she didn't ask.

"How was the rest of the family?" Anders asked.

"Fine."

"Did you use my name for anything?"

"No. I handled myself," Thali said.

"Good."

They wandered through the library books again. Anders gave Thali a list of questions about different animals he'd made while she was away, and she answered them all—for the low, low price of a cup of coffee. She felt relaxed and at ease by the time she left Anders to return to her ship. She had some chores she had to get to because they were leaving the next day.

"Miss Thali." A voice interrupted her as she was about to leave the main hall.

Thali turned and saw Phoen standing in the shadows.

He approached her, and she felt her heart rate jump. "I'm sorry if I startled you. Would you walk with me in the gardens?" Phoen asked.

Thali agreed only because the gardens were a public place and Anders was still in the library that overlooked the gardens. "Of course."

He offered his arm and Thali took it out of politeness. She didn't really know why she was so nervous. She tried to remind herself that she had really liked Phoen the other night when they had danced together.

"I'm very sorry about my brothers. They're all brutes, but I was hoping Vol would be too busy to come out. The younger ones all appreciated the lesson. But Vol is just ...the worse of us."

"It's not the first time, and it probably won't be the last time, I've encountered someone like him," Thali said.

"Then I'm sorry that brutes exist around the world," he said.

Thali noticed the flowers starting to bloom on the low hedges. There were a few people in the gardens, bent over and smelling the flowers, but Thali and Phoen were too far away to be overheard. Still, it comforted her some to be in public.

"I ... I have something to confess," Phoen said.

Thali swallowed hard. She tried to focus on how she would turn down a proposal.

"I was planning to ask for your hand in marriage."

Thali opened her mouth, but then closed it, realizing he had used the past tense. She waited for him to continue.

"I thought a marriage to someone from a family as famed as yours would help my family."

Thali narrowed her eyes, trying to figure out where this was going.

"But I think I'd much rather be your friend."

They continued to walk. Thali finally asked, "Not that I'm not grateful, but can I ask why you decided not to ask for my hand?" She had felt relief at first, but now she wondered if there was something wrong with her.

"At first, I told myself it was because you were still young. But seeing you with your brother, the way you fight, I think it would be cruel to shackle you to one place—even if you had thirteen brothers to beat to a pulp." Phoen grinned, as did Thali, at the thought. "I don't think you could be happy here, staying in one place with warriors who aren't even your equal to spar with."

"Thank you for thinking about it so thoroughly," Thali said.

"You would have said no?" he asked.

"I would have done so in the gentlest way."

They walked along for some time. Thali was more comfortable than she would have thought now as they looked around them.

"Will you marry Anders?" Phoen asked.

Thali choked on air. "No."

"You seem surprised."

"I am. Anders barely likes me."

"I've known Anders my whole life. He has never been as friendly with anyone else."

"We share a common interest. But no. I do not plan to marry and stay in one location."

"You haven't given it much thought, have you?" Phoen asked.

Thali giggled then. "Is it that obvious?"

"Yes. You're beautiful, and even though you're only fourteen, I imagine many suitors will be lining up for your attention."

Thali giggled some more. The thought made her stomach flip and gave her an icky feeling.

"You may not believe me, but think of how little time you've spent among people your own age, or of marriageable age. You spend your time with old sailors and your brother mostly?"

Thali nodded; she loved her family.

"Well, if you're ever looking, know that I asked you first," Phoen said.

Thali smiled. "I do hope you find happiness."

"That is all anyone can ever hope for."

He walked with her back to the ship, and she curtsied and thanked him. She boarded her ship, turning away from Phoen.

"Did he propose?" Rommy asked as she boarded.

"No. He admitted to thinking about it though."

"What changed his mind?"

"I'm not sure. Something about my happiness."

"That was thoughtful of him."

"I thought so too."

"Well I'm ready to head to the next market. You?"

"Definitely." She followed her brother to their family's quarters.

"Anders had this dropped off this morning," Rommy said, pointing to a package on the table.

Thali looked. It was wrapped in oilcloth. She grabbed the edge of it and two objects clattered to the desk. She scrunched the oilcloth in her hand and discovered the two objects were daggers. "These are nice," Thali said as she picked one up and examined it.

"One for you and one for me," Rommy said. He reached over her shoulder and plucked one from the desk.

"Hey, what if they were supposed to be a matching pair?" Thali and looked carefully at the details of the dagger in her hand. A small blue jewel was set in the pommel, and the handle was made of twisted, welded, wire. A small crow was etched into the base of the blade and only visible at certain angles. It was sharp and Thali smiled. She liked this one.

"Then I guess you and I are matching pairs." Rommy said. He grinned and danced away with his new dagger.

Thali rolled her eyes.

The next day ...

Thali started her day in the library as she always did. It was her last day with Anders, and the plan was to catalog as many of the different animals and plants in various regions as they could.

She walked into the same chaos she'd left yesterday. Anders was already there. He'd pushed four large tables together and spread out stacks of books; parchment pieces were strewn all over open books, the table itself, and tucked inside closed books.

Anders pointed to the coffee as Thali walked in, and she rolled her eyes as she went to pour them both a cup.

She bit her tongue though. If she said something snarky to him now, she knew she'd be in for a whole morning of grumpy Anders. Thali sat down next to him and placed his cup in front of him. He was studying a map and had three bird drawings in front of him.

"Here," he said as he plunked a box on the table.

It was a tiny box. Thali wasn't sure what it was, so she took it and opened it. She gasped.

Inside was a tiny silver ring. It was beautiful. It looked like leaves intertwining to support a sort of spikey ball at the top. Maybe it was a thistle? Thali swallowed, trying to remember if a ring was supposed to represent marriage in this kingdom.

"It's not marriage, unless you need it to be," Anders said. He still hadn't looked up from the birds and the map.

"What does that mean?" Thali asked. She knew Anders well enough that she felt comfortable being blunt.

"Mother thought it would be a nice gesture for me to give you a thank-you gift. Girls like jewelry, therefore, a ring. Thank you." He looked up briefly, but he was starting to sound annoyed.

"And what do you mean 'if I need it to be'?"

Anders sighed, closing his eyes. Thali was definitely in for grumpy Anders today.

He sat back, weaving his fingers together and placing them on his stomach.

"I'm grateful to you, for this, for all of this," Anders said as he waved his hand over the table, then waved his hand around the rest of the library.

"And ..." Thali said. She was still confused. She knew she'd never be as intelligent as Anders, so she didn't mind asking stupid questions.

"If you need a man to marry for officialness, then this can be a marriage proposal. If you need to pretend I'm your husband, this could be a wedding ring. Now, or later, or whatever."

"And how will your future wife feel about that?"

"I don't plan to marry."

"Don't you need to continue the family line?" Thali asked.

Anders shrugged. "Why?"

"You're telling me your family is *not* expecting you to marry?"

"When my father dies, I'll be lord. Who's going to make me marry?"

Thali blinked. "What if, say, you do find a wife and want to marry?"

Anders took a deep breath and heaved a long sigh as if he was speaking to someone truly unintelligent. "Then it shows you are a friend of this kingdom. And I will let you know. But should you call on our aid, we will come. I will come."

"I don't know why I would need your aid," Thali said.

"Take it or leave it. It's there. I don't care anymore."

Thali was silent. She didn't have words to express her gratitude to him, not that she could ever imagine a situation where she would need to call upon an entire population for aid. "Thank you," she said more quietly than usual because she was worried she would cry and nothing made Anders more uncomfortable than crying. She rolled the ring between her thumb and index fingers, making the little thistle catch the light as she composed herself.

Anders mumbled something and waved at her. He went back to looking at the birds. "Which one did you say came from where again?" he asked as he pointed to a page full of birds with tiny, hooked beaks.

They turned to the work in front of them. Thali slid the ring on her pinky finger.

TEACUPS AND TALES

ELRIC COUGHED AND THALI blinked, coming back to the present moment. She gently placed the ring back in its spot in her armoire. Her relationship with Anders had evolved since then. He was still smarter than she was ever going to be, but she was glad for it. He always answered her questions no matter how stupid they might seem. She made a mental note to check for Anders's next letter tomorrow. It should be here any day now.

A knock on their door brought Thali back yet again.

"Come in," she said automatically, and Tilton coughed as he entered the room. He always stared at the floor when he first walked into their bedroom, no matter that she'd invited him.

"I've got your list of meetings for tomorrow, and I thought you two might like some tea," Tilton said. He shuffled in with a tray on a little cart behind him.

"Do they want snacks?" Daylor's voice floated in from the other room.

Tilton closed his eyes briefly. "Sorry, he hasn't seen you in a few days and he misses you."

"Come in, Daylor," Thali said.

Daylor appeared with two trays: cookies and pastries on one and savory items on the other. "What are you two up to?" he asked as Tilton set up the tea service on a small table and Thali slid closer to the bed.

"Thali here has been regaling me with stories from her past," Elric said as he took the offered cup from Tilton.

"Do you want to use this one or that one?" Tilton asked as he pointed to a chipped teacup with tulips inside the armoire.

Thali smiled. "The one in your hand is fine."

Tilton turned away, and Daylor made himself comfortable. He dragged a chair closer to the table where he'd placed the trays, then slouched low in it.

Tilton shot him a look, and Daylor blinked, his mouth stuffed with a scone as he glanced at Elric. He slowly sat up. He'd always been fully himself with Thali and Tilton, but not Elric.

Elric waved it off. "It's fine. Don't be uncomfortable on my behalf."

Ana slowly crawled over the bed to Daylor. She hung suspended, back paws on the bed, front paws on the arm of Daylor's chair, as she reached out and licked Daylor's crumb-covered chin.

"Come on up, sweet girl." Daylor patted his chest as he lay across the chair. In a single motion, Ana was sitting on his chest, hunched over and licking the crumbs from his cheeks.

"Is that cup from one of your friends?" Tilton asked, tilting his head at the tulip teacup. He held out a normal palace cup filled with tea.

"It is," Thali said. She rubbed her thumb on the delicate tulips painted on the outside, the gold rim interrupted by the chip it already had when she had received it. She placed it on the top of the armoire and thanked Tilton for the hot cup of tea. She glanced at a chair, and he raised his eyebrows in a silent question. Thali nodded.

TULLIKA

T HALI SAT ON A barrel, trying to catch jumping dolphins with her toes. She was at the ship's bow, two rice sacks folded under her bum and her heels on the railing's edge. She'd pulled her boots and socks off and spread her toes wide as the wind passed through them like tiny sails. The dolphins were plentiful here. They had swum along Thali's parents' ship the entire last hour of their journey into port, and Thali's mouth had dropped when they had arrived.

Their ship had sailed right up to a dock that doubled as a street. Closer to the water than she'd ever seen anywhere before, rows and rows of buildings lined the edge of the water. They were so close to the market here, Mouse could point out the edge of tables through a narrow gap between two buildings that Thali wasn't sure she would have seen if he hadn't shown her. Instead of unloading and guarding all their merchandise at the market tonight, they would unload their goods onto the street in front of the ship tomorrow morning. This was the first time she had been allowed abovedeck as they neared this port, and she was loving every sight.

"The whole street turns into a market," Mouse said. "That's the edge there, but tomorrow, it'll be a market as far as you can see both ways."

Thali didn't say anything. She was too surprised. Rommy looked around, as if he could already see it.

"Why are the buildings so close to shore?" Thali said.

"Lots of people live here, and most work with the market in some way," Mouse said. "Each building has two, maybe four families. You'll see all kinds of folk at the market. Well, this part is where the fancier folk live, but you'll still glimpse all walks tomorrow."

Since they didn't have to haul the goods now, they had a rare afternoon off. They had already waterproofed all wooden surfaces and prepped all the goods to go out tomorrow morning. So now Thali had time to lean back and stare at her toes, tipping them to the left as if to touch the buildings that went down the shoreline before disappearing into the ocean.

A mop of blond hair caught Thali's eye between her feet as a tall girl came around the corner. Her hair was the color of gold, the sun reflecting off it like a competing sun.

Thali watched the girl as she skipped down the street. She had a crown of flowers in her hair, and she daintily avoided bumping into people like a dolphin darting through the water. The girl skipped halfway down the road before slowing, then looking around. When she caught Thali staring, instead of scowling like most would, she smiled brightly and waved. Thali looked behind her and didn't see anyone, so she waved back. She was surprised at how friendly this girl was. The golden-haired girl turned back toward the road and continued to skip away until she was out of Thali's sight.

Thali went back to watching the dolphins farther out in the bay as they swam and jumped and played with each other. It was a quiet, peaceful port.

"Thali!" her father yelled.

Thali startled and leapt up to see what he wanted, hoping it wasn't more chores. She clambered down to where the gangplank connected the ship to the dock.

"A letter just came from the duke. His daughter has invited you to tea this afternoon," her father said, holding a thick, cream-colored letter.

"Who?" Thali asked.

"The duke's daughter. You've met the duke once, though I think his daughter was away then." Her father scratched his beard.

"Do I have to go?"

"Do you have anything else to do?"

"No, but ..." Thali wiggled her bare toes. She'd have to put shoes on.

"You wanted to start meeting our acquaintances, and you should start making your own too." Lord Ranulf nodded like it was final.

Thali considered fighting him on it, but he would no doubt find some chores for her to do if she refused. "When?"

"In about an hour. You'd better hurry and change into something appropriate," he said.

"How will I get there?"

"She's sending a carriage."

Thali turned around, ready to head back down to her family's quarters to change. She rolled her eyes, wishing she could at least walk there. She found her mother in their quarters, parchments spread out everywhere as she responded to some of the letters that had been waiting for them when they had arrived that morning.

"Did I hear your father correctly? You're going to tea with the duke's daughter?" her mother asked when Thali walked in.

Thali nodded. Her mother continued. "You should wear that light-blue dress we brought, with the slippers. I'll do your hair when you've changed. If I remember correctly," which her mother always did, "Tullika is quite lovely, if a little older than you. And she's kind and thoughtful from what I could tell."

Thali ducked into the more private area to change into the blue dress her mother had suggested. "I've never met her, so why would she invite me?" Thali asked through the sliding paper wall.

"She's probably just inviting you at the request of her parents."

Thali hoped Tullika was at least an interesting person, not too boring like most nobles.

"Are you sure you've never met her?" her mother asked.

Thali heard only silence outside; evidently her mother had paused her correspondence. "Yes. I'm quite sure I've never met anyone named Tullika," Thali said. She was getting impatient as she hopped up and down, coaxing the dress up her body. She came out of the tiny space and let her mother tie the back up, then sat on a barrel so her mother could style her hair.

Thali stepped out of the carriage in front of a little row of shops. She looked left and right and didn't see a place to eat or an inn anywhere. She checked the card that had been in the letter for her father. It asked her to meet for afternoon tea at the pudding shop. Thali looked around again and saw some brightly colored cakes and breads in a window one door away. She guessed that was the pudding shop and pushed the door open. The smell that greeted her made her mouth water and stopped her in her tracks as she took in another long breath.

"You'll be wanting to head up the stairs, miss," an older woman told her. She pointed to the stairs on the right that seemed to leave the shop. "All the way to the top."

Thali thanked her and started ascending. *People must live in the rooms above the pudding shop*, Thali thought as she looked around. She heard children playing behind one door, a consistent banging as a spoon stirred something in a pot from behind another, and quiet coughing behind yet another door. Wondering how she would know which door to knock on, she paused when she saw light hit the staircase in front of her and remembered the lady's direction: "All the way to the top," she'd said. Thali quickened her pace around the corner. The sunlight hit her face and she stopped with her foot on the first step, breathing in and closing her eyes. She smiled. If Tullika was meeting her on the roof, she already liked her. Roofs reminded Thali of her ship's deck and the freedom of the ocean.

She ran up the last few steps and saw a quaint little table on the wooden roof and the girl with golden hair she'd seen earlier that day.

"Ah! You found me!" the girl said, and she stood up and ran over to Thali.

She was surprised by the hug, especially considering the other girl had to bend over to put her arms around her.

"I'm sorry if that was too forward. My parents always tell me that not everyone likes to be greeted so warmly, but since I saw you this afternoon, I knew we'd be good friends."

"I'm honored, Lady Tullika."

The other girl laughed. "Oh please, Tullika is plenty. Tulli is even better. Too many syllables." She looked up at the sky. Thali turned to look and saw a seagull making a wide turn back to the marina, probably for the fish guts most fishermen tossed.

"Please, come sit with me," Tulli said. She took Thali's hands and led her to a seat before taking her own seat across from Thali. She used a tiny spatula to place a little cream cake with red jelly on a small plate, then a puffy pastry with icing sugar on it, and finally, the tiniest chocolate cake Thali had ever seen. Tulli gently handed Thali the plate with both hands. "I hope you'll like them. These are my favorites." Her eyes glistened as she smiled, and Thali wondered how a person could be so sparkly. Tulli reminded her very much of a gem twinkling in the sunlight.

"Doesn't tea usually start with milder pastries, then sandwiches, then dessert?" Thali asked.

"Oh yes. But I like to eat dessert first. Don't worry though. I've saved a couple more of my favorites for our real dessert. Now we'll get to have dessert twice!" She squealed the last word, and Thali couldn't help but smile.

Thali finally spotted Tulli's help; there was a man and an older woman standing beside one of the chimney stacks with several baskets of what Thali could only imagine was food. The older woman came over with a teapot and served tea after Tulli had already devoured two pastries. Thali was surprised to see a tiny chip in her cup, just along the farthest edge. She glanced at Tulli's cup and there was another chip, a bigger one.

"My mother gave me this tea set right after I got Jo. Jo and I used to pretend to have tea together. I mean, he doesn't really drink tea, but no one would have tea with me, so it was just us."

Thali nodded, assuming Jo was a stuffed animal or doll. Thali waited for Tulli to bite into another pastry before biting into her own. She started with the same one Tulli had: the pastry with icing sugar on it. She was pleasantly surprised to feel her mouth fill with a sweet cream. Tulli's eyes opened wide as if she was tasting it for the first time like Thali was.

The older woman cleared her throat quietly and looked at Tulli as if reminding her of her manners, and Thali wondered if this old woman was Tulli's nursemaid. She was a little old to have a nursemaid, but it was possible that Thali had miscalculated her age. The woman's look was the same look Thali's own mother used to chastise her.

"Thank you for inviting me to tea, Tulli," Thali said.

"You looked so relaxed, but also kind of bored, when I saw you today. I asked Father about you, and he said you'd be too busy tomorrow for tea, so if I wanted to ask, I'd better get on it quickly."

"Thank your father too. It's very kind of your family to welcome us to your city."

"Oh, Father adores when merchants arrive. He can't wait to see and hear about the newest things from other places. And Mother is always so happy when she can purchase a few new exotic things. I was just curious about you since I saw you earlier today. It must be so exciting to meet so many people all the time, to be on a ship with so many dashing gentlemen." Tulli's eyes sparkled again as she stared into the sky.

Thali was proud of herself for not choking on her pastry when Tulli described her version of Thali's life. She took a moment to swallow her second bite of the cream-filled pastry and thanked the woman who filled her cup with tea before she spoke. "Most of the men on our ship are my parents' age. They're like uncles really." Tulli looked like she was patiently waiting to hear more, so Thali continued. "And I've only just started being allowed to meet people. My family thought I was too young and it was too dangerous before, so I spent much of my childhood hiding on the ship."

"Still, you must see very different landscapes? Not just the same one all the time? No matter where I go, it's pretty much the same sight." Tulli waved her arm over the side of the roof, and Thali looked at the coastline. Buildings surrounded them, but she also saw the harbor and cove. Across the way, behind Thali, was the opposite coastline; buildings lined it too. Beyond the harbor was the open ocean, sunlight shooting stars into it like it was a multifaceted gem polished to perfection.

"It's beautiful here," Thali said.

"Oh yes. This is my favorite spot. But still, I'm sure you've seen something *else*. Other beautiful things too, right?" Tulli asked. She gripped her teacup with both hands, and Thali understood that she wanted to hear about some of the other places in the world.

"There are sandy places, and jungle places, places with trees as thick as houses. Ones with castles made of stones on beautiful green hills. There are lots of different kinds of beautiful places," Thali said.

Tulli clapped her hands together like she was encouraging a performance. A cough interrupted them, and Thali watched Tulli freeze a moment. "I'm sorry. I get all caught up in adventures. I don't mean to be pushy," she said as she glanced at the older woman.

"That's all right. Thank you for your curiosity. Not many people are interested in learning more about other places," Thali replied, though at that moment, a few other people popped into her head, people she had befriended because of her knowledge of other places and ability to tell stories about them.

"Please, I've prevented you from eating. Let's finish these off so we can get to second dessert sooner!" Tulli said. She stuffed the last one—the tiny chocolate cake—into her mouth and stared out at the open ocean.

Thali took a bite of the second pastry and turned to follow Tulli's gaze. Dolphins jumped in the distance, and Tulli tensed and clapped her hands, then held them in a praying position as she squinted, watching the dolphins carefully.

Tearing her gaze away from the dolphins, Thali finished her own tiny chocolate cake—which was the best bite of cake she'd ever had. The moment she placed her hand back under the table, the older woman ambled over with a plate of tiny sandwiches and another of plainer pastries.

"This one is cucumber, this one is fish, and this one is chicken," Tulli said. She waited for Thali to take the first one this time and then stuffed a whole one into her mouth. The old woman coughed again, and Tulli chewed slowly, looking guilty. "May I ask you another question?" she asked, her mouth full. It prompted another cough from her nursemaid.

"Of course," Thali said. She wanted to put Tulli at ease, and answering questions was a lot easier than coming up with conversation.

"Oh! How about we play a question game? I'll ask one, then you can ask one. We'll go back and forth until one of us can't answer. And that person will have to ... finish their plate before they can talk again!" Tulli said.

Thali thought that wasn't much of a punishment because the tiny bites of food were delicious, but she smiled and nodded.

"What's the most scared you've ever been?" Tulli asked. But the older woman gasped, and Tulli's cheeks turned pink. "Sorry, that was inappropriate. I mean, what was one of the most exciting things you've done?"

Thali's eyes slid over to the older woman. She didn't mind answering the first question, but she didn't want to get coughed at, so she decided to answer the other question. "There's not much in my life that's exciting. I guess the last time I was excited was this morning when I realized that we didn't have to do all the chores we normally have to do when we arrive at a port since we'll be setting up right outside the ship tomorrow."

"You were excited to do nothing?"

"Yes." Thali saw how this could be a strange thing to be excited for. "So what do *you* find exciting?"

"Adventure! Running! Danger! Something new and ... unknown!" Tulli said.

Thali thought for a moment. "I guess meeting you today fits most of that."

"Me?!" Tulli asked. "Meeting me is exciting?"

Thali had definitely said the right thing. Tulli was glowing with excitement. "Yes. I've never met you before, so that's new and unknown. I had to run up those steps to get here, and there's a little danger because I came here alone."

"I'm exciting!" Tulli said, turning to the old woman. "Did you hear that, Livi? I'm exciting!"

The old woman smiled and nodded, glancing and nodding at Thali.

Tulli turned back, smiling. "Oh yes. Now it's your turn."

"Right." Thali thought about what she could ask without offending Tulli by accident or having her misunderstand it. "What's your favorite color?"

"Pshaw! That's such a safe question. Green! Like the color of that house there." Tulli pointed across the way to a green house the shade of seaweed dried in the sunlight. "Was that your brother beside you this afternoon?"

"Yes. His name is Romulus. Do you have siblings?" Thali asked.

"No. It's just me." Tulli said. She started to hum a lively tune, then stopped and asked, "Do you have any pets?"

"At home I do," Thali said, "Do you?"

"Yes. I have a Jo." Tulli said.

"Oh," Thali said as Tulli looked at something above and to Thali's right. Thali turned, expecting to see a bird or something, but there was nothing. She turned back to her food and took another bite. *Tulli is a little strange,* she thought, but she had met many people from many different cultures, and she recognized that she was more comfortable around Tulli than most other people she'd met. "Who's turn is it? I can't remember anymore."

"I think it's mine. I'm sorry. I was just thinking about Jo," Tulli said. She blinked a few times and then refocused on Thali. "Where did you come from before arriving here?"

"We came from the north. It's not as pretty as it is here, but it has a lot of green, lots of trees and grasses and moss. And the buildings are much farther apart, but also a lot bigger. Everyone lives in one giant building of stone instead of here where families live separately. It's also very cold there. I'm glad we went earlier in the winter."

"What do you sell there? Oh, sorry, it's your turn."

"That's all right. Mostly we sell things people have a difficult time making or finding themselves, fine ceramics, fresh foods," Thali explained. She paused then, thinking of another question. "What kind of pet is Jo?"

"Jo is a Jo. He's my pet. I'm not really sure how to describe him. He was a gift, and I can't say I've ever seen anything else like him. You'll meet him tomorrow though, when your family comes over for dinner," Tulli said.

Thali hadn't known they had plans with Tulli's family.

"Oops, as I left to come here, Father said he was sending the invitation. I hope you'll come to dinner. Then you can meet Jo."

"That would be wonderful." Thali said.

"What do you do for fun?" Tulli asked.

"I draw. Or watch the whales and dolphins. I like to play card games too," Thali said.

"I've never played a card game."

"I'll teach you one tomorrow night if you like."

"Oh, maybe we can play in front of Jo. He loves being included. How many people can play a card game?"

"There are games for all numbers, from one person all the way up to a dozen," Thali said.

"Ohh ..." Tulli said. She clapped her hands together in excitement.

Thali's brother had warned her that most of the card games they played with their crew weren't appropriate for children or for respectable society but he had mentioned the few that were, so Thali was grateful she would have something to teach Tulli. Thali took another bite of a small sandwich, looking out over the ocean.

"It's your turn to ask a question," Tulli said, staring at the buildings behind Thali.

"Oh right, I'm sorry. I very much enjoy your company, Tulli."

"That wasn't a question."

Thali was a bit surprised Tulli hadn't acknowledged her compliment but knew it could make some people uncomfortable, so she asked a question instead. "What do you like to do with Jo?"

"We like to play, pretend to walk in the city—especially along the coast. Everyone is so friendly here, and I love watching the dolphins. I wish I could swim with them."

"Have you ever tried?"

"It's my turn."

"Right, my apologies."

"Have *you* ever gone swimming with the whales or dolphins?"

"I have with the dolphins. They're very fast though, so you have to be careful. But they're also very playful." Thali smiled, remembering it was her turn. She asked Tulli the same question.

"I don't know how to swim. Father says that if I can learn to swim, I could swim with the dolphins, but I don't really understand how to swim. I've had seven teachers, and no one has been able to teach me successfully."

Thali's brows knit together. She wondered why Tulli hadn't been able to learn yet.

They each finished their last pastry, one with cheese on it, and Tulli asked another question as Livi came and placed the last plate on their table. This one held a dessert too, but it was much larger than the previous desserts. This looked more like a mini cake; it was double the size of the chocolate cake they had eaten. And this cake was frosted beautifully. Thali wasn't sure she wanted to cut into it because it had been shaped to look like a tulip. The base was wide, but it was tapered, and the frosting had been shaped and colored to resemble the soft pink of a tulip head with a darker streak of pink in the middle.

"This is beautiful," Thali said with a sigh.

"Not a question."

"How is this made?"

"Oh, that's easy. I've helped make it before. It just takes time. We have so many tulips in the garden, they're practically burned into my memory. You just swirl the icing around and then dab the top of it with a wet finger. It's like a sculpture made of foam," Tulli said. She took her fork and smooshed the whole tulip down before cutting it into small pieces and putting it in her mouth. "How many uncles do you have?" Tulli asked between bites.

Thali knew she must be talking about her crew members, but she added more information anyway. "If you mean the crew members on my family's ship, there are twelve. If you mean related to me, I have three uncles on my mother's side and a bunch on my father's side." Then it was her turn, so she asked, "How many uncles do you have?"

"I don't have any," Tulli said. "I have one aunt. She lives with us, but she's much older than my mother, so she doesn't really do anything interesting."

They finished the rest of their cakes in silence as they looked out at the ocean.

Livi came over and leaned down to whisper something in Tulli's ear. Her face fell, so it was apparent their time together was coming to an end.

Tulli took the chipped teacup in front of her and her napkin from her lap and wrapped the teacup up carefully. She pressed it into Thali's hands. "This is a sign of our friendship. We'll have tea together every time we meet, and we'll bring this set together." Tulli glanced at the rest of the tea set.

Thali thought it was strange to separate the set, but she wanted to be Tulli's friend so badly she was glad they had an excuse to come together.

Tulli pushed her chair back. "I'm so sorry, but I have to get going now."

"That's all right. I'll see you tomorrow," Thali said as she rose and curtsied before turning and heading for the stairs.

Tulli caught up and wrapped her arm around Thali's elbow, and they traversed the stairs together until they reached the shop below. Outside, two carriages awaited them.

"I knew we would be such good friends," Tulli said, then she pulled away and disappeared into the first carriage.

Thali fiddled with her skirts again as her mother wrapped a hand around hers. Then Thali patted the lumpy pocket she'd gently placed her teacup in. Her family stood in the receiving hall of the duke's home, Thali fidgeting because she hated this style of dress the most. It was so itchy and awkward to walk in as her skirts were so wide, she barely fit through a doorway.

"They're about to arrive. You need to stop your fidgeting please," Lady Jinhua murmured under her breath.

Rommy took Thali's hand and wrapped it around his elbow. With that hand occupied, Thali took her other hand from her mother's and rested it on the one on Rommy's arm so she wasn't tempted to pull at her skirts again. Satisfied, her mother nodded and stepped ahead just as the click of doors opening made them turn to face their hosts.

The duke had an enormous mustache the same color as Tullika's hair, and the duchess was an older version of Tulli herself. Tullika stood just behind them, looking demure with her eyes cast downward as they walked into the room. Thali wondered for a moment if Tulli was angry with her because she didn't look up even once.

Thali smiled and curtsied when it was time to and turned her attention politely to the duke and duchess. She focused on keeping her hands still as the duke spoke. After they were all acquainted, the duke guided them to a sitting area tucked into the side of the hall. But before he sat, he glanced at Tulli. "My daughter was hopeful that Lady Routhalia would join her while we visit, if it's all right with you?"

"Of course. I know she had such a lovely time yesterday," Ranulf said with a nod at Thali.

Thali released her brother's arm and followed Tulli as she walked quietly away. It wasn't until they were past the doors and in the hallway that Tulli scooted closer to Thali and took her arm. They walked silently until they went through another set of doors. Tulli took a deep breath in and out and turned to Thali. The spark in her eyes came back, and Thali grinned. Her friend was back.

"I'm sorry for the formalities, Thali. Father prefers that I behave as an exemplary lady would when we have guests."

"That's all right. I understand," Thali said. She looked around the room. It was expansive. Thali spotted the tea set—her cup missing from it—on a table nearby. She gently took her cup out and placed it on the empty plate.

Tulli grinned and poured each of them a cup of tea. They sat silently as Thali's gaze roamed.

Tulli's room was as big as the foyer, but even more impressive was the large glass aquarium that took up the short side of the room. The aquarium was quite plain, without much inside besides a rock and a wooden platform with a bowl atop it. But the creature inside it was remarkable. At first, Thali thought it was a seal. But it was too short to be a seal. She approached the glass as it swam back and forth.

"Thali, this is Jo. Jo, this is my new friend, Thali," Tulli said. "Jo, why don't you come up to the rock over here and show Thali what you really look like." Tulli took a small fish from a box on the floor and placed it in the bowl.

Jo swam up to the rock and scrabbled with his legs as he landed on his belly. Thali's eyes widened as she took it in. Jo had a large bill like a duck and webbed feet like an otter, but also the wide, flat tail of a beaver. His body was mostly round. Thali narrowed her eyes as she realized that his legs emerged from the side of his body, unlike most animals with fur but rather like amphibians.

"Jo is incredible," Thali said.

"See why I struggled to describe what kind of animal Jo is?"

"Yes, definitely," Thali said.

Jo turned to look at her with dark eyes and tilted his head as Thali peered at him.

"My father said you have many animals," Tulli said.

Thali nodded. They had started to flock to her. Her father had even built a barn at home so they wouldn't be in the house all the time.

"I think Jo is unhappy, and I was wondering if you knew anything about his kind, or if you had any insight as to what might make him happier," Tulli asked. She spoke quietly, and the soft words sounded like a plea to Thali's ears.

Thali took another sip of tea and decided she wanted to do the thing that she wasn't supposed to. She closed her eyes and reached for the door she had built in her mind. She slowly cracked it open and saw a coral thread that must be Jo's. She connected to it, and images started to flood her mind: a river, a riverbank with crayfish, and rocks on the riverbed. She saw branches to climb on, small fish, and tiny frogs. Thali felt her body start to waver, and she closed the door in her mind.

When she opened her eyes, Tulli was holding her arm and guiding her to sit on an ottoman nearby.

"Are you all right?" Tulli asked.

Thali nodded. "You mustn't ask me how, but I think Jo needs small pebbles at the bottom of his home, and a hidey hole like a mini cave. He needs branches that come out of the water so he can climb on them. And he likes the fish but would also like crayfish and worms once in a while."

Suddenly, Thali was lying flat on the plush bench as Tulli had thrown herself into Thali's body and hugged her close. "Thank you so much. Jo is my whole life. I can't even understand how I love something so much without even knowing what it is."

They discussed the different animal parts Jo seemed to have until they were called for dinner. Thali was exhausted, but they had rested on the wide bench together, so she knew she'd make it through.

Tulli jumped up when the messenger closed the door and rushed to the side table. She reached out and took a box off it. "Here," Tulli said. She opened it. The soft fabric inside was dented in the middle. Tulli took the chipped teacup Thali had returned and placed it in the box.

"Are you sure I should take this with me?" Thali asked.

"Absolutely. This is my personal tea set, and I want you to have a piece of it. Then you'll always know that you'll have a right to visit me, no matter where we both end up," Tulli said.

Thali narrowed her eyes, wondering what Tulli was imagining. "Thank you," she said as she accepted the box with the teacup inside, nestled in a handkerchief.

The next year...

Thali hated masked balls. She had a tough enough time trying to guess people's motivations by their facial expressions and movements, and at a masked ball, she could only use their body language, and even that was constricted by inflexible corsets and boxy jackets in this kingdom. She wiped her hands on her own skirts, patting them down. Of all the fashions, the super-tight corsets and voluminous skirts of this land were her least favorite. At least the skirts had ample pocket space though. Thali patted the one with her teacup in it. Mia and her mother had made this particular dress for her using some pictures Thali had drawn for them of the fashion. Her only consolation was getting the chance to see her friend, Tullika. She hoped they were still friends. It had been a year since she'd seen Tulli, and people could change a lot in a year.

"That's a very pretty dress," a voice from behind a column said.

Thali jumped.

The girl moved around the column until she was directly in front of Thali. She wore a deep-purple dress, her golden hair half pinned up. Brown eyes like polished wood peered at Thali through the mask. Tullika had become even more beautiful. She looked much more serious and sterner than Thali remembered though.

"Your dress is also very pretty. That's one of my favorite colors," Thali said. She smiled, remembering her manners and being careful of what she said in case Tulli's feelings toward her had changed.

Tulli bowed her head and Thali did the same. "Have you ever wondered what the stars might be made of?" Tullika asked, looking up.

"Actually, yes," Thali said. She looked up and noticed that through the glass roof she could see the tiny specks of light.

"And what do you think they're made of?"

"Light. Fire maybe."

"I think they're the souls of all the people we've known watching over us."

"There are some cultures that believe they're heroes that conquered evil, forever immortalized in the sky to watch over us."

"That's very comforting," Tullika said. She turned back to Thali. "Would you like to take a better look at them?"

"Please," Thali said, welcoming any excuse to leave the room. She would much rather be out looking at the stars than in the stuffy ballroom, getting nervous at every twitch in her direction.

Thali followed Tullika to the edge of the room. There, with a look back in Thali's direction, Tulli slid behind a screen, and Thali followed. She glanced around the room on her way out and noticed her brother tracking her movement. He nodded ever so slightly to acknowledge that he saw her, and she did the same.

Thali slid into a hall with plush carpet. Tullika had taken her shoes off, so Thali did the same. She hated wearing the shoes that accompanied the skirts, so removing them was a relief.

"I'm so glad you're here." Tulli turned and her smile was bright. Even though she had left her mask on, this was the Tulli that Thali remembered. Thali's shoulders lowered, and she relaxed as she followed Tulli down the carpeted halls.

"Is it true you have a pet rat?" Tullika asked.

"Yes." Thali had had to leave Tika on the ship. Her mother had insisted there was no room for her in her dress. But Thali was aware enough to know that rats weren't often recognized as pets.

Tullika skipped down the hall, zigging this way and that way.

They passed only a few guards, and Thali noticed they all smiled at Tullika as she passed them. "Where are we going?" Thali asked.

"You'll see," Tullika said. She turned abruptly into a dark doorway and started climbing some stairs.

Thali followed her. She was excited to get some exercise. The corset was so tight it didn't let her breathe properly though, and she found herself having to stop to catch her breath.

"Is your corset too tight?" Tullika asked.

Thali only managed to nod.

Tullika spun her finger in a circle, indicating Thali should turn around.

Thali did so obediently, grasping the rail with her hand as the lack of air combined with the spinning had unbalanced her. She felt deft fingers pull at the ties of her corset. Suddenly, her ribs allowed her to suck in the air her body wanted.

"The trick is to put something underneath it when they fasten it," Tullika said. "I have this wooden board I like to put on my stomach. I made it myself so it curves around my body. Then when they're done, I pull it out and have space to breathe normally. No one's really noticed."

Thali just focused on breathing properly. Tullika was quiet while Thali caught her breath.

"Ready?" Tullika asked.

Thali nodded. She followed Tullika up the last of the stairs, and when her friend pushed open the door, Thali sucked in a welcome breath of air. This was one of the highest points of the castle. She followed Tullika to the edge to peer over the side. They saw some latecomers arriving and some already leaving, furtively looking around before jumping into a carriage together.

"They never think to look up," Tullika said. "That's my cousin. He's married but likes to find a new woman to play with at every ball. His wife is nice, but she's as stupid as a brick and doesn't understand how she loses track of him every time."

"I'm sorry."

"Oh, don't be. He's happy and she's happy. He's a bit of a scoundrel of course, but his wife doesn't seem to mind just sitting and enjoying the music. She gets her fair share of attention at these things anyway."

"Oh." Thali wasn't sure to make of that.

Tullika suddenly went to the middle of the roof and sat down, then flopped back. Thali smiled when she saw the tea set on a little table between them. Thali removed the cup from her pocket and sat it with the rest of the set. Then she took the pot and poured them each a cup, putting one beside Tulli. Thali followed Tulli's lead, putting her own cup on the ground, then stretching out beside it and looked up at the stars.

"Do you know any of the star-hero stories?" Tullika asked after a few minutes.

Thali told her one about a great hunter who had taken down a large boar to feed his village, of how he had been the first to clean the boar and the last to eat it, and of how an old woman rumored to have magic used the last of her magic to immortalize him in the sky as she died later that year.

"That's a beautiful story. You've met many different people. Are there other beliefs about stars?"

"Well, one group thinks the stars are actually places as big as the sun, but far, far away."

"That seems unlikely. Or if it's true, then I wonder if we glow to someone out there too."

Thali smiled; she liked the way Tullika thought, how she was so open-minded.

"Sorry for interrupting you. Father says I need to practice thinking before I speak."

"It's refreshing actually," Thali said, then continued sharing the other tales of the stars she knew of.

When she got to one where people were banished to the stars for crimes they'd committed to forever learn their lesson as they watched their families grow old, Tullika stopped her. "It's interesting, isn't it, how some people think of immortality as a reward and others consider it a punishment?"

"Yes, actually. What do you think?" Thali asked. She took a sip of her tea, which was already cooler than she expected.

"Hmm ... I think it would appear as a reward at first to me, but then it would feel like a punishment. After my family had disappeared in death, what would the point be? I wouldn't have any loved ones to watch over." Tulli sat up and drained her own cup.

"Do you think you could love your extended family from afar? Like your children's children?" Thali asked.

"Perhaps. But maybe I would just feel numb after awhile, watching all those people dying over and over."

"True. I suppose my perspective would shift. Maybe I'd love the trees or the mountains instead," Thali said, thinking of things that might exist longer.

"Perhaps indeed."

They didn't say anything for a while after that as they sat, lost in their thoughts as they considered immortality.

"Do you think a life is called a life if there is no end?" Thali asked quietly.

"Yes, because I think even a life without an end would have the possibility of an end eventually," Tullika replied.

They continued staring up at the sky, the music from the ballroom softer from their position. A knock came at the open door, and both girls turned. An old woman stood there, her head held high even as her shoulders rounded forward; she was clearly fighting the shriveling of old age.

"Miss, your father is requesting your presence." The woman curtsied.

"Thank you for covering for me, Liv," Tullika said.

They stood, and Thali tucked her teacup inside its handkerchief and back into her pocket. The girls started back down the tower to return to the ball, slipping their shoes on their feet right before turning into the last hallway before the ballroom. Thali watched Tulli's posture change. Gone were the loose, skipping, swinging steps, and in their place were the stiff-backed, small steps of a lady. A sober pout replaced her bright smile.

Rommy's gaze caught Thali's the moment she came back in, and she nodded to let him know she was all right. He nodded and continued his conversation with some young ladies. They flocked to him now, wherever they were.

Tulli linked arms with Thali, and they toured the room. Thali felt everyone's eyes on them and wondered what Tulli was doing.

The music stopped suddenly, and Tulli let go of Thali, but not before she realized that Tulli had placed her near her brother. Rommy edged nearer, and Tulli patted her hand as she left Thali and started to weave her way back to the front of the room.

Her lord and lady parents stood waiting for her, and everyone turned their attention to them. Thali knew the lord and lady here were quite respected. Their people were all warm and friendly, and Thali liked that they seemed kind and warm in return.

"It is with great honor that we have an announcement to make," the lord began. Tulli stepped behind her parents, standing between them.

The lord's eyes gleamed as he gently took Tulli's hand and brought her forward. "Our very own Tullika is betrothed to the prince of Henkram!" he said and the whole room erupted in cheers.

Thali watched her friend's face carefully. Tulli gave nothing away. She smiled politely and demurely, her cheeks flushing as her parents hugged her. Thali concluded that she and Tulli weren't very good friends after all. How could they be, when they'd only ever spent a few hours together? Even though they'd continued writing letters to each other, Tulli hadn't said anything about courting the prince of Henkram, so this announcement caught Thali off guard.

Yet Tulli was so busy accepting the congratulations of all her guests that Thali didn't have time to speak with her privately to dig deeper.

Early the next morning, Thali spotted Tulli's messenger carriage drive up, and Thali hoped it was a message from Tulli, asking to meet. She jumped off the ship, happy she'd just finished her morning training, though they were starting to unload their goods.

The carriage rolled to a stop, and Thali went over to meet the messenger, but when the door opened, she was thrilled to see Tulli herself had come. "You're here!" Thali said.

Tulli nodded. "Do you think you can get away for an hour or two?"

Tulli stuck her head out and waved at Thali's mother and father, who were organizing all the goods, as Thali looked over her shoulder at them.

Thali caught Rommy's gaze. She glanced at Tulli and then held a finger—then another—up. He nodded and turned to their mother, translating Thali's request. Thali's mother held up one finger as she made eye contact with Thali.

Thali nodded, then turned back to the carriage. "I've got an hour," she said as she climbed into the carriage with Tulli.

The carriage started to roll as soon as Thali closed the door and sat across from Tulli. "Congratulations on your betrothal."

Tulli took a deep breath and sighed. "Do you hate me for it?"

"Why would I hate you for it?"

"Life after this is going to be so different. You'll have to come visit me in a palace, and we'll be watched constantly. I have to be 'princess' instead of just Tulli."

"Then why did you say yes?"

"I didn't really have a choice. And I mean, Prince Sailen seems nice enough."

"Your father wanted the status of your betrothal to royalty?"

"Daddy would have said no if I really didn't want it."

Thali waited for Tulli to continue. There had to be a reason she'd said yes.

"Sailen sent a young noble to come live with my family for a couple of months, his cousin or something. I know now that he was spying for him because of what the marriage proposal had included."

The hair on the back of Thali's neck prickled with suspicion. "What did it include?"

"It included a place for Jo. He's the first suitor to promise a place for Jo. He guaranteed several large aquariums would be built in my bedroom, my sitting rooms, and public receiving rooms."

"That's good, right?"

"It is." Tullika sighed.

"So what's wrong?"

"I've never met him. I *hear* he's nice, but I don't know that," Tulli said.

Thali blinked. She knew of arranged marriages—her best friend in Bulstan had been promised to another when he was just five—but her parents had met, fallen in love, and built a life together. "Well if he's not, you can run away with me," Thali assured her, grinning and sitting next to Tulli.

"Thank you for your friendship, Thali," Tulli said.

"Thank you for yours." Thali felt like Tulli was saying goodbye.

"You will visit me in the palace, yes?"

"Why does it feel like you're saying goodbye?"

"The palace is a day's ride inland. It's going to be a long journey, far away from your ship, to come and visit me."

Thali grinned. "Well, I don't know if you're worth it, but Jo certainly is." She winked.

Tulli grinned then. "Truly?"

Thali nodded. She felt the loneliness Tulli was already feeling and felt terrible that her friend was moving alone to a palace where she knew no one. "Are you scared?" Thali asked.

Tulli nodded but smiled a small smile. "Livi will come with me. But the palace is much bigger. And the nobles won't be happy. I'm an outsider. I've never been to court before, and they've grown up there."

Thali didn't need to ask about court, though she hadn't been to court for more than a couple of days at a time, and not even recently. Her mother and father were too busy as working nobles to bother with being at court if it wasn't for trade purposes. She'd only glanced at the nobles from a distance in a random hallway or from afar on the lawn as they were picnicking when she was coming or going.

Then she had a sudden thought. "Oh, I almost forgot. Tulli, meet Tika," Thali opened her sleeve as she held her arm steady. Thali's rat poked her head out and her whiskers danced as she squeaked at Tulli.

"Oh hello, little Tika. It's so nice to meet you. You and Jo would be such good friends," Tulli said. She smiled wide and Thali was glad she could at least bring a smile to her friend's face.

They continued to exchange stories about Jo and Tika until the carriage rolled to a stop and Thali knew their time was up. "Write to me and if you need to escape, I'll help," she said.

Tulli nodded. They squashed each other in a hug and then the door opened. Thali hopped down with Tika on her shoulder.

"Safe travels, Thali," Tulli said.

Thali smiled at her friend, worried for what her future might hold. She closed the door. The carriage rattled off, and Thali returned to her family, helping them stack the rest of their goods for the next leg of their journey.

A year later...

Thali worked through the night to finish her chores and begged her parents to let her and Rommy ride to the palace so she could see Tullika. They let her go only because Rommy had agreed to go with her. She knew they wouldn't let a fourteen-year-old girl undertake a day's ride inland on her own.

"Thank you for going with me," Thali said.

"I'm just glad not to have to do chores," Rommy said.

Thali had had to do his chores and hers to convince him. Yet he was still getting the better end of the deal because he would be left to his own devices once they arrived at the palace.

Rommy slowed his horse to a walk, then paused before they reached the palace's entrance. "Ready? Put your decorum mask on, and re-member, ultimate politeness. She's a queen now."

Thali nodded. It was crazy that her friend had not only become a princess, but then the queen of Henkram in a single year.

They lined up with the guards just as everyone else did. But as soon as she gave her name, as Tulli had told her to, three guards peeled themselves out of the lineup and led her and Rommy across the lawn to the side of the palace. "You can leave your horses with me and enter through those doors there. They will show you to the rooms the queen has chosen for you."

Thali didn't know what she'd been expecting, but this was a lot more formal than what she had ever associated with Tulli. Rommy waited for her to follow the footman, and when she did, they were led through many hallways. Finally, the footman opened a set of double doors for her, and they stepped through to a large common space. There was a fireplace and two sitting areas with couches. A table with chairs and a few desks scattered throughout the space sat ready with writing implements.

Thali was about to open her mouth when she saw more doors on the far wall, three of them.

"The queen wanted to ensure you were comfortable and knows you like to stick together. You'll find two bedrooms behind the doors and a bathing chamber behind the third," The footman said. "I'll leave you to settle in."

Thali could only visit for one night and would have been fine sleeping in the stable with the horses. This seemed abundantly luxurious. The sitting area alone was more spacious than her families' quarters onboard their ship. Everything was cream colored, and she wondered how it all stayed clean. She was afraid to sit down because she didn't want to get anything dirty.

"Well, this is nice," Rommy said. He plopped his travel bag onto one of the creamy chairs, and Thali cringed, hoping it didn't leave a mark. "If you're so worried about making something dirty, why don't you go bathe?" He asked as he sat and put his booted feet on a table. He wouldn't have dared if their mother was here, but he made himself at home quite easily now.

Thali nodded and went over to the three doors. She opened one to find an equally plush bedroom with a high fluffy bed, a nightstand, another desk, two sets of drawers and armoires, and a dressing screen. She poked her head into a second door then and saw a large claw-footed tub, a raised chamber pot, and a decorative sink. Thali went to the tub to explore how to fill it with water using the levers above. There were three, and she didn't know which one was for what.

A cough from behind her made her spin around. An older woman stood waiting. "May I?" she asked, and Thali nodded. The woman approached and pulled the two outer levers, the right one only briefly but the left continually as the water came flowing out of two pipes in the side of the wall right into the tub.

The tub was full and steaming in mere moments. The woman bowed her head and disappeared through a back door Thali hadn't previously seen. She went back to grab the clean clothes she'd brought, then returned to peel off her travel clothes and sink into the warm bath after carefully placing a handkerchief-wrapped package on a chair.

Thali reveled in the warm water until it cooled. Next, she dressed—ensuring she put the package in her pocket—and emerged from the bathing chambers. Food had been brought already, and Rommy was digging in. He hadn't filled a plate yet but was plucking out a few of the meats and cheeses. As always, he waited for Thali to fill her own plate before he took his share, not that they would have to share today. The spread before them was way more than they could eat in two days.

There was a knock on the door, and it opened as a guard stepped through. He eyed the room before he stepped aside, allowing Tulli to enter.

"Tulli!" Thali shouted. Rommy elbowed her, and her eyes went wide as she coughed and corrected herself. "Your Majesty!" She sunk into a curtsy next to her brother, who was already bowed over.

"Please," Tulli said.

It sounded like Tulli, but a much more reserved Tulli than Thali remembered. She stood up again and examined her friend, dressed in the finest of fabrics and draped in gems.

The guard closed the door but stayed inside.

Tulli went and took Thali's hands. "You are looking well. Thank you so much for coming to visit me," Tulli said. Even though it had only been a year since they'd seen each other, she looked so much more grown up in Thali's eyes. Tulli turned to Rommy. "And thank you, Romulus, for accompanying your sister on this journey to visit me."

"It is my honor," Rommy said, and he bowed his head.

Tulli's eyes sparkled then, and Thali recognized her friend again. "Romulus, once you're ready, my husband would love to meet you," Tulli said.

Rommy's eyes lit up. Thali's friend had certainly said the right thing.

"Lady Routhalia and I will go for a walk," Tulli said. She offered her hand to Thali.

Thali wasn't sure what she was supposed to do, so she took her friend's hand.

Rommy opened his mouth, but when Tulli glanced at him again, he closed it.

"I will bathe quickly then, Your Majesty, and meet with the king. And I'll see you later, sister." He bowed and remained that way until they left the room. Thali was glad for the double doors because she and Tulli would have had to shimmy sideways through them, side by side as they were, and she didn't think that was particularly queenly or elegant.

Tulli guided her down the hallway to the private wings. Thali could only tell they were such because there were more guards than people. Tulli turned to a door that a guard opened, and the friends stepped through into what Thali assumed was their private library.

Except one wall was now a giant aquarium.

"Jo!" Thali exclaimed as she let go of Tulli and ran over to the aquarium. Jo climbed out onto a large rock and waved his bill at Thali as she approached.

Thali turned to see the door was closed and it was just her and Tulli again.

"I thought you'd like to see an old friend," Tulli said.

Thali pulled the handkerchief-wrapped teacup from her pocket and gave it to Tulli. She smiled and took it to the table and poured them both a cup of tea.

As she came back to stand next to Thali, Tulli's shoulders relaxed. She pressed the cup into Thali's hands, then cradled her own. Thali started walking along the aquarium. Jo had both water and land options dotting his habitat. It continued the length of the library, and as Thali walked, Jo and Tulli accompanied her on either side. Eventually, they walked into a study, where the aquarium continued the length of another entire wall. "This must be the biggest habitat I've ever seen, for any creature." Thali was amazed.

Tulli grinned. "I'm so happy I got to show it to you!" She gripped her arm then, so Thali spun around, and Tulli embraced her tightly. "Sailen is so good to me. Only the aquarium in the library was built when I arrived, but he's been building Jo more and more spaces so he can go wherever I go and be comfortable," Tulli said. She was grinning from ear to ear. "I even have a little water-filled cart he can hop into that I can bring into any room in the palace, though I hate making people bring it up or down stairs."

"That's fantastic," Thali said. She took a sip of tea. She was filled with so much happiness for her friend.

Tulli went to a box on the side of the aquarium, took out a crayfish, and fed it to Jo. The little creature swam to the bottom of his aquarium with it, pulling some pebbles with him to mash up the crayfish as he munched on it.

They lingered, watching Jo quietly as he darted this way and that, not out of boredom the way Thali had seen him do the first time she'd met him, but seemingly to show off.

"Being a queen suits you," Thali said as she turned to Tulli.

She refilled their cups and smiled, but then nodded sadly. "I thought I'd have more time as a princess, but his parents' carriage flipped en route to their summer home, and they never fully recovered. Then we had a terribly cold winter and they got sick. One morning, Sailen and I were woken up to all our staff bowing and curtsying, shouting, 'Long live the king and queen!'" Tulli shook her head as if trying to push the memory away.

"I'm sorry about Sailen's parents. It must have been quite a shock and transition."

"I've had a hard time believing this is my life most days." Tullika shook her head. "You know, you'd make a good queen."

"No, thank you," Thali said earnestly.

"I mean every word of it. You probably don't realize it yourself but traveling the world, it helps you understand people. And being a merchant, you understand politics and the delicate ways of conversation. You also understand trade and resources and how a country makes their money. Being a traveling merchant makes you a perfect candidate for royalty."

Thali felt the heat flush from her neck to her cheeks. "I want to sail the ocean."

Tulli nodded. "I can understand that. But if you'd like to be introduced to some royal princes, let me know. Sailen has friends." Tulli winked as she grinned and elbowed Thali in the ribs.

Thali shook her head. "I can hardly believe you're married, never mind that you're a queen. I don't think I'll ever be ready for any of that. I'm happier sailing the free seas!"

Tulli and Thali shut themselves in the queen's rooms for the whole day before emerging at dinner. Thali was leaving the next morning, so it was her only real chance to meet Tulli's husband, the king.

"How's my dress?" Thali asked her brother as she stood outside his room.

"It's fine," Rommy said, though he didn't even look at her as he emerged from his room.

"What's he like?" Thali asked. Rommy had spent time with Sailen already, and she was nervous about meeting him.

"He's like any other prince. He likes the outdoors, maybe more than others though." Rommy shrugged.

That didn't give Thali much reassurance.

"Ready?" he asked as he offered his arm to her. She nodded and took it. There was a knock on the door, and Rommy opened it before the guard had a chance to.

"If you'll follow me to dinner tonight," he said and turned on his heel.

Thali let Rommy guide her as she looked up and around at the palace's decor. Tulli's home had been opulent, but this took opulence to an entirely other level. Only when Rommy nudged her in the side did Thali remember herself. She closed her mouth and faced forward.

They reached another set of grand double doors, and the guard opened them. Thali and Rommy stepped inside onto a huge mezzanine. It boasted a huge domed ceiling and detailed paintings of war scenes, most victorious. Thali thought it was odd they would have dinner here when war scenes seemed more appropriate for a training space.

Tulli and Sailen had not yet arrived, so Rommy led her to the edge of the balcony. Thali stared down at the giant space below. It was likely the biggest open space she'd seen in her life.

"Their Majesties," a runner said, and Thali and Rommy turned around to watch as Sailen and Tulli walked in.

Tulli's arm was wrapped around Sailen's, and they leaned close together as they walked. As they neared Thali and Rommy, Sailen straightened and smiled at them. "Rommy, it's good to see you again, and Thali, thank you for giving me my wife back. She has enjoyed your time together immensely," Sailen said as he nodded.

Rommy elbowed her gently in the ribs as Thali was trying to put together something to say. "Thank you ... for ... allowing us to spend time together," Thali managed before she cringed. She would have preferred to say something that didn't suggest Sailen possessed her friend.

Sailen was gracious and only smiled and nodded as he waved his arm to invite them to the table.

Thali was seated on Sailen's right, and Tullika sat to his left. Rommy next to Thali. Thali knew enough to know her seat was a place of honor, but she did kind of wish she was next to Tulli.

Dinner was more enjoyable than Thali had expected, and certainly more engaging than dining with any other royals she'd encountered. Sailen was an animated storyteller, and Thali's favorite part was watching him dote on Tullika. She glowed as she looked at him, and he seemed to have a special smile only for her. Thali looked away as Sailen and Tulli often shared an extra moment when their eyes met. Thali wondered for a moment what it would be like to have someone stare at you that way, what it would be like to know you were loved as much by someone as you loved them.

Rommy coughed, and Thali looked back to her plate and focused on finishing her food.

"Sorry for being distracted. Tullika and I just can't get enough of each other." Sailen smiled at them. At Thali's nod, the king continued. "Thali, I know Rommy already has someone special in his life, but I wondered if you did. Tulli told me it was none of my business, but I have some friends I think you'd get along with quite well."

"Oh, thank you, Your Majesty, but I don't plan on settling down. I'd like to take to the ocean and travel as my family has," Thali said.

Sailen glanced at Rommy, then smiled at Tulli again before turning back to Thali. "Well, if you change your mind, you'll have to let us know." Sailen smiled and switched topics.

If Thali really thought about it, she imagined she'd meet another sailor, or another merchant with his own ship, and she imagined they would sail from one place to another working for her parents, then her brother. They'd experience all their days at seas and markets, visiting her friends in one place or another. She smiled as she imagined someone next to her as they sailed into a friendly port.

"Whoever's put that smile on your face is the person you should go after," Tullika said.

Thali felt her cheeks heat, and Rommy raised an eyebrow, clearly waiting for her answer.

"Not someone, something. I can't imagine a better life than the one I live now, sailing, friends, markets." Thali forced herself to meet Sailen's and Tulli's gazes.

"Cheers to finding your life's purpose then," Sailen said. He lifted his glass. They all joined in and then listened avidly to more stories about Sailen's kingdom.

MORE AND MORE MEMORIES

"**D**O YOU REMEMBER WHEN Sailen and Tullika came to our wedding?" Elric asked.

Thali smiled and thought back to that meeting, a rare time when Thali and Elric were both present to meet their foreign guests.

Tullika had swept Thali up into a hug the moment she'd walked in the sitting-room door. "I'm so happy for you, Thali. I always knew you'd be royal," Tulli had whispered in her ear.

"Sailen, it's good to see you. Thank you for coming so far for us." Elric had embraced Sailen.

"So you two know each other?" Thali had asked. Tulli wasn't letting go of her, but that had suited Thali just fine.

Sailen had grinned as he'd glanced between Elric and Thali. "Actually, do you remember that conversation where I told you I had a few friends I could introduce you to? I was thinking of Elric."

"No! You mean you two could have been together years ago?" Tulli had pulled back and taken Thali's hands. Hand in hand, they'd sat together on one couch, Elric and Sailen following and taking a seat on the couch opposite.

Thali had smiled at Tulli, thinking a younger Thali wouldn't have liked Elric. She'd been adamant she'd sail the ocean as a merchant. "How do two princes meet anyway?" she had asked.

Sailen had grinned as he'd glanced at Elric. "I believe my father, as a prince, came to your father's wedding and coronation, and they hit it off so they kept in touch. Then they thought it was a good idea for us to start writing to each other."

Elric had patted Sailen on the shoulder. "My father thought it was a good idea to have us all connect as children so when we grew up, we'd be more likely to work together as kingdoms."

Mia broke into Thali's reminiscing as she poked her head in the room. "So, do you write to all the royalty around the world then?" She bustled in then with a bag overfilled with fabric and patted Indi on the head before she sat down.

"Not all," Elric replied. "Some correspondence from childhood has dropped off, mostly just because we get too busy. Sailen, though, has always returned my letters within a month, and I do him the same courtesy."

Mia had settled on one of the trunks against the wall next to the armoire and was mending some trousers.

"Want anything to eat?" Daylor asked her.

Mia shook her head. "No, but I've always loved Thali's stories, so I couldn't help but move my work in here when I heard you all." As she crossed her legs, she bumped the armoire.

Something brown rolled out and Daylor squeaked and jumped up onto the chair he had been sitting on, hugging Ana to his chest as he looked around for the brown thing.

Tilton bent down and grabbed something from underneath his chair. "It's just a bracelet." He held it out. It was a brown braid tied in a circle and held together with a leather band.

"Oh, I ..." Daylor stuttered. "Ana startled, so I startled with her." The curly-haired dog's long legs dangled outwards, and she looked around as if wondering what was happening. Daylor sat back down and arranged Ana's limbs across him. Ana just placed her chin over his shoulder and went back to sleep. "So, who gave you what I assume is a horsehair bracelet? Or is it more like a bear-hair bracelet?" he asked.

"It's horsehair. And it's actually Arabelle's mother's tail hair," Thali replied.

Tilton handed her the bracelet, and she ran her fingers carefully over the braided hairs, careful not to pull them out as her fingertips traveled over the bumpy strands overlapping each other.

PINTO

"ARE WE THERE YET?" Thali asked.

"You can see as plainly as the rest of us that we're not," Rommy said. He began to roll his eyes, but a look from their mother stopped him short.

They stood on the deck, Thali practically hanging off the edge of the ship, as they approached land. She squinted, hoping to see the horses on the island.

"We'll be there in a few hours," Crab said from behind her.

"Why don't you go get your bag ready?" her father suggested.

"Done."

"What about your chores?" her mother asked.

"Done," Thali said. She was vibrating as she awaited their next port. They'd been there a few times before, and it was one of her favorites. Some of the most beautiful horses in the world called it home, and the locals had told her that next time she came, she'd be able to ride the horses. She was more than excited do that. They looked so smooth as they ran, she could only imagine what it would be like to be astride one.

"Lass, sit," Crab said. He pointed to the barrel next to him and she sat.

She knew if she continued being annoying, her mother would make her train. Even though Thali was stronger than most other eleven-year-olds, she didn't want to have to run laps or do pull-ups. She had dressed carefully in her most appropriate riding clothes and didn't want to get them all sweaty.

Her feet wouldn't stop *tap-tapping* on the edge of the barrel, but her family ignored it. She figured that was probably because they considered it a victory that she was sitting instead of dangling half off the ship. Soon though, her fingers joined her feet as they tapped the top of the barrel on either side of her.

She watched the island get closer and closer. They would have to keep their distance and lower the smaller boats to get there. Her family would go first, then some of the crew would including Mouse and Dog, to stretch their legs. "Crab, I wish you could come with us."

"I'll see you at supper, lass. Someone needs to make sure the rest of the crew does what they're supposed to—and that no one steals the ship," he replied. He winked at her. Crab had told her the story of how their ship had been stolen once when everyone had disembarked to go to the market. They had been lucky that a friend was docked too and taken them out to their ship to face the thieves and get their ship back.

"All right, I think we're as close as we can get," Thali's father said.

Thali leapt off her barrel, bag already slung over her shoulder, and ran down to the smaller boats, leaping off the side to land in one. "I'll help!" she said as she ran grabbed the ropes.

The boat rocked a little after she leapt into it, but she was ready to help lower it, making sure the oars did not fall out as it descended to the ocean.

Her brother leapt in right after she did. He was lanky at fifteen. His limbs had decided to grow before the rest of him, and he was now almost as tall as their father, towering over their mother and Thali.

"You look like a goat," Thali said.

"And you looked like a hummingbird flying across the ship so quickly. I think Mouse is still spinning."

They lowered the boat together and then their mother and father climbed down the rope ladder to join them. Mouse climbed in after them and Dog, and they headed for shore. Thali was tempted to leap into the water and swim because she thought they were moving too slowly; instead, she took in the beautiful island as it neared. A few small horses grazed on the grassy sand just beyond their landing point. The horses looked up and stood quietly alert, watching them as they came closer and closer. The chestnut stallion, a red-brown horse closest to them, flared his nostrils. Thali hoped he would run away instead of choosing to charge them.

"Stop," Thali said. Mouse and Dog immediately stopped rowing. Thali knew the stallion was weighing whether to charge or run and rejoin his herd.

"Run away, friend. Run away," Thali murmured under her breath.

Their little group was silent as they watched the stallion pace back and forth, then turn and run away, keeping an eye on them after he turned his head back in their direction.

"All right, we're safe," Thali said. Mouse and Dog began rowing again, and her father and Rommy patted her shoulders. The horses disappeared into the trees beyond the grass. As the boat neared a sand dune, they couldn't see the forest or anything else beyond the grassy, sandy hill. She leapt out with Rommy to pull the boat as high as they could so her parents wouldn't have to get their boots wet.

After they were all out of the boat, Mouse and Dog pulled it with them up the little hill. Thali was surprised to see the Pony People standing there, awaiting their arrival.

They wore dresses and tunics of leaves they had strung together. The men wore large leaves that covered their bottom halves, and the women tended to wear much smaller leaves strung together in a net that they wore like a dress. Thali thought the dresses looked beautiful and showed the intricate craftsmanship. The group that had come to welcome them included the chieftess, her husband and daughter—Pinto was Thali's friend—and two young men from their village who looked like guards. As soon as Thali saw Pinto, she ran ahead. Pinto met her halfway, and they hugged gleefully.

"Did you make a new dress? It's so beautiful!" Thali said.

"Your hair is so long now!" Pinto said.

Their parents caught up to where Pinto and Thali had collided, while Rommy hung back. The chieftess only had a daughter and no sons, so Rommy usually spent his time with the adults or some of the young men in the village.

Thali's mother and father embraced the chieftess and her husband. Rommy stepped up to greet them and then Thali turned around dutifully and greeted the chieftess and her husband too. Even Pinto turned dutifully to her mother and father.

After the formalities, Thali and Pinto turned to their parents, Pinto's expression mirroring Thali's hope that they would be released from the business stuff so they could go do their own thing.

The chieftess glanced at Thali's parents and nodded. Jinhua nodded a moment later. Rommy grabbed Thali's bag before the girls took off.

"Thanks, Rommy," Thali said as she slipped out of her bag.

He added her bag to his own slung over his shoulder.

"Do you want to come too?" Pinto asked Rommy, her cheeks turning pink as she spoke.

"No, thank you. I'll let you ladies catch up. I'll see you at supper," Rommy said, smiling. He added a little bow to Pinto and then turned back to follow the adults.

Thali grabbed Pinto's hand and tore off into the forest with her. She wanted to find the horses. "What was that about?" She asked when they found themselves alone in the forest.

"What?" Pinto asked.

"You've never asked my brother to come with us."

"Your brother is very handsome. I couldn't resist."

Thali rolled her eyes, then stuck her tongue out. She could never think of her brother as handsome.

They slowed their pace as they got further into the trees. It was a strange kind of forest, with light-gray tree trunks as thick as her legs curved away from their path and leaves like balls on the treetops. Those leaves provided lots of shade for the moss that stretched across the path. The curvier trees had small leaves, and the straighter ones had bigger leaves. When she looked up, she saw a strange mix of small leaves and giant leaves woven together like a handmade basket of green and purple. She'd never seen purple leaves until she'd come here. Even now, she wondered why they were that color but didn't bother to ask.

They quieted their steps. Pinto walked as quietly as Thali. They usually used their silent steps to sneak up and scare some of the village children. But now, it came in handy as they tried to watch the wild horses.

They crawled to the top, sticking their heads over the edge until they could peek over. Pinto flattened herself along a small hill, and Thali did the same. There, on another beach, was that same herd of ponies Thali had seen earlier: the chestnut stallion and two other ponies, one black and one brown.

"Did you see them run away when we landed?" Thali whispered.

"I did. I knew you'd arrived when I saw them running. It's funny because he's never run away before. He always charges."

"Did you name him?"

"Mama doesn't approve as they're not ours, but I named him Isral."

Isral turned his head in their direction, and they ducked back behind the hill.

"Let's go. One of the mamas is about to have a baby," Pinto said.

They crawled away from the ledge and started to walk quietly back toward the village. Thali looked behind her and saw that Isral had come up to the ledge they had just vacated and stood there, nostrils not flared but watching them attentively. She tapped Pinto on the shoulder, but by the time Pinto turned around, Isral had descended, only his tail visible as it swished in annoyance.

As they walked back, Thali's gaze was drawn up to the treetops again. The mix of greens and purples looked like a kaleidoscope as she turned her head this way or that, seeing different shapes in the colors.

As Thali and Pinto walked into the village, Thali breathed in the smell of cinnamon and saw the many low bushes outside every home with their green and red leaves, some with yellow edges and tiny flowers. She was excited because this was the home of cinnamon, one of her favorite spices. It was her favorite because it lent itself to sweet dishes, and Thali loved sweet dishes more than savory.

The homes were huts of clay with a network of large leaves connecting the layers and acting as roofs. The homes were set up in familial circular groups, with their horses in the middle. Each family had a group of homes, and everyone took care of the horses. Thali and her family stayed with Pinto and her family. Though the houses were made of clay, some were impossibly large and intricate with all the many designs carved into the walls. The interiors contained multiple rooms and were much cooler than the blazing heat outside.

There was only one real rule on the island—stay off the black lands. Half of the island had black ground; even the beaches had black sand that sloped into the water. The legends of the Pony People said the summit of the black earth had given birth to both their people and the ponies. Though the locals called them ponies, they were some of the finest horses Thali had ever seen. The Pony People never tread on the black lands in respect for their origins. Thali had heard of stories where terrible things happened to those who dared to.

She ran ahead of Pinto to the center of Pinto's ring of huts. There, thin branches and rope attached one house to the next. Thali stayed respectfully outside the rope. She was always amazed that the horses stayed within the confines of that small rope. On one visit, Pinto had left the rope undone and the horses had stayed in the center even though they could have escaped. These horses clearly loved their people as much as the people loved their horses.

She stood quietly by the rope, and one of the younger horses came over and sniffed her, nosing her hands as she looked for food.

"That's one of the babies. She was just born a couple of months ago."

"What's her name?" Thali asked.

"She doesn't have one yet, though her mother's name is Bell because the light part of her leg looks like a bell." Pinto pointed to Bell's hind right leg.

"How about Arabelle?" Thali asked. The name had popped into her head.

The horse tossed its head up and down as if in agreement.

"That would be a good name." Pinto laughed.

Thali stretched her neck up as more horses started to crowd in, and she tried to remember all their names.

"That's Tide, and that's Waves, over there?" Thali asked. Pinto nodded. "And Isla and Isra?" Thali asked, pointing to two red-brown horses. Pinto had told her that Isral was the only chestnut stallion on the entire island, and the people considered themselves lucky that he had come to breed with one of their mares. When the twin horses had come out looking exactly like him, the people knew for sure Isral had sired them.

One horse, a dark-gray one, pushed its way to the front of the herd as they gathered around Pinto, stretching their noses out to be scratched. It was so peaceful. Thali expected one to squeal and bite another one, but it never happened. She felt their calmness permeating the air she breathed. They were all patient, sharing Pinto's attention. It was strange to see so much calm in ordinarily flighty, jumpy animals.

The little reddish-brown horse nosed its way through the crowd, but instead of going to Pinto like all the others, she went straight to Thali. She pushed her nose right into Thali's belly, and Thali smiled as she pet the demanding baby horse, holding in her laughter. Some of the other horses switched their focus too, as if the little horse had stamped her approval on Thali, so she too could pet and scratch them in just the right spots. Thali could have stayed there for hours.

Suddenly, a whistle sounded, and all the horses turned around and ran away.

"It's feeding time," Pinto said. Thali's belly rumbled, so Pinto laughed and said, "For us too."

Thali smiled and followed Pinto to the giant firepit beside the corral. The pit was as large as a building and had a tall crackling fire burning. It was only about half its normal size now, but Thali saw folks tossing logs into it. To keep it contained, a mote had been dug and filled with water. Thali followed Pinto to one of the repurposed troughs outside of the corral and they washed up, scrubbing their hands with the salve on the trough's edge. Once clean, Pinto and Thali moved closer to the firepit. A group of people were moving logs from one place to another, so the girls jogged over to help. With so many people, Thali and Pinto only had to lug logs back and forth a couple of times before all the wood was moved.

Then they followed the dirt path around the mote and found their parents by a wall of fish. The Pony People had once asked Ranulf and Jinhua to bring them two poles of metal as tall as they could manage.

Ranulf had had to tie them to the mast to transport them, but now they sat buried deep in the ground with a huge net—its strands covered in wax—strung between them. Woven into the net were fish. It was a literal wall of fish that would serve as their supper.

Rommy was helping whittle branches into pointy sticks with his knife, and when she neared, he looked up and raised his eyebrows. Thali nodded. She turned to her mother, saw her watching them, and smiled. She went over to tell her about the new baby horse and how she'd had the opportunity to scratch them all this time.

"Ranulf, I think we'd like to ask you to bring two more poles, if you can, the next time you come to see us. I'm afraid these may wear down soon," Pinto's father said.

"Consider it done. We should be able to return in half a year. If they break before then, send a bird, and we'll bring them as soon as the poles are finished," Ranulf said.

The other man nodded. He was bald and carried a staff topped with a horse tail like a tiny, fancy mop.

"Father, Mother, the new filly has taken a liking to Thali," Pinto said.

"Oh?" Pinto's mother said.

Thali admired Pinto's mother. She looked like the grown-up version of Pinto. They both had long brown hair that reminded Thali of a horse tail blowing in the wind. They shared tan skin and were tall and thin. Pinto could wrap her legs around some of the smallest ponies the last time Thali had been here, and they'd been nine then.

Pinto stretched up to whisper in her mother's ear. Thali glanced at her brother. He was watching Pinto's lips closely even though he could only see them from the side. Thali reminded herself to ask Rommy to teach her how to read lips. Thali watched as Pinto's mother raised her eyebrows and nodded. Pinto looked around, blushing as she saw Rommy's eyes on her.

"I think we're ready to eat," Pinto's mother said.

Pinto walked with her parents, and Thali with hers, to take their places around the fire.

Their third day on the island, Thali could barely contain herself as she woke and leapt out of bed. She could sense the horses outside her door before she even opened it. A couple of them had taken to waiting for her in the morning. This morning particularly though would be one she was sure she'd never forget. Pinto had said she could ride one of their ponies today.

The people of this island worshipped their horses. They were special creatures not seen as a mode of transportation or piece of equipment as they sometimes were back home; instead, they were seen as creatures of beauty from whom the locals would be lucky to receive attention.

The little chestnut horse's mother had bestowed her attention on Thali, and she was in rideable form. Thali couldn't wait. She waved as Pinto came to join her, a small herd of horses following her as they met halfway. Thali helped change the freshwater troughs for the horses, then helped feed them various grains. It was almost lunch time before Pinto finally asked, "All right, ready?"

"I've been ready for ages," Thali said.

"Well, let's get started."

They took out brushes, some that the Pony People had made and some that Thali had brought from other lands, of various bristle lengths and stiffness. The girls began grooming the horses, running the brushes over their legs and bodies following their hair. Thali used her fingers to comb through the pretty mama horse's tail and mane.

"So today, we'll just walk around the corral here. Your only job will be to stay on," Pinto said.

Thali nodded. She had made sure to wear trousers today.

"When she sighs, she's ready for you. Bell is smarter than most, so she'll move to the rock over there so you can climb up on her easier."

Thali nodded again at the instructions. She tried to keep her beating heart calm.

Then Bell let out a big sigh and slowly started to walk away. After three steps, she turned her head to look at Thali. Thali put the brushes away, then followed the mare to the big rock. She climbed up on the rock and waited for Bell to come closer and stand still. When she did, Thali put her hands across Bell's broad back. It looked like a big leap from where she was.

"Just toss your middle onto her back. Then swing your leg over," Pinto said.

Thali glanced over and saw Pinto already astride her horse and she wondered how she had gotten on so quickly. Thali calmed her racing heart and put her hands on Bell's back. The horse was standing almost unnaturally still, as if trying her best to help. Thali counted to three and leapt, almost overshooting and sending herself hurtling over the horse instead of onto her. She caught herself in time and quickly threw her leg over, scraping her foot along Bell's back end. She sat up, and Bell turned to look at her as if wondering why she'd had to kick her.

"I'm sorry," Thali said. Bell huffed and Thali moved around on Bell's back, settling herself in place behind the withers but ensuring her legs didn't hit Bell in the shoulders.

Bell turned around again, then started off slowly as if afraid that this human would topple off. Thali grinned. The ride was so smooth, she barely noticed when Bell placed a hoof on the ground. The other horses got curious and started to meander in and around Bell and Thali. Thali had gotten to know these horses and felt their calm trying to wash away her uneasiness. Some bumped up against her leg gently, and some made sure she had some space so as not to squish her legs. Thali finally heaved her own sigh and felt a lot better for it. She let their calmness move through her and focused solely on following Bell's movement as she walked. She liked being in the middle of the herd, so much so that she closed her eyes to feel it all instead of worrying about where or what they were doing.

"They really like you," Pinto said.

"I love them," Thali said. A familiar little nose poked her in the calf, and she peeked open an eye to see the little chestnut filly trotting next to her. She'd taken a position next to her mother and wasn't letting anyone else butt in. "You're a bold little one," Thali said. She reached to scratch the little nose, and it reached up as high as possible. Thali smiled before closing her eyes again and enjoying the wandering.

Then they started to pick up the pace, and before she knew it, they were trotting in a wide circle along the ropes. Thali had been riding horses since she could walk—just not bareback and tackless. She didn't have a problem staying on, but Thali grinned from ear to ear as she was filled with pride at being able to handle a faster pace without any equipment.

After a few laps, the horses slowed, and Pinto made her way to Thali. "I've never seen them take to someone so quickly, more quickly even than to some of our people," Pinto said.

"I'm grateful. They're all so beautiful," Thali said. Even at eleven, she understood how special these horses were and how much it meant that she could ride them.

"I've asked my parents to consider Marking you," Pinto said.

Thali had no response because she couldn't believe it. She looked at her friend.

"The horses respond to you as well as any of us, so why not?" Pinto said with a smile.

"I want to hug you so badly right now," Thali said. She had learned quite young that most every culture had some rite of passage into adulthood, and for the Pony People, it was the Marking. Thali still remembered when she had asked what was required to become an adult on this island, and Pinto had explained that they called upon the spirits of the horses. If one or more horses came to the person and let that person ride them, if the person could demonstrate their ability to ride without interfering with the horse, they would be Marked. While Thali didn't really care to think of the rest of it, she would love to ride and be recognized as a capable rider.

"Mama's considering it," Pinto said. She grinned again, then added, "I'm hoping they can do our Markings together."

"You don't want your own Marking ceremony?"

"I want to share the memory of the Marking ceremony with you," Pinto said.

Thali felt honored. "You are too kind, Pinto."

Bell stopped suddenly. Pinto's horse stopped next to Bell, and they both raised their heads to look through the trees. Pinto and Thali's attention snapped immediately to the trees, where the chestnut stallion, Isral, stood in a clearing on a hill.

"You're definitely getting Marked now," Pinto said. She grinned and the horses resumed their trot. A few laps later, the horses walked, then stopped, so the girls swung their legs over and slid to the ground.

"Nervous?" Rommy elbowed Thali in the ribs.

"Jealous?" Thali asked as she looked back at her brother.

"When you win, I win," Rommy said as he grinned at her.

Thali shook her head. He placed a reassuring hand on her left shoulder as she pulled at her simple dress for the hundredth time. After she pulled the bottom, she readjusted the top. Her mother had laid this dress out for today likely because it was at once simple and elegant.

Thali and Rommy stood in the forest with their parents behind them and a bunch of other families on either side. Pinto peeked around a tree and waved at Thali, and she waved back.

"What if no horse chooses me?" Thali whispered softly so only Rommy could hear. She was, in truth, nervous.

"From what I hear, a pony and its mother have taken to you. Why do you think they won't pick you?"

"Maybe it was Pinto they were following?"

"Then they would have approached Pinto. But they approached you. You've got nothing to worry about. Even if you aren't chosen, we pack up and leave this place afterward. There aren't any consequences," Rommy said. He shrugged.

Thali wished she could be as confident as her brother. He was so sure of himself and didn't seem to care if he failed at anything.

Pinto's father and mother stepped into the meadow. The ponies all galloped into the open space from the other side.

The world was silent but for the beating of hooves on the ground as they started to circle the meadow. Everyone stepped in, and Thali followed suit. She took five steps forward as Pinto had instructed her. The families stayed back, only taking three steps. Everyone was out of the treeline now and standing in the meadow as the horses ran another circle around the large meadow before slowing and making another lap. They did another three laps before slowing to a walk. Then they spread out and grazed on the grass around them. Pinto had told her to stand still, that there would be a lot of waiting. Thali didn't mind; the horses were beautiful, and she was so tempted to open the door in her mind to see their thoughts, but her mother had warned her not to. And her mother was standing two steps behind her.

Suddenly, the horses all stood at attention, their heads shooting up from the grasses to look up and back toward the forest they had come from. They all watched, nostrils flared and ears pointed in one direction.

Isral stepped out from the trees, his shiny red-brown coat glinting in the sun, his head held high as the other horses watched him. Everyone froze. Isral whinnied then and ran out, galloping a large circle around the other horses before returning to the forest and disappearing.

"He has given us his blessing," Pinto's father said. The other horses' ears were flicking back and forth now, so Thali didn't dare move.

Some horses shook their heads and whinnied; then all the horses started to move, some at a trot, some at a walk. Ten horses neared Thali and Pinto, but the others moved further away, creating a line in the meadow. The horses that had walked away went back to grazing on the long grasses, and the ten horses that had come their way turned directly toward the people.

Pinto, as the chieftess's daughter, had the option of a private cere-mony, but she'd decided to join everyone instead. There were twelve hopeful teenagers here—and only ten horses. Thali swallowed as she wondered if she would be left out. She was often left out: because her family never stayed anywhere very long, because of how she looked, because of her name. There were so many reasons that she was left out.

"Now we will place the markings on you, and if a horse chooses you, you may mount. Once all the horses have chosen, the new pairs will ride around the meadow three times," Pinto's mother said.

Two members of Pinto's community walked up to Thali and Pinto carrying shallow bowls and short, thick brushes. Thali swallowed as she watched the woman in front of her dip the brush into the bowl and pull it out again, the brush full of red paint. She brought the brush toward Thali's chin but then paused and raised an eyebrow. Thali nodded. The woman brushed a line down to the base of Thali's neck, then down the middle to her belly button. Thali glanced over to see that the other woman had done the same to Pinto and had continued down the line of young hopefuls.

Thali turned her focus to the horses. The ten had all stopped a dozen feet away, watching as the young humans were marked with red paint.

She spotted a couple of familiar horses, and something in her chest eased as she spotted Bell. Her chances increased significantly if Bell was already part of the ten. The two Pony People women melted back in with the rest of the families, then stood and watched.

A black mare that Pinto had ridden before approached first. She walked confidently up to Pinto, stopping so her face was directly in front of Pinto's. Then she lowered her head and nudged Pinto's chest, essentially transferring the red paint from Pinto's chest to her own face. The horse slowly lifted her head, the red paint like a bright blaze on her face. Pinto's arms went gently to the horse's cheeks, and she pressed her forehead to the red paint on the horse. Pinto closed her eyes, and the horse did too, as they breathed together slowly.

A soft step in the grass near her had Thali turning back to the horses to see that Bell had approached her. Bell stood three feet away, and Thali wondered if this was going to be a rejection. But then Bell's little filly came out from behind her and closed the distance carefully. The filly was already as tall as Thali. She lowered her head to Thali's chest height and slowly took a few steps until her head was pressed into Thali's chest. A thread materialized in Thali's mind—outside the door she'd learned to always keep closed, outside the wall she'd built.

Thali closed her eyes, and the filly raised her head. They pressed their foreheads together. Thali felt the wet paint squelch onto her forehead, but more importantly, she felt the thread in her mind establish itself and start to glow.

Then she felt it, this little horse's joy and happiness at finding a partner. Thali didn't know how long she stayed with her forehead pressed to the filly's, but when she blinked and they finally stood up properly, she saw that Bell had bowed down. The filly moved around to duck her head under Thali's arm, then led Thali to Bell. Thali looked around at the other chosen humans climbing atop their horses. So Thali leaped and swung a leg over Bell, and the little filly whinnied and followed as the horses all took off around the meadow.

Thali laughed and heard her own laughter mirrored by the others—Pinto's especially—as they all rode in a wide circle around the edge of the meadow, around the other horses, and around the folks who had come out to watch. Finally, the horses slowed, then stopped, and Thali slid off Bell as the others dismounted as well.

The horses left, and when they joined the grazing herd, they all took off into the forest.

Pinto came and looped an arm around Thali's shoulders. Pinto's forehead and chest were splashed with paint, but Thali knew hers were too. As they turned back to their families, Thali saw that her parents were talking with Pinto's, their heads close together.

"What do you think they're talking about?" Thali asked. Her heart started to sink as she wondered if she'd be able to take the filly home. The foal was too young to leave her mother yet, and maybe Thali's parents hadn't thought she would bond with a horse.

"One way to find out," Pinto said.

As they walked closer, Thali's steps slowed.

"Once a bond is formed, it's unbreakable. That's the highest law here," Pinto said, and she dragged Thali forward to join their families.

The discussion ended as soon as they arrived. Rommy had been listening in and placed a hand on Thali's shoulder. He drew the symbol on her back with his thumb that told her it was going to be all right. She relaxed as she looked at the adults.

Pinto's mother turned to Thali. "Arabelle is too young just now to be separated from her mother. We were discussing whether it would be better for Bell to join you and her filly temporarily, or if you'd prefer we keep Arabelle until she's of an age when she can leave on her own."

It was the first time Thali had ever been asked to make a big decision like that, and she wasn't sure how to reply. Her mouth gaped open until Rommy tapped her on the shoulder blade again. "I think she'd rather stay here until she's older," she said.

The adults nodded. Her parents hugged her from each side, surely to avoid the red paint. Then they all walked back to the village together for the celebrations that night.

Thali was sad. She knew it was better for Arabelle to be with her mother for now and easier on her mother to stay with her horse family. She also knew Pinto would take extra good care of Bell and Arabelle, but Thali still felt like she was leaving a piece of herself on the island.

"I'll take good care of them, I promise," Pinto said.

"I know you will. It's just not easy to be apart from her," Thali said.

Pinto hugged her tight.

The horses had come to the beach to say goodbye too, and Bell and Arabelle were standing a few feet away. Thali went over, and Arabelle pressed her head into Thali's chest again. Thali wrapped her arms around the filly's big face. "Grow up well and listen to your mother and Pinto, all right? I promise I'll be back for you." The thread that had rooted itself in her mind glowed, and she felt the filly's joy and sadness at the same time.

Bell came to nudge the filly away and placed her chin on Thali's shoulder, her eyes level with Thali's. They breathed together, and Thali could have sworn she felt a wave of comfort from her.

Bell backed away and they joined the rest of the herd. Rommy placed a hand on Thali's shoulder, and she looked behind to see that everyone was on the ship; it was ready to go. Even her parents had said their goodbyes. Thali turned to Pinto once more.

"Here, so you'll always have her with you until you really do," Pinto said. She wrapped a bracelet made of Bell's tail hair around Thali's wrist and secured it. Thali saw a tiny streak of orange in it from Arabelle's barely there tail.

Thali carefully stroked the hairs in the braid with a finger. "Thank you."

"You're family now," Pinto said.

When Thali turned away from Pinto and the rest of the herd, Rommy was waiting for her a few feet further ahead. He put an arm around her shoulders to bolster her emotionally. But he looked behind him and tapped her once on the shoulder. Thali turned to her right and saw the herd. Arabelle had reared up and was kicking out a foreleg as if waving goodbye. It was such an anthropomorphic thought, Thali shook her head and smiled as she turned back to the ship.

Human Tales and Dragon Tales

A RABELLE TUGGED ON THE thread in Thali's mind now. Thali reminisced by sharing some of their early memories together with Arabelle. A soft nicker from her stall across the grounds was the reply, making Thali think tomorrow would be a great day to go for a ride in the forest behind the palace.

She put the bracelet back into the armoire, next to the ring Anders had given her. She pulled out the shallow drawer to its right and took out a box, popping the lid off to reveal a beautiful lace necklace. It was wide at the center and depicted two rearing horses and a myriad of creatures in its swirling pattern. It was still the most beautiful piece of lace she'd ever seen in her life.

A knock on the door interrupted her thoughts. At Elric's invitation, Alexius entered and stood at the door. "I noticed you were all gathered and wanted to make sure everything was all right," he said as he looked around.

"Pull up a chair, my dragon friend. Thali is telling stories!" Daylor pushed a chair by the window out with his feet and offered Alexius a snack from the tray closest to him.

Alexius glanced at the tray and grabbed a pastry, but as he went to sit down, he stood again when he saw what was in Thali's hands. He went to join Thali, and she held the lace up for everyone to see. Alexius squinted as he took in the lace. "Where is this from?" he asked.

"The Island of Four. It's a healer's island. My friend, Jify, gave this to me," Thali said.

"This is a cockatrice, and a manticore, and there's a minotaur, and a dragon," Alexius said.

Thali squinted at the intricate lace too. "I always thought they were ordinary creatures, like a snake, a chicken, a cow, and a lizard."

Alexius grinned. "Don't let them hear you say that."

"You mean those lace creatures are real, and we shouldn't be talking about them in front of them?" Tilton asked. He swallowed and his eyes went wide as he glanced back at the lace.

Alexius shook his head. "No, no. You tell your story first, Thali, then I'll tell mine." Alexius had a wolfish grin that Thali took to mean there was some grand coincidence or joke that amused him greatly.

She sat down and handed the piece of lace to Mia, who was certain to want to see it more closely. Mia handled it like it was a delicate piece of glass as she gently set it on top of her mound of fabric. She moved her head this way and that as she took it in from different angles, then gently flipped it over and looked at it closely again. "I don't know how you thought these were normal creatures, Thali. They have wings," Mia said.

Daylor leaned closer and squinted at it too. "Hurry and tell us your story, Thali. I need to hear Alexius's too."

JIFY

THALI PATTED HER DRESS for the tenth time. She pulled at the fabric to make sure it was straight, trying her best to unwrinkle it. She didn't even know why she was nervous.

"Ready?" Rommy asked. He offered his arm, and Thali looped her arm through it.

"When did you get so tall?" she asked as she realized her arm was floating a lot higher than the last time she'd looped her arm through her brother's.

Rommy shrugged. Her father was doing up the last couple of buttons on the back of her mother's dress. Thali looked at her mother's impossibly slim form with envy. Why didn't she look more like her own mother? Instead, she was thick where her mother was slim. Turning her head sideways to look at her brother, she realized he had gotten the best of their parents. He was tall like their father and slim like their mother. She clenched her teeth in frustration before going back to pulling the fabric of her dress down.

"You look great, Rou, like a real lady," her brother said, patting Thali's arm.

"Of course she looks wonderful! She's my daughter!" her father announced. He grinned at his children. His large frame filled a room, just like his voice did.

"You look beautiful." Her mother had turned and scanned her from head to toe. She reached out to adjust Thali's collar, and Thali felt herself deflate a little. If she was so beautiful, why was her mother still making adjustments?

"Let's get going then," Ranulf said. He took his wife's hands in his and kissed the backs of them before winking at Thali and ducking out the door, headed for the deck.

Thali followed her brother but was pulled back by a weight on her dress. She turned to see Indi sitting on her skirts, licking a paw innocently.

"Indi, I'm sorry, but they're afraid of tigers. We'll get you out tomorrow for a run, but for tonight, you and Ana have to stay in here." She looked at her dog sprawled on her bed, belly up, all four paws in the air. It made her smile. Ana could sleep anywhere.

Indi growled low in her throat and stood up, then hopped up on the bed, scrambling with her back legs to avoid Ana. She carefully tucked herself around the curly-haired dog, avoiding the legs in the air. Thali checked her dress for tiger fur, then left their family's quarters.

Rommy was at the stairs, eyebrows raised in question.

"Indi's upset that she can't come with us," Thali explained.

Rommy nodded and proceeded up the stairs. Indi liked fanfare and being stared at, so being left out of any opportunity to be fawned over upset her. The family strode along the deck, their crew assembled as usual to see them off. Thali was too nervous to fully register the crew's proud expressions as they accompanied the family to the gangplank. Besides, she was too busy not falling over or catching the dress on anything. Hoop skirts were not made for navigating tight spaces.

As they walked down the gangplank, Rommy tapped her arm twice with one finger, which was their code for "look left." So she looked left and saw enormous columns lining the middle of the dock. The dock was not only nicer than most, painted white and built extra wide, but its great white marble columns caught the attention of seagoers and landlubbers alike. They reached beneath the dock, so Thali realized they must be buried deep in the ocean floor. Apparently here, they tied ships to the giant white columns rather than to cleats along the dock's edge.

As if that wasn't enough, the sparkling city beyond was magnificent. Rows and rows of white buildings—some domed, some square, some tall or squat—lined dusty hills, and adorning each steep hill was a staircase of white, interrupted only by the horizontal surface of the road. It was as if a great white ribbon festooned the mountainside all the way up to the most palatial building of them all.

"They really like their columns here," Rommy whispered out of the side of his mouth.

"And white," Thali said. As they walked along, she counted twelve white columns supporting the domed entrance to a wide building with several domed roofs at the end of the dock. Thali gaped.

Rommy chuckled. "That's not our destination tonight. We're headed for that one up there, at the top of the tallest hill." He jutted his chin in that direction.

Thali gasped. "Are we walking up those steps?" she asked in a whisper.

"No. They usually send a carriage."

They continued walking along the dock until Thali finally saw what Rommy was talking about. A perfectly square white carriage awaited them on the road. Billowy white fabric covered the top, and four muscular white horses pulled it. Thali suddenly felt very self-conscious about the blush-pink dress she wore. "Why is everything white?" she asked Rommy after they'd settled into the carriage. Her parents sat facing the inclined road, so Thali and Rommy were left traveling backward.

"It gets so hot that the white helps reflect the sun, keeping the buildings cooler inside," Rommy explained.

With a gentle jerk, the carriage started to roll forward, then upward. Thali put her hand on the side of the carriage to brace herself. Her legs were too short to reach the floor, and her backward position and the incline meant she'd slide off in no time. Her mother grabbed one of the cylindrical pillows and tapped Thali's knee. She lifted her knees up, and her mother slid the pillow under her thighs. It stuck to the seat, preventing her from slipping off the bench.

Thali turned to look at Rommy. He was biting back a laugh. She smacked him, then turned away from her family to watch the landscape as their carriage rolled on, taking a wide turn and continually climbing, but gently. She saw the staircase up close and realized that in reality it meandered rather than climbing in a straight line. Then she marveled at the road's width. It was wide enough for two carriages to pass each other, which was extraordinary given the buildings had been built right into the hill. They continued up and up the winding path as Thali watched the ship getting smaller and smaller.

When the carriage finally stopped, Thali shifted her glance to the palace that wasn't a palace in truth. No one of noble blood lived there, just a merchant family, much like Thali's family. The difference was that they lived on an island and likely employed most of the island.

The columns of this home had looked grand from the dock, but up close, they were so wide, she didn't know if her whole family could link arms and still reach around a single one. Thali's father helped her down from the carriage and then her brother took her arm again. He tapped again and she looked to the right as they walked along the cool marble floor, slowly passing the great columns. A garden filled the distance to the right, but four statues beyond the shrubbery caught her attention. They stood tall and stately and were lined up in a long row like trees in a field. The white statues dotted the greenery and looked as if each guarded their own courtyard. The closest one had the torso of a woman and the lower half of a cow. Further off was one that looked like a giant chicken but with wings like a bat. She couldn't make out the other two but hoped she would have the opportunity to look at the strange, muddled creatures.

"They worship them," Rommy whispered in her ear as they strolled along behind their parents.

She was marveling at all the white stone walls and marble columns when they stopped at a set of white doors triple their height. Her mother ran her palms along the sides of her dress, and Thali did the same, surprised that even her mother was nervous.

The doors opened from the inside, and Thali was awed by the sight before them. The largest sitting room she'd ever seen loomed before her, the ceiling towering to at least the height of two of the doors she'd just slipped through. Several sitting areas dotted the room, lush couches and carpets softening the vastness of it. How many sitting areas did one family need?

Rommy followed their parents and led her past two sitting areas to a trio of people standing before one of the longest and most ornate tables she'd ever seen. It was carved out of white marble, but every crevice, swirl, and etching was filled with gold. Even the table edges were gold. An intricate design like a tapestry was carved into the marble tabletop, with various dyes in the grooves depicting an image. She couldn't make it out though, as the three awaiting their arrival blocked it.

The woman and man looked about the same age as her own parents, maybe a little older. The third person, Thali thought, must be their daughter. She was a little younger than Thali, maybe eleven or twelve. Thali was pleased to see that the two women were dressed as she and her mother were, in giant hoop skirts with slip bodices and sleeves and high collars.

"Lady Jinhua, Lord Ranulf, it's an honor to see you again, old friends." The man came forward. He smiled as easily as her father did and embraced him like an old friend.

"Ranulf, Jin. We're so happy to have you stay with us for a few days." The lady's voice, reminding Thali of a flute, floated over to them as she approached Thali's mother to embrace her. Thali and Rommy waited silently.

Finally, her mother stepped back and to the side. "You remember our son, Romulus. And this is our daughter, Routhalia."

"My, you've grown so tall since last I saw you! I can barely believe you're the same young boy we saw two years ago!" the man said. He stuck a hand out, and Rommy shook it and smiled. Rommy was a natural charmer, so he was all smiles and compliments when they were presented to people. Thali was always more awkward, and this was her first time visiting these people.

The woman turned to Thali. "You'll have to excuse my husband's bad manners. He's terribly fond of your family and gets excited when you all come to visit. We are Lord and Lady Okshin, but please, call us Kir and Elsjo. It's our pleasure to finally meet you, Thali." She wrapped Thali in a hug. When she pulled back, she said, "And this is our daughter, Jify," Lady Okshin said. She gently nudged Jify forward.

The young girl stiffly extended a hand. Thali took it and shook the limp offering politely. She smiled at Jify, but the girl looked down at her shoes immediately. Thali turned her attention back to Lady Okshin, seeing a brief frown cross her face before the smile returned.

"Jify, why don't you show Thali around? I'm sure Rommy wants to join us since he's likely learning about the business?" She cocked an eyebrow at Lady Jinhua, who smiled and nodded.

Thali knew a dismissal when she heard one, and while she was glad not to have to sit and listen for the next several hours, she wasn't sure Jify wanted anything to do with her. But when Jify slid away from the group and headed for a side door, Thali closed her eyes and took a couple of deep breaths before plastering a fake smile on her face. When she opened her eyes, she was surprised to see that Jify had paused there, waiting for her.

When Thali caught up to her, Jify said, "Hi. I'm honored to accompany you. Is there anywhere you'd like to see? Or should we just wander until suppertime?" Jify sounded like a stiff automaton, as if she was rehearsing lines out of a book.

"I'd like to see the garden, if that's all right with you. I've never seen statues like those before," Thali said, hoping she hadn't offended Jify with her phrasing.

Jify's shoulders seemed to relax, but the smile was still plastered on her face like a mask. Without saying anything else, she suddenly turned down a corridor, then at the end of it, turned right when they hit a wall and continued toward a doorway at the end. Thali was impressed with how quickly such a small girl could walk. Being on a ship for so long was starting to show as Thali's breaths came faster.

Jify looked sharply to the right and her pace halved. It was kind of Jify to slow down for her, but now Thali felt like an invalid. They pushed through the doors, Jify holding the door for Thali as they emerged outside.

Thali stopped suddenly the moment they exited. Two rows of lilac bushes made an aisle from the door to as far as the eye could see. She squinted to find the end of the pathway, but it went beyond her sight. Thali was tempted to use her other gift, but when she glanced at Jify, the younger girl was staring at her, so Thali threw the idea behind her mental wall. Her heart racing, she swallowed and tried to cover her anxiety with a question. "Jify, if you don't mind my asking, could you tell me about the statues I saw to the right when we came in?" She knew she was being ridiculous. Jify wasn't a mind reader, so there was no way the girl could have guessed what Thali had been thinking of doing. Her mother was right; she should just keep it buried.

"Of course. It'd be my pleasure." Jify smiled that mask of a smile again and started down the pathway. Quite suddenly, an opening on the right appeared, and Jify stopped. "This way please." She stuck her hand out stiffly, her elbow glued to her side.

"Thank you," Thali said, walking through the gap in the bushes. A wall of bushes on her left rose as high as the walls of the house. To her right was a wall of tall, skinny trees. They were almost as high as the smallest mast of their ship, but even then, it only reached the tail of a cow statue standing upright on two legs. She looked again at Jify, who was again staring at her. When Jiffy didn't say anything, Thali asked, "Would it be all right if I looked at it straight on? Are there specific rules about this place?" Thali had been taught to be cautious, for offending people of different cultures was all too easy.

"Yes. You may go anywhere here. Only women are allowed in this temple. But please do not touch the flowers, seedlings, or the statue itself. We pray to the minotaur for fertility. It is said that if you plant a seed in the dirt at her feet, you will be blessed with healthy children," Jify said, still smiling mechanically.

Thali nodded, wondering whether Jify was extremely nervous, really didn't want to be here, or just plain crazy. Shoving the rude thoughts to the back of her mind, Thali eased around the billowy trees to the statue's front so she could examine the minotaur more closely. As she did, she stopped dead in her tracks as she took in the field of flowers before her. The flowers weren't arranged in any particular way; there were just flowers of all colors and kinds in jumbles. Here and there were patches of grass. Thali realized women likely chose any free patch of soil to plant their seedlings. It was one of the most beautiful things Thali had ever seen. She had to walk ten long steps to the right to get safely to the edge, where there weren't any flowers.

Thereafter, she ensured she stayed on the edge of the field of flowers until she finally turned the corner and could see the front of the statue. She walked along the grass border, keeping a respectful distance from the flowers, a few other women carefully choosing the right spot for their seedlings, and the statue itself. When Thali reached the center, she looked up and saw a beautiful stone woman with the lower body of a cow. It was a large cow, more muscular then ordinary cows, but a cow nonetheless. She'd heard of minotaurs before; she'd seen drawings of them in some books in her friend's library, so she wasn't completely surprised.

But she was awed. Thali looked up at the statue again, at the pure white stone; the woman was beautiful and fierce. She had hard, intense eyes, but her sharp, angular features were strong. She looked as if she might start moving, the stone being a perfect medium to show off the angles of her face. Her cheekbones were high, and her lips full. Thali smiled. She didn't look particularly motherly, but she looked like someone women should look up to.

"Would you like to see the others?" Jify asked.

Thali smiled at her host and followed Jify as she led the way out of the first courtyard and down another long aisle.

"Jify, is there another entrance to the temples?" Thali remembered the word the girl had used to describe what she would have called a courtyard.

"Yes, our people must navigate a maze to visit the temples. That is part of the pilgrimage they must make." Jify walked very slowly, and it made Thali feel awkward as she slowed her own pace to match the startlingly deliberate steps Jify took. "But we will take the shortcut so we can return for dinner."

"What are the four temples called?" Thali asked.

"They are the Temples of the Four. We believe they control life and death and are therefore the gods we devote our lives to."

"So ... that one is the god of women?" Thali asked. She hadn't wanted to say cow woman, and she wasn't sure she was a true minotaur.

"Yes. Vadentia is the god of females."

"And the others?" Thali asked.

Jify stopped. "There is also Yagaron, the Manticore, God of Water; Talmaro, the Cockatrice, God of Family; and Xenon, the Dragon, God of Metals."

It looked like Jify was waiting for her, so Thali just nodded. Jify led them through some tight spaces that Thali wasn't sure they were even supposed to go through.

The other statues were equally as gigantic. The God of Water's statue included flowing water and a series of small bridges so people could get closer. The God of Family had groupings of statues with groupings of mushrooms around those, and the statue of the God of Metals reminded her of the minotaur's temple, but instead of flowers, coins and various metal instruments were scattered in the shallow rivers running around the edges of its temple.

They were leaving the last temple—for the God of Metals, which reminded Thali of a huge, shiny snake—when she misstepped and rolled her ankle. "Ouch!" Thali leapt up as she tried to bounce away from the pain.

Jify was beside her in the next moment. She grasped Thali's arms to steady her. Thali was impressed at how strong Jify was. The small, slight girl hadn't looked this strong.

"Do you think you can hop to that bench there?" Jify asked. With her chin, she indicated a stone bench intertwined with coins that looked as if they were emerging from the bench legs.

"I think I can walk on it—" Thali started to put her foot down.

"No," Jify said, stopping Thali in her tracks. Jify's sudden sternness surprised her. "You could injure it further," the younger girl said. "It's best if we play it safe until we know what we're dealing with."

Thali nodded. She hopped carefully with Jify until they reached the bench and sat down.

"We're going to carefully put your leg up here along the bench and then take your boot off." Jify narrated everything she was doing before she did it, and Thali realized it made it a lot easier when she knew what to expect. Jify removed Thali's boot and her sock and then started to poke and prod at her ankle. She carefully moved it one way, then another, and stopped immediately when Thali flinched. "It's not broken, but I believe you've sprained your ankle."

"That happens all the time—" Thali started to say.

Jify shook her head. "You'll need to stay off it for a day once we apply a poultice and wrap it. It'll feel much better by tomorrow."

Thali looked up and realized they were at the temple farthest away from the main building.

"Don't move. I'm going to get someone to bring a litter to carry you back," Jify said.

Thali felt embarrassed. She really didn't want to cause trouble or inconvenience anyone. Her mother had taught her it was almost a sin to inconvenience someone else.

"Please, let me do this. I know what I'm doing," Jify said.

Thali was still stunned at how much sharper, clearer, and more enthusiastic Jify suddenly was compared to earlier. It made Thali nod to see her come alive and not be the dull, bored version of her previous self.

It wasn't long before Jify returned with a litter and two young men who carried her back on a piece of fabric between two poles. Jify walked alongside them as they headed back to the main building. Before entering though, they turned and went around back to a fountain depicting all four gods together and a building with gold trim.

"This is where we take care of the sick and injured," Jify said as they proceeded inside.

It was much nicer than any sick house Thali had ever seen before. There were streams and fountains and large glass windows or open-air spaces. As they entered, they went left, which, guessing from the statue at the end of the room, was the space for the God of Women.

Thali didn't know why she was feeling so brave, but she asked Jify, "Is there a God of Men?"

Jify shook her head. "Women have much more complicated bodies and ailments." Jify turned away then and spoke to someone as the two young men transferred Thali to a bed. There weren't many people in here, which was nice because it meant she didn't have to be right next to anyone.

"I've sent for your family, but we should start with the poultice now," Jify said. She went to the shelves behind the statue of the female minotaur and started to put some dried herbs into a mortar she pulled from the wall. When she was done, she brought it back with a pitcher of water and started to grind the mortar's contents into powder. She added some water, and soon a paste formed.

Thali's family arrived and gathered around her. Thali was embarrassed she'd interrupted their business dealings.

"Are you all right?" Lady Jinhua asked as she looked Thali up and down.

Thali nodded as Rommy made his way around her bed, looking carefully at her two naked ankles—one swollen—before sitting carefully on her other side. "It's just a sprained ankle."

"Which will be treated seriously so it doesn't get any worse," Jify's mother, Elsjo said as she arrived with Kir. They supervised their daughter as she created the paste.

"May I?" Kir approached her swollen ankle, and Thali nodded. On her ship, she would just have been told to rest up, and maybe she would have wrapped it, but Jify's family was taking this far more seriously than Thali was used to.

"Father specializes in muscles and tendons. What he's going to do will hurt, but it will make you feel a lot better much quicker," Jify said. She sounded proud of her father, making Thali wonder how this girl was the same girl who had shown her the temples.

Thali didn't have much time to think about that though as Jify's father's thumbs dug into the soft spots of her ankles, and her body nearly arced out of the bed in pain. Thali turned to her parents, but her mother took her hand on one side, and her brother took her hand on the other side.

"It's pain now for gain later," her mother said.

Thali swallowed whatever she'd wanted to say and looked, wide eyed, at her brother.

"They're the best, Rou. Just squeeze my hand. It'll be over soon," Rommy said. He didn't break eye contact with her as the next wave of pain came. This time it wasn't as bad, maybe because she knew it was coming, but she still had to fight her body as it wanted to retract, to pull away from the pain being inflicted on her. Thali was fighting so hard that she didn't realize she was about to pass out until the world went dark.

Thali woke to a much quieter place. It was darker, though the room was well-lit with candles strategically placed on reflective surfaces. She blinked and saw her brother in a chair next to her. He reached over and drew a couple of letters with a fingertip on the back of her hand. She smiled and nodded. It was a quiet, cavernous space, and Rommy rose quietly to pour her a glass of water. She drained it and he took it from her.

"Does it throb now?" Rommy asked as he glanced at her ankle.

Thali tested her ankle out. It was stiff, but it wasn't painful and not nearly as sore as she'd expected it to be.

Jify came around the corner and spoke as she neared. "Sorry, I forget sometimes that our healing methods are not well practiced around the world. But I'm glad you're feeling better."

"Thank you, and thank your father," Thali said. She was proud of herself for remembering her manners.

"Is there anywhere I might fetch some soup for my sister?" Rommy asked.

"If you go down the stairs through that door there, you'll find the kitchen," Jify said.

Rommy glanced at Thali, who nodded.

"I'll be fine. Jify here will help me with whatever I might need," Thali reassured him.

He stared at her for another moment before finally turning around and leaving.

"It's sweet that he cares so much for you." Jify took a box out of her sleeve. "Thank you for giving me a chance to practice making poultices. Here, this is for you. I believe your family is leaving tomorrow, and I have to leave tonight for a retreat, but I made this for you, so you'll always be recognized as a friend of the Island of Four."

"Thank you," Thali said. She accepted the box and opened it. Inside was a beautiful golden lace collar. She gasped at the intricate designs. Tiny animals were woven into a scene as pretty as any painting. "How is this even made? It's so beautiful!"

Jify said, "Thank you. We healers spend much of our time watching patients overnight. It's become a sort of common hobby to craft lace."

"It's incredibly intricate. You're very talented," Thali said. She half wondered if her parents knew about this beautiful lace. Her merchant wheels were spinning as she thought of those customers who liked pretty, exotic things and what kind of price something like this might fetch—not that she would give this one away. This one would be hers forever. She'd already spotted one of her favorite animals: two horses rearing up, their hooves connected like they were creating an archway.

Jify's gaze followed Thali's when her brother returned. The young girl smiled. "I hope you heal well, and I look forward to your next visit." Jify bowed her head and Thali thanked her again. Jify turned to leave, nodding at Rommy on her way out.

"We've got vegetable with lentils, or vegetable without lentils—I think." Rommy held two bowls of soup. They looked exactly the same.

"With lentils?" Thali said. She didn't really care; she'd never really been a picky eater. No sailor could be.

Rommy handed her the bowl, but before she took it, she carefully placed the lid back on the lace collar's box and tucked it under her pillow.

A SHARED MEMORY

A PURPOSEFUL TINKLING OF glass pulled everyone's attention to the window. A bat was hanging inside the box Thali had installed along the windowpane.

She went over and opened the window, then slipped the box from its holder and petted the bat inside. She held a finger so the bat stepped out of the box, onto her finger. After taking the note from its leg, she reached into a little glass jar sitting nearby and fed the bat a cricket before getting it to hook onto her finger, thanking it, and sending it back home.

She'd left the box of lace on the bench in front of Elric on the bed, and when she turned back to her friends, she saw Indi had gotten a paw stuck in it. Indi shook her paw, but the box was stuck on, and Elric scrambled to grab it before she flung it across the room. Just as he almost reached it, the box broke free and went flying.

Nasir thankfully caught it before it hit him square in the face.

"When did you come in?" Daylor asked.

"I couldn't resist a good story," Nasir replied. He took a few steps in and handed the box back to Thali. Daylor offered him a plate of snacks, and he took one and stuffed it into his mouth as he took up his post, leaning against the door.

Indi sauntered over to the bench, licking her paw as if nothing had happened. Thali narrowed her eyes and realized the tiger wasn't actually licking her paw but had somehow draped the delicate lace around her paw.

"Indi, stop." Thali rushed over and asked Indi to extend her paw. Thali carefully extracted the lace from the claws and examined it closely, her heart racing; she hoped it wasn't wrecked. She sighed when she saw it was undamaged and returned it to its box and the box to the armoire.

Daylor turned to Alexius. "Didn't you have a story to add to the one Thali just told?"

"Thali, you said your friend comes from the Island of The Four?" Alexius asked.

Thali nodded.

"Well, I know The Four. Actually, you've all met one—well except you, Elric," Alexius said.

"What are you talking about?" Mia asked.

"Xenon is the dragon—or the snake-on that lace and a member of The Four, the deadliest group of warriors in history, along with Talmaro, Vadentia, and Yagaron," Alexius said.

"Wait, The Four—" Mia started.

"So named because even now, I believe, in Cerisan culture, the number four is synonymous with death," Alexius explained.

"You walked us into a death-warrior's home and didn't think to tell us?" Mia asked.

"Well, technically, he's only one-quarter of the deadly group." Alexius glanced at his feet.

"I thought he was also your brother-in-law?" Daylor asked.

Alexius nodded.

"I thought I had a strange family tree," Elric said.

Alexius shrugged. "When you live for a long time, it eventually gets complicated."

Thali looked over at Indi staring at Ana under Daylor's feet. Thali glanced at Ana. The dog was licking something under the table, clearly trying to be as quiet as possible. That told Thali Ana had something she wasn't supposed to have. Thali used her threads to peek at what Ana was licking, then said, "Ana, please give that back." She held her hand out.

Ana sagged and tried to tuck her prize under one paw as she looked up at Thali, wondering through her thread whatever she could mean.

"Ana, please." Thali kept her hand open. "Let's trade."

Thali glanced at Daylor. He picked a nice, simple cookie for Ana and held it in one hand. Ana stood and delivered the item to Thali's open hand before running over and leaping into Daylor's arms, taking the cookie, then flipping upside down on top of him to eat a second one that he put right in her mouth.

"I don't even understand how she got this out of the armoire ..." Thali said as she looked at the tiny blue figurine of a knight in full armor.

Nikolai

THALI GROUND HER TEETH together. Her brother had woken up on the wrong side of the bed this morning and had been taking it out on her all day and night. From unloading the ship to moving all the goods to market, he'd done nothing but bark and snap at her. It had turned her mood sour, and she'd started throwing crates on top of each other.

"Move, Rou," Rommy said. He held three crates and had almost run into her.

"Fine," Thali said. She put her crates down on the floor right where she was. It was still pitch black out, and it would be hours before people started to arrive for the market. She grabbed her staff and started walking away from their stall. "I'll be back for market," she hissed through clenched teeth at Mouse as she kept walking. Mouse caught up with her and popped a hat on her head. She tucked her hair underneath it. Part of her was looking for a fight, but the logical, more well-behaved part of her knew that if she caused trouble, it would only lead to more trouble. With the hat on, she'd pass as a boy and lecherous characters would leave her alone as she walked through the streets at this hour.

She headed toward her ship, but before the stone stairs that met the wooden dock, she unconsciously made a sharp right turn toward some of the darker, more questionable streets. Her heart started to race, and she felt the thrum of blood through her veins as she readied for a fight. Her darker nature had won. She rolled her shoulders in toward her chest, pulling her hat down low over her eyes, and slowed her walk almost to a shuffle, using her staff as a walking stick. Thali slowed as she walked into the most likely place to get accosted. It was an intersection where a street ended, leaving a small clearing between buildings that had no windows facing it. She bent over in the middle of the space to tie her shoe and sure enough, she saw three boys close in from three dark nooks. Without needing to look, she knew there were another three behind them, keeping watch down the quiet alleyways.

"Well, what do we 'ave 'ere?" one boy asked. The boys weren't much older than Rommy, but from their gait alone, Thali could tell they weren't experienced fighters. She almost felt bad for them. She felt her heart beating faster, letting the killing calm take over her body and hoping they wouldn't be completely disappointing opponents.

Thali stayed in her crouched position, her face down. She didn't want them seeing the calmness on her face. Let them think she'd frozen.

The boy on her left darted in and grabbed the hat off her head. "Oh look, boys! We're going to have some fun this morning."

Thali's hair fell over her face, and she growled. She knew what a group of boys would do to a girl. She growled on behalf of all the girls who didn't have her skills. Her heartbeat was so loud, she thought for sure they would hear it. Then her hearing dulled. She twisted her staff, so slowly that no one noticed the blade that slid out of the top and bottom.

"STOP." The voice was clear and strong.

Thali was startled when she looked up at an older man dropping from a rooftop to the ground.

The boys immediately dispersed, but the man caught one by the sleeve, turning him around to grab the back of his jacket. "Know that I saved your lives just now. That—" He pointed at Thali. "—is a warrior. Did you even see the blades slide out of her staff?" the man asked.

The boy's eyes went so wide, Thali could see the whites all the way around his irises. He shook his head violently before the older man let him go and he ran off.

Thali ground her teeth. Her body was thrumming with energy, and now she had nowhere to focus it.

"Come with me," the older man said. Instead of walking off like she thought he would, he turned and ran.

Her body reacted without thinking, and she sprinted after him. He ran down the streets and made a few sharp turns until he was running along the seawall. Thali wasn't stupid enough to run further away from the sea and her ship, but she was glad to expend the energy. She stretched out her legs, elongating her gait. Her body had been ready, joyful even, to do what it had been itching to do. She continued to follow him along the seawall until, ahead, she saw a gate, a manor tucked behind it, and a stone wall. The older man stopped and walked to it. He opened the gate and tied it open, using the lock to keep it that way.

Thali didn't feel threatened by him. She recognized the steps he was taking to make her feel at ease. She could scale the wall pretty easily too if she had to.

"There's a wooden dummy you're welcome to hack at over there. I'm going to get tea. I'll be back in ten minutes." The older man disappeared to the left, and Thali scanned the area before stepping through the gate.

The seawall continued past the gate to a lookout. A wooden floor with a couple of wooden dummies bolted into it lay a few feet from the edge. She looked out beyond the wall to the ocean and the beach to the left. It was a beautiful spot to train.

She felt her muscles want to work, want to hit something, so she took her energy out on the wooden dummy. *Clack, clack, bang, clack, bang, clack, clack!* She let her body slip into the rhythm of a pattern she'd been working on lately. Thali didn't care if anyone saw, though she never felt eyes upon her. She did see the old man come back with a tray and two cups and sit at a table further along the seawall. He sat facing her but looking out at the beach.

Thali had been panting when she started, and now, drenched in sweat, she stopped and let her lungs gulp air greedily. She turned to look out at the ocean, sneakily taking peeks at the older man. He was well-dressed, not in the fancy way of flashy nobles, but in the expensive way of quality fabric. His clothes were well-worn but cared for. She noticed he was more muscular than she had originally thought, and as she looked around her, she guessed that he himself was a warrior.

Her breathing calmed, and she felt her body starting to settle. Her anger had melted into annoyance, though she knew it was best she hadn't badly beaten or killed those boys. She calmly ambled to the little table and saw the towel he'd left her. She thought it odd that she had never met this man though she'd been to this city half a dozen times before. Once she got closer, she saw that he had a scar from his right cheek to his left forehead, into the hairline. It was faded and blended into his wrinkles, but still it was there.

He turned to her, smiling gently. "I don't believe we've had the pleasure of meeting. Nikolai." He stuck his hand out, not palm up like gentlemen did for ladies, but thumb up to shake her hand.

Thali took the hand and shook it. "Thali," she said. If he wasn't going to use his title, then she wouldn't either.

"Please, have a seat," he said. He moved the chair in front of her with his foot.

Thali sat down, intrigued by this strange man. He hadn't asked her any of the questions one normally would.

"You're an outstanding warrior," he said. He had turned his attention back to the waters and cliffs below.

"You must be too," Thali said.

The man smiled. "I had my day. I do it mostly for exercise now." He turned his attention back to Thali, gently taking the teapot sitting between them and filling the two cups he'd placed on the table. There were a few biscuits too, ones Thali recognized from the market with their signature red jam in the middle, dusted with sugar, and cut in the shape of stars.

Thali narrowed her eyes. Had the teapot been steaming before she sat down? She peeked into the cups and saw their metallic interior. She recognized this metal as one that indicated the presence of poison. He'd carefully chosen these cups so she'd know he hadn't poisoned anything.

She took the teacup, noticing the swirls of heat above it. How had the tea stayed hot all this time? She took a tiny sip after watching the man bring a cup to his own lips. A familiar tea filled her mouth, and she let it warm her throat. The ocean breeze was cooling the sweat on her skin, and she was starting to feel grateful for the hot tea to keep warm.

"There's a blanket on the chair if you like," Nikolai said.

Thali turned around and was surprised by the blanket draped over the chair. She didn't remember it being there when she'd sat down. Had it appeared out of nowhere? "Thank you," she said, wrapping the blanket around herself.

The man smiled into his teacup. They sat sipping tea, looking out to the ocean for many minutes. Thali didn't feel awkward or pressured to speak. When her cup was empty, the man refilled it. She was surprised that the tea hadn't cooled at all. It had stayed hot. Every additional cup had the same steam curling above it.

"Thali," he said finally, as if he had been rolling her name around his mouth for a time. "May I offer you some wisdom to consider, warrior to warrior?"

Thali didn't know what to say to that, so she nodded, letting him continue.

"It's not often that warriors develop a killing calm. I've fought in wars and skirmishes, and I can tell you I've only ever witnessed it a dozen times or so." He snuck a peek at her, so she kept her expression blank.

"I lived in a killing calm for years. And I would advise you to live in it as little as possible."

"Why?" The word escaped her lips before she had a chance to clamp it down. It felt good to be in that state, powerful.

The man looked out at the ocean. He stared at the horizon for a few minutes.

Light was filling the sky now, and it was beautiful. Thali wondered if he was expecting someone or if she should just leave. She decided she'd just sip her tea.

"This silence. Is this what the killing calm feels like to you?" he asked.

Thali nodded slowly. She wasn't really sure she should be admitting so much to a stranger.

"This—" He raised his hands, not spilling a single drop of the tea in his left hand. "—this moment, this scene, is filled with emotion. The killing calm is not."

Now it was Thali's turn to be quiet. She sat thinking about what he'd just said. It didn't seem to make sense at first, and just when it did, she wasn't sure if it lost its logic or not.

"When you stay in it for too long, you turn off your feelings, your emotions, your connections to the world around you for too long. That's what makes us human ... I—" He sat up, refilled his tea and hers in two quick movements, then turned back to stare at the ocean. But Thali had seen the tear that slipped out of the inner corner of his eye.

He coughed. "I lost my family because of it." He turned to her then. "You're young. There will be plenty of times you're going to feel angry and will want to physically take it out on someone. But life is precious. Let killing be the absolute last solution. You're skilled enough to let your opponent try first and fail before you make that decision. You've been well-trained."

"What do you do when you're angry then?" Thali asked.

"I take it out on those." He slid his gaze to the wooden dummies. "I meditate."

Thali looked at her tea. Her mother had tried to get her to meditate, but she'd never really understood what that meant. She mostly just sat there quietly until the other person moved. "What exactly is meditation?"

He grinned. "It's like nothing. You clear your mind and try to leave it blank. If thoughts won't go away, you acknowledge them and push them aside. It's trying to clean your mind like you might clean or polish your weapons."

Thali nodded. So she *had* been doing it right. It just didn't seem useful.

"How are you feeling now?" he asked.

"Calm."

"May I be so bold as to ask what made you angry?"

"My brother. He's grumpy today, and he's been taking it out on me."

"You're lucky to have a brother so close to you."

"Do you have any siblings?"

"I did." His lips tightened into a line. "He was a good brother. I was not."

"What would you do if your brother made you angry?"

"Probably what you did," he said, then continued. "Now I wish I could go back and tell myself to hug him, especially when he was angry, to just love him and hug him."

Thali snorted. "That's ridiculous."

"Is it? Maybe that's what he needs? I'd been very close with my brother until an argument set us on diverging paths. I went to become a warrior, and he stayed behind to look after our people. He was so busy keeping it all afloat, he never learned an ounce of what I did as a warrior, so when they were attacked in the middle of the night..."

Thali opened her mouth to say something but didn't. She closed her mouth again and thought about the difficulties of the last day. Maybe her brother did need a hug. Suddenly, she felt the urge to do just that. She stood, scraping her chair on the ground. "Thank you for the tea, and for your ... advice." Thali said. She put the cup down and gave him a small bow. She folded the blanket and gently placed it back on the chair.

"You're very welcome." The man stood too and returned her bow.

"Is there anything I can do to thank you for your time?" Thali asked. She looked around, wondering if there was something she could do in return.

"Live your life," he said. "And live it well."

He shooed her away, and she gave him a second quick bow before grabbing her staff and running back down the seawall to their booth at the market. She made it to the edge of the market before literally running right into her brother.

He was scowling, but then a look of relief filled his eyes before it turned to annoyance. "Where have you been?" he demanded. "I've been looking everywhere for you."

She didn't even say anything. Thali brought her arms around her brother and squeezed him with her whole being.

He tensed at first but then eased into her hug and hugged her back. "Are you all right, Rou?"

"I am. Are you?"

"I am now," he said, sounding calmer now. "When did you learn to give such good hugs?"

She was silent as she held onto him for another minute. When he finally let her go, he slung his arm around her shoulders, and they walked back to their stall together.

It was a busy place now. There were people in all the aisles, some rushing around and some leisurely strolling. But their area wasn't as busy as usual.

"Where did all the carpets go?" Rommy asked. Bringing the giant stack of carpets to their stall all night had been one of the worst tasks, and now there were only three left.

"Someone with a scar came by and bought them all. Your parents even went to meet with him," Crab said.

"What? Who? I was gone for like five minutes." Rommy asked.

Thali guessed who it might have been. How he'd done it so quickly was beyond her. "I think I know. Come, you'll like him," Thali said. She took Rommy's hand, and they ran back the way she had come to the manor along the seawall.

Except this time, she went around to the front of the manor, only now realizing how grand it was. They had to slow to a walk as they walked along a winding path through a garden full of well-tended plants. Thali took some time to look around at the pretty flowers. They were combinations of ones she knew; some were the shape of a rose but the color of a daisy, some were the shape of a daisy but the color of a gardenia, and some had swirls of color as if a painter had dipped their brush into a cup of water, then swirled the watercolor right onto the petal.

When they finally reached the front door, Thali was about to knock, but the door opened as she raised her hand.

"Miss, if you'll follow me." A man she assumed to be the butler was simply dressed, but she noticed the quality of his clothes, as she had his employer's earlier. Thali had learned long ago to look at the clothing of the help to determine the quality of the person who employed them.

As they traveled down a hall, Rommy gripped his staff, readying to fight their way out even as Thali relaxed her own grip on her staff. She noted the stone walls, warmed with tapestries and rich wooden furniture. It didn't look at all like she would have imagined Nikolai's tastes to be.

They finally stopped at the open doors of a study. This was more like what she had imagined. The furniture was simple, and though books didn't fill the wall-to-wall shelving, it was clear he was trying.

And in the middle of the room stood her parents, chatting with Nikolai, who was standing behind a desk. Rommy looked stunned but quickly hid his surprise.

"Ah, children," her father said. "Nikolai said you'd come to find us. Please, come and meet Master Nikolai." He ushered them closer, and Nikolai shook Rommy's hand. Thali went in for a hug. "Thank you," she whispered.

When she backed away, she saw surprise in her father's face but not her mother's. Jinhua was surprisingly at ease for a mother who had just seen her daughter hug a complete stranger. At the same time, her staff was horizontal on the floor; she truly trusted this person.

She smiled as Thali glanced at the staff and then her. "Nikolai and I knew each other when we were children," she said.

Thali turned around, looking at Nikolai again.

"I'm sorry I didn't say anything. I wasn't sure your mother would remember me."

"How did you come to know each other? Were you in Cerisa?" Ranulf asked.

"Nikolai came to my family when he was three. My family rarely took in students from other families, but Nikolai was part of our family for six years." Jinhua smiled fondly and looked down.

Was her mother blushing? Thali was taken aback.

Her father picked up on it right away. "Oh? How old were you?"

"I was six when you arrived," she said, proving to Nikolai that she remembered him.

"I never thought I'd see you again. Imagine my surprise when I came across your daughter—who is your spitting image—in the city," Nikolai said.

Her mother and father quickly glanced at Thali, a clear question in their eyes.

"She was about to beat three boys senseless," Nikolai said as he smothered a laugh.

Thali felt a little betrayed at his words, but no one noticed. Her eyes went to a drawing of a man who looked like Nikolai, with children and a wife standing in front of the manor.

"She's a lot like you when you were younger." Nikolai raised his eyebrows at her mother.

"They deserved it," Thali's mother said. She laughed, bringing Thali's attention back to her.

"Ranulf, Jinhua, please say you'll stay for lunch. Give an old man an excuse to use more than one room in this place," Nikolai said.

"Don't call yourself old!" Jinhua admonished. "If you're old, then I'm ancient!" She smiled.

That put Nikolai between a rock and a hard place. "Time has been ever better to you than I," he said. He came out from behind the desk to show the hobble in his gait.

Thali's eyes narrowed. He hadn't had that hobble an hour ago. She was just about to open her mouth when she saw her father stand a little taller. Now Thali understood. Nikolai was faking his injury to put her father at ease. He was a very kind person.

"Come along, let me show you where I plan to put all these carpets," he said. Thali jumped in front of her mother to take Nikolai's arm as he led the way out of the library. They walked down the hall and Thali saw a small rocking horse in one of the rooms they passed. Thali whispered to Nikolai, "This is your brother's home, isn't it?"

Nikolai nodded. The decor was extravagant, over the top even, and it was kept immaculately clean. Normally, bachelors' homes had a fair dust build-up, but not Nikolai's house. She wondered what Nikolai's brother had been like.

They ended their tour in the dining room, and Thali refrained from looking around until she was in her seat. The floor was of stone yet covered in carpet until halfway under the table, which was also of stone and shone as brightly as a coin. Giant shells behind the candlesticks on the walls reflected more light than the metal disks she'd seen used in other homes to reflect the light. "It's beautiful," Thali said.

"Thank you. I collected those shells by hand in a faraway place," Nikolai said.

After that, he turned back to her parents. He tried to include Thali and Rommy when he could, but her mother and father moved so quickly between topics that Thali and Rommy gave up. They had been to many meals like this and knew there would be many more.

"How do *you* know him?" Rommy leaned over to ask.

"I was ... angry and ran off. He stopped me from beating on some boys looking for trouble. His back courtyard has wooden dummies, and he let me take my anger out on them. Then we had a little chat over tea. It's beautiful back there, you know. He has a view of the ocean."

"Oh?" Rommy said.

Thali knew he was wondering about the hundreds of things that were wrong about what she'd just said and was wondering whether she'd truly been that stupid. "I know, don't trust strangers, but he ... he knew things. He's a warrior," she explained.

"All the more reason you should have stayed far away."

"I was careful. He made sure I always had an escape route, that I was never pressured into anything. He even drank his tea before me."

"All right," Rommy said slowly, though his eyes still narrowed with suspicion. He was always the one to give her a chance and trust her abilities. Even if he was still suspicious, he trusted her more than her parents usually did.

Thali suddenly noticed the quiet in her head. There was nothing clamoring for her attention, no animals in the house. She wondered why a man so lonely wouldn't have any animal companions. She searched a moment in her mind and didn't even find a rat in the walls. "That's strange," she said.

"What's strange?" Rommy asked.

"There are no animals here, not even rats or pigeons or seagulls."

Rommy narrowed his eyes, suspicion shining again as he straightened his spine. It was so unusual to have no animals near that Thali began to wonder if maybe they should be more suspicious. She could count on one hand the times she'd been in a place with no animals.

The meal was nearly over now and they were savoring dessert. Thali gulped hers down, trying to look down into her lap as if she were bored. She wasn't supposed to, but Thali went into her mind to crack open the door a tiny bit to see if she could see any animal threads anywhere. Within this room, within this entire manor, there was nothing, not a single other creature except the humans in this room and a handful of humans in the kitchens. A small staff for a single person was not unusual, but to have no creatures at all—not a dog or cat or mouse—was very strange. Even if Nikolai didn't have a pet, usually one of the kitchen staff had a dog that hung around the kitchen waiting for scraps or a cat on mouse duty.

"We must be boring you two to death. If you'd like to explore the manor, please do. There's nothing dangerous here, except perhaps the excessive and embarrassing amount of dust." Nikolai's eyes glinted as he looked at Thali, almost as if he was challenging her. He immediately turned his attention back to her parents before she could ask him anything.

"If you two would like to walk around, I don't see the harm in it," her mother said. Her father nodded.

The implication was clear to Thali. They were to stay together and not go poking their noses in closed doors.

"Thank you, Nikolai," Thali said as she stood. Rommy looked like he wanted to stay, but Thali dragged him from his chair, and they left.

"What? Why'd you drag me away from my dessert?" Rommy whispered.

"Don't you feel something off? Why are there no animals, not so much as a rat?" Thali asked.

"Not everyone collects menageries of animals like we do. Haven't you ever been to a place where there were none?" Rommy asked.

"No. Well, maybe? I don't always look. Mother says not to. I just happened to look this time because it was too quiet, and I was bored." She didn't tell Rommy that she often checked when they were in new places.

They walked along the plush carpeted hallway until it forked in three directions. Looking down the hallways, Thali couldn't decide which way to go. They all looked similar.

"Let's stick to outside for now," Rommy suggested. They took the left hallway, the one with all the windows.

Thali stopped at the first window to look outside and saw the courtyard from earlier. "Look Rommy. That's where I was earlier today. Look at the view." Thali pointed to the ocean.

Rommy stopped and looked out the window. Then he stared and gaped. "Did you see that?"

"See what?" Thali asked, squinting and trying to see what he was seeing. She swept her gaze along the seawall, in front of it, and along the courtyard. She didn't see anything out of the ordinary.

"Never mind," Rommy said. He blinked, then turned away from the window. They continued to walk down the hallway but stopped to look out each window, Thali searching as Rommy stared at the same spot in the ocean.

Thali turned her attention to the tapestry on the opposite wall. Half the doors were open along this hallway, but when they poked their heads into each one, they discovered only plainly decorated bedrooms, nothing of true interest. She stopped at a tapestry hanging opposite a bed in one room. It was very strange looking. It depicted a large argent dragon on it next to another, smaller, blue dragon. It was strange because the silver dragon was more snakelike, whereas the blue dragon was more crocodilian, except with a large rear end. The strangest thing, though, was a man in armor not facing the dragons but standing with them. Both dragons faced a stone archway bigger than even them and many, many times bigger than the armored man.

Dragons weren't real, but she'd seen depictions in tapestries all over the world, snakelike ones in Cerisa, and heavy-bottomed crocodilian ones in her father's family castle. Tapestries often showed knights battling dragons, but to be standing harmoniously with them? And two so very different ones? She shook her head. "That's kind of strange, isn't it?" Thali asked when Rommy came up behind her.

"It's just a tapestry," Rommy replied, though he couldn't seem to tear his own gaze away either.

Thali looked at the rest of the tapestry for clues, but the rest looked like any other, with vines and flowers and leaves embroidered along the edges like a border and a background of trees and a sandy beach. She looked at the dragons' feet and saw a familiar courtyard. "Rommy, doesn't that look a lot like the courtyard out there?" She pointed with one finger to where the dragons and the man stood and out the door of the bedroom with another.

"It could be any courtyard."

"I suppose so," Thali said hesitantly.

Finally, Rommy tore himself away, and they left the bedroom and continued down the hall. They were silent, lost as they were in their own thoughts. Instead of heading outside as they had intended, their feet took them back to the dining room just as their parents were leaving it with Nikolai.

"Perfect! We were just coming to see how far you'd gotten," Nikolai said. He glanced at Thali, and she could have sworn his eyes were searching. Nikolai walked them to the front door. "There are a few gifts I'd like to give your family," he told Thali's parents. He ducked into a side room and came out with two small boxes. He gave a purple one to Thali and a green one to Rommy.

Thali undid the ribbon and opened the purple box to find a small blue metal figurine: it was the knight in the tapestry.

She glanced over at Rommy. His longer green box held a beautiful but strange quill. It had no feather like most did but was thick and compact.

"This quill holds ink inside. You can write an entire letter without dipping it in more ink," Nikolai explained.

Rommy looked at it with wonder and gently put it back in the box. "Thank you," he said, bowing to Nikolai.

"And that is something to help you remember this place," he told Thali.

Thali thought Rommy's gift was much more exciting but put on a bright smile and thanked Nikolai anyway. She'd been taught to be grateful and show appreciation for gifts given.

Nikolai led them out to where a carriage waited to take them back to their ship.

After they had said their goodbyes and climbed in, Thali sat quietly as her parents discussed the items Nikolai had asked them to look out for and bring back should they come across them.

She slumped in her seat as Rommy took his pen out and tried to use the candlelight inside the carriage to see through the pen and figure out where the ink would go. Then she shrugged and opened her box again. When she lifted the tiny little knight out, the candlelight shone on something along the inside edge of the box. Thali lifted the tiny, soft pillow the knight had been laying on.

Written on the bottom of the box was, "Should you ever need assistance, tap me three times and ask." Thali replaced the cushion and took a closer look at the little knight. It was extraordinarily finely detailed. She could see every link of chain mail and the grate on his helmet. Astonished, and touched, she put the little knight back in the box and tucked it carefully in her inside vest pocket. She would keep the little knight with her most precious things.

Echoes of Gratefulness

W HEN THALI PLACED THE little blue knight on top of the armoire, Elric asked, "Are you sure you want him staring at us?" Elric asked.

"You're probably right." Thali smiled though she only half believed anything would actually happen if she did what Nikolai asked her to. She gently moved the tiny blue figure inside the armoire, standing on the shelf so he would greet her when she opened it.

"Alexius, what happened there?" Mia, sitting next to Alexius, asked.

When Thali turned around, she saw Mia poking at his forearm. Everyone turned to look.

Alexius rolled his sleeves back down. "It's nothing. I scratched myself when I was training."

Thali felt it wasn't the truth as color flushed his cheeks to match the hair on his head.

"What weapon scratches dragons?" Daylor asked.

"In human form, I'm as delicate as you are," Alexius said.

"I'm pretty sure I've seen you take hits that would have crushed my bones," Tilton piped in.

"Okay, almost as delicate then," Alexius amended.

Thali watched her friends banter and grinned. This was just like when they were in school. Yet here they were in a palace, surrounded by luxury. She felt so happy they were all still friends.

Elric crawled over Indi—carefully. She'd almost bitten him once when he'd crushed her tail by accident. Daylor moved the tray to help, and Elric snatched a couple of the pastries, then sat back in the bed. Indi just flicked her tail—in acknowledgment of his care, Thali knew.

"Thali?" Daylor offered her the tray, and she took a couple of cookies before they were all gone. She suspected Daylor was offering so he could have a free-for-all of whatever was left.

"Thanks." Thali took a bite of cookie and a sip of tea. Everyone had a teacup, and Thali wondered just how that had happened. Even Nasir had one now.

"Some useful magic," Alexius said as he followed her gaze.

"I'll say," Mia said. "Can you make more of those cream puffs appear?"

"Just for you." Alexius grinned and two cream puffs popped up next to her cup of tea.

"Why don't you use it all the time?" Daylor asked.

"A person can only hold a finite amount of magic, and given the threats we've been under, I try to keep my reserves full in case we need them," Alexius explained.

"Well now I feel terrible for wasting it on cream puffs," Mia said.

"I use less magic moving something that already exists," Alexius said.

Daylor opened his mouth, but Tilton shot him a look. Instead, Daylor rose and went to the armoire. "What about this one? It reminds me a bit of that ring." He pulled out a silver cuff with vines that swirled this way and that around little amethyst gems embedded in the cuff; silver crowned each gem. Daylor turned it over and squinted. "To Scratchy from Hammy," he read out loud. He looked up again at Thali, confused.

"I didn't realize it had an inscription," Thali said. And she shared another story.

Hammy

"**H**ELLO."

Thali spun around and quickly schooled her expression, hiding her surprise. "Hi."

"May I join you?" a young man asked, gesturing to the tiny table she was huddled at.

"Please," she said, smiling her most pleasant smile. Thali glanced at the empty seat. She didn't dare let go of the warm mug she held. She was so cold, and the mug was the only thing keeping her from turning to ice.

"I've heard a lot about you, and if you'll forgive me, I couldn't wait to meet you." He smiled and she swore she saw a spark of light glint off his teeth.

She pressed her lips together as she kept smiling. She hated being known here.

He looked down, making her wonder if he'd noted her lack of enthusiasm.

"How do you like our little party tonight?" he asked, swiftly changing the topic and glancing around the room.

There were quite a few people here, but not nearly enough to heat the room made of ice. It was a novelty that her cousins had spent months planning. They'd created blocks of ice to build a small ice castle. Thali hated it, but this party was theirs, and she didn't want to be rude. "It's ... cold," she said.

His lips quirked up on one side. He glanced back at her hands holding the mug so tight it might actually break. In one swift motion, he reached up to his shoulders. Then with a smooth twirl, he swept his fur cloak off and onto her shoulders. Thali immediately sank into the warmth.

"My apologies, I should have noticed." His smile was now a little hesitant.

Thali, finally not shivering, relaxed and said, "Thank you. It's very kind of you to lend me your cloak."

"It would please me if you kept it. This is the beginning of your stay here, I believe, and I think it would serve you much more than I."

Thali's eyes narrowed. She never trusted generosity. If there was anything she had learned as a merchant's daughter, it was that everything had a price. If not in money, then in favors. "Sorry, what did you say your name was?"

The stranger's cheeks turned pink, and he glanced down. There was something very familiar about him. He chuckled. "I'm very much off my manners tonight. I owe you another apology. I am Lord Dougal. But I'd rather you call me Hamish."

Even without his cloak, Thali saw that he dressed appropriately for his station. She racked her brain to remember what she knew about the different lords here. It was hard enough keeping track of her cousins—and now her cousins' kids—but there were also other lords here. By his clothing alone, and his willingness to part with a fine fur cloak, he must be a powerful, wealthy lord. He stood and swept into a low bow, so Thali felt obligated to offer a hand in greeting. She forced herself not to curl her lip in disgust as he kissed the back of it. She thought this particular greeting was disgusting, men kissing ladies' hands. She always surreptitiously wiped her hand after.

"It's an honor to make your acquaintance, Miss Routhalia of Densria. We don't often have guests from far off lands, and you are famous."

"My family is famous. I have yet to make a name for myself," Thali muttered. Hamish's eyebrows raised, and she cursed herself for being heard.

"Surely you do not doubt your skills and abilities, having been trained by two of the best in the world," he said, a laugh hidden in his smile.

She looked at him then, really looked at him. "I'd like to be known for my own merits."

"I think you will be. With knowledge and skills like yours, how could you not?"

Thali started to wonder how she could extricate herself from this conversation. She looked around the room for Rommy. She was used to dealing with people who thought she was older than she was, but Lord Dougal was close to her age, so she felt uneasy.

Lord Dougal leaned in, closer to Thali than she liked. "So ... how am I doing, Scratchy?"

Thali's eyes went wide, and she turned her full attention back to Hamish. She really looked closely at his face this time. "Hammy?" she whispered, jaw dropping in shock.

Now he grinned wider than before, with real crinkles around his eyes.

Thali leapt over the table and threw her arms around him. "I can't believe it's you!" She backed up again and looked him up and down. It had been six years since she'd seen Hammy, and he'd changed completely.

Hammy grinned. "Turns out the fat redistributed as I grew taller." Not only had Hammy become tall and slender, but a full red-brown beard covered his face now.

"How did you grow such a beard since I last saw you!" Thali asked. She continued to look at Hamish, blown away by the difference in his appearance.

Hammy shrugged.

Remembering their conversation, if Hammy was now Lord Dougal, that meant his father had passed. "I'm sorry about your father," she said.

Hamish looked down. "It was a couple of years ago. He just ... died, in the middle of the night."

Thali reached for his hands to comfort him. "It's never easy," she said, feeling awkward. "I can't believe I never knew your full name."

Hamish laughed. "It never really mattered then. But at least I had Mother. She knew a lot about Father's job, so she helped me with the transition." Hammy squeezed her hands back.

"I should visit your mother. My family should at least," Thali said, dutifully.

"I would love if you came to visit us." He grinned.

"Don't start again with that noble blither-blather. I was considering tackling you just to get out of the conversation, and now I know I could." Thali grinned back. She put her elbow on the table and slumped over it, relaxing more and more as the cloak kept her toasty warm.

"You never even knew that my nickname came from my actual name, did you?" Hamish asked, still facing her.

"No." Thali said.

"How long are you here this time?"

"A couple weeks," Thali said. She snuck a glance at Hamish. She still had a hard time believing this suave, slender man was the same boy she'd had to push over the wall to escape the cows chasing them.

"I own two thousand head of cattle now," Hamish said. He must have been thinking of the same memory.

"No way," Thali said. Hamish had been terrified of the cows after they'd been chased.

"The cows and I have reconciled. Plus, if they're truly terrible, I just eat them."

Thali's eyes went wide.

"Don't be like that. They serve a purpose. They have a great life before then."

"I understand."

"This room is something else," Hamish said, looking around again at the blocks of ice.

"I just hope we're not buried alive," Thali said. She shivered as she glanced around them, then beyond the ice room to the snow that covered the ceiling.

"I'll dig us out." Hamish opened his vest and showed Thali the ice pick he'd hidden in his pocket.

Thali laughed. He was definitely still the same Hammy.

A few years earlier ...

Thali sighed. She'd tucked herself between two stone columns in hopes that her little cousins wouldn't find her.

"Ahh ..."

"*Shwing, shwing, shwooong!*"

"No! It's *clink, clink, clink!*"

Thali pulled her legs in and around and dropped off the other side of the short wall, pressing up against the rough stone and turning her head so she was completely hidden, she hoped, from the other side.

The voices quieted as the little boys swung their swords at each other and continued along the wall. She counted to ten before she stood up. The angle of the ground made her scrape her entire arm on the rough stone wall, and she cringed.

"Do you normally injure yourself on purpose?" a voice asked from behind her.

She turned to see a round boy with a mop of straw-colored hair standing a few feet away from her. He looked more curious than malicious.

Before Thali could open her mouth, the boy's eyes went wide, and he looked in the direction of another archway before he put his finger over his lips, then skirted the wall and the horses in their smaller day paddocks. Thali followed, now curious about who this boy was hiding from, considering she had just been hiding from someone herself. He was a full head shorter than her, but perhaps he was the same age? She wasn't sure. She followed him around the paddocks and the barn. They finally stopped at the corner of the barn that faced the bigger pastures.

"Who were you hiding from?" Thali asked.

"Well, Scratchy, I was hiding from the older boys. They like to pick on me when given the opportunity."

"Scratchy?"

He gestured to her arms, and she looked down to see that her arm was indeed completely scratched up.

"And what should I call you?"

"Hammy," the boy said. She thought it was a little too on the nose, but he puffed his chest and stuck a hand out.

"So what do you normally do around here, Hammy?" Thali asked. She was trying to figure out if Hammy was one of her cousins. Her father had so many siblings that it was hard to keep track of all her relatives. It was overwhelming here, but at least it was friendly, for the most part.

They heard yelling and ducked behind an old trough. The boys sounded like they were a distance away, but Thali wanted to be sure. Fear flashed through Hammy's eyes.

"I'm sorry the older boys pick on you," Thali said. She wondered if her brother was one of the boys who picked on him.

"It's all right. I'm an easy target. And it's not like it's unique to me." Hammy shrugged. But he looked away, and Thali wondered if it hurt him more than he liked to admit. He changed the subject then. "Would you like to come fishing with me?" he asked.

Thali shook her head. "Do you know how to skip rocks on the river?" Thali asked.

Hammy shook his head.

"Do you want to learn?"

Hammy nodded.

I'll teach you then," Thali said.

They looked left and right before running into the cover of the trees and to the river.

"It's getting late and I should get back. They'll come looking for me," Thali said.

Hammy nodded. "Thank you for today."

"I appreciated it too. My cousins are so loud. It's nice to have some quiet." Thali turned her face up to the last warming rays of the sun.

"Would you like to go riding with me tomorrow?" Hammy asked.

"I would." Thali smiled. Another quiet day would be blissful.

"I'll meet you at the stables tomorrow after breakfast?"

They had left the river's edge and were walking back through the woods to the main house. Thali nodded, and they walked in silence the rest of the way to the stables. It was quiet now. Her cousins loved to eat, and the dinner table was like a battleground. Thali knew Rommy would make sure she had something, so she wasn't too worried about that. Hammy waved as he split off away from the stables, and Thali waved back as she kept going to the castle. She used the side entrance and took a deep breath as she washed up in the trough her aunt had installed by the door. She heard the cacophony of her cousins and aunts and uncles and took a deep breath before pasting a smile on her face and sliding into the dining room.

A long rectangular table that everyone was gathered around filled the room. Rommy always managed to secure a seat by the end of a bench and had saved her enough space to slide in. He slid a plate from his lap to hers. "I got some of your favorites before they were all gone."

"Thanks," Thali said. She kept the plate on her lap because she'd learned the hard way that anything on the table was fair game unless she could defend it. She ate quickly and pretended to put one or two things on her plate on the table, so she didn't draw the suspicion of the others. Even Rommy had to stand a few times to grab some roast meat freshly placed on the table. He cut it in half, then stuffed half in his mouth and put the other half on the plate on Thali's lap.

Thali looked around the table. All her cousins were surely here because if there was one thing her mother's and father's families shared, it was that everyone ate dinner together. The whole family's males all looked like her father, with hair that ranged from straw blond to dark auburn. The men were all bearded. Hammy wasn't here though. She'd suspected he wouldn't be when he hadn't followed her in.

"Where did you go off to today?" Rommy asked.

"I met a new friend. Do you know Hammy?" Thali asked.

Rommy nodded. "Rounder boy, blond hair?"

Thali nodded. "Do you and the others make fun of him?"

"We're not laughing *at* him. He's just funny!" Rommy said.

Thali shook her head. "I don't think he thinks so."

Unfortunately, one of her cousins called to Rommy then, so she didn't think he heard her. She sighed and looked up to see her father in his element. He was laughing with a couple of his brothers at the head of the table, but her mother was wearing her fake smile. She hated this, Thali knew. It was chaos. Jinhua's eye twitched every so often as she glanced from cousin to cousin. If Thali or Rommy had half the bad manners their cousins had around the dinner table, they'd be practicing drills for three days straight. But Lady Jinhua smiled and nodded politely as she spoke with some of Thali's aunts. Many of Thali's uncles and aunts didn't sit together, but her parents always did. That always made her smile and wonder if she would find someone like her mother and father had.

The next morning after breakfast, her cousins scattered for chores, so Thali knew she could sneak away without much notice. She was an early riser and had already trained, done her chores, and breakfasted.

Thali had told her parents where she was going and now walked down the front steps. She saw Hammy approaching well before he arrived. He was a terrible rider and bounced up and down in the saddle as the chestnut horse beneath him pinned its ears with every third step. He held the reins of a gray horse who was following and tied by a rope to the saddle on which he was bouncing.

The horses seemed to sigh as they stopped in front of Thali; she had covered the rest of the distance so Hammy's poor horse didn't have to go further.

"Good morning!" Hammy said.

"Good morning!" Thali smiled at her new friend. "Do you ride often?"

"Not at all."

"This isn't your first time on a horse, is it?" Thali asked.

"No, it's my third," Hammy said.

Thali blinked. She took Hammy's reins, untied the gray mare, and walked both around the stables to the field out back. "All right, I'm going to teach you then," she said. She also took a moment to pet both horses and crack open the door in her mind that connected her to the animals. She wasn't supposed to, but after Tariq's mother had died when she was struck by a young horse, Thali had told herself it was her duty to check on the horses she or anyone she cared about was interacting with.

She sent thoughts of calm and patience and friendliness to the two threads she saw there, hoping to buy them enough patience to get Hammy through the morning.

"All right, let's start," Thali said. She swung up onto the gray mare. She showed Hammy how to position his legs and tried to express how his body should feel and what it should do when the horse moved.

Only an hour later, they were riding out in the fields with some of the shaggy-looking cows. Hammy was a quick study and looked like a much better horseman than he had riding up the driveway. Thali thought it strange that he hadn't been taught to ride like most nobles. She didn't question him though; she was only glad to help him now. "You're doing much better. I'm confident you can keep your seat now."

"Thank you for teaching me," Hammy said. He squared his shoulders and kept his attention ahead as he adjusted his hands again.

Thali was just about to open her mouth to respond when they heard a moo and Hammy's horse spooked. He startled forward, but his hindquarters buckled down and his front tipped up. As if in slow motion, Hammy's arms pinwheeled. His horse took off, and Hammy tumbled off the side.

Thali's gray mare looked over at the other horse as if he was an idiot and didn't move as Thali dismounted and ran over to Hammy. "Hammy, are you all right?" she asked as she knelt by him.

He was lying on the ground and staring up at the sky. "I think I got too cocky." He moved his feet back and forth, moved his knees up and down, then finally sat up with Thali's help.

Thali looked into his eyes; he seemed all right. He blinked a few times, and she let him lean on her. "Every rider falls at some point," she said.

"And it's important I get back on the horse, right?" Hammy said. He seemed in good spirits, if not a little dazed.

Thali nodded. She looked over and saw his chestnut gelding trotting back toward them, the gray mare still standing where Thali had left her. "Maybe you should ride my horse though."

Hammy nodded, and they stood and sorted out their reins. Thali was impressed the reins on Hammy's horse were still intact and swung them over his head. Then she felt the ground start to rumble and wondered if it was her stomach. Or was it her mind playing tricks?

"Scratchy, do you feel that?" Hammy asked from the other side of the gray mare.

Thali poked her head around to see a herd of cows rushing toward them. "Hammy, we have to go."

Hammy's gaze followed hers and then he looked back at her. He looked truly scared. "I can't get on fast enough."

The cows were closing in. Thali didn't think she could stop that many even if she threw open the door in her mind. "Leave the horses. Let's go this way." Thali left her horse and grabbed Hammy's hand. They ran the opposite way to a stone fence ahead. They could make it if they ran and climbed over the fence. She pulled Hammy along, and they ran as fast as they could. When they got there, they were both panting.

"Over, get over the fence now!" Thali yelled.

The stones had mortar between them, so they had footholds. Hammy tried to scramble up.

Thali looked over. The cows were only fifteen feet away and not slowing down.

"Hurry, Hammy!" Thali shouted. She couldn't wait any longer or she'd be trampled. She climbed up, and when she reached Hammy's behind, she shoved her shoulder into it and continued to climb, pushing Hammy further and further until they were over the wall.

Luckily, they landed on soft grass on the other side. They lay there, catching their breath as they listened to the many hooves stomping past on the other side of the fence.

"Thank you," Hammy said.

"Maybe we should stick to the river," Thali said.

They were quiet then. Thali wondered if she'd offended her new friend, but then Hammy started to laugh. It made Thali laugh too, and soon they were both laughing until they had to stop to breathe again.

Thali smiled at the memory of how she and Hammy had become friends as she and Rommy prepared for an official visit to Hammy and his mother a few days after the party in the ice castle.

"You didn't know that Hammy was Hamish Dougal, the son of our family's oldest friend?" Rommy was giving her a hard time as they dressed.

"No. How would I know that?" Thali asked.

"Because you two have spent so much time together. Did you never talk to each other?" Rommy sounded amazed.

"Yes, we talked, but we just never talked about titles, I guess."

"He knew yours."

"Of course he knew mine, Rommy. Everyone knows who we are before we even open our mouths." Thali retorted. She was getting annoyed that he was pestering her over something that didn't matter to her.

"Remember when they were cute and little and didn't fight?" Thali's father remarked from the other side of the desk in their family's quarters.

"Ah, but remember the diapers and getting peed on?" Thali's mother crinkled her nose as if she remembered the smell.

"Eww, Mother!" Thali exclaimed. She was thankful that at least they were alone on the ship, except for Crab. He always stayed on the ship now.

Thali and Rommy led the way as they disembarked and headed for the carriage that would take them to Hammy's home. Thali was surprised she'd never seen his home before. They'd always played or met by her cousins' castle.

"Is it strange that Hammy never took me to his home?" Thali asked Rommy.

Rommy shrugged. "Ask him why."

They passed the Dougal family estate and then the familiar fields of cows and trees. Surely Hammy's house wasn't far if he always walked to meet her. They pulled around a hedge Thali had never gone past and saw a massive castle.

"That looks bigger than Papa's." Thali said without thinking.

"Do you know nothing?" Rommy asked. He shook his head. "The Dougals are one of the original families in this kingdom. They sold part of their property to our family in exchange for the farming labor like five generations ago."

Thali scowled and turned away as the carriage continued rolling up toward the house. She didn't like not knowing things that Rommy knew.

Once they arrived, an attendant helped them all out. Thali was surprised Hammy wasn't here to greet them himself. But the attendant showed them into the castle and into one of the rooms to the right of a vast hallway. The room was full of seating options, so Thali wasn't sure where they should sit. Her father chose one closest to the windows, so Thali and the others followed. All they could do was sit and wait. Again, Thali was surprised Hammy wasn't already here waiting or they hadn't been shown to wherever Hammy was.

Rommy was just leaning toward her when the double doors opened.

"Marquis Dougal," a footman announced. Thali's family rose, then bowed and curtsied. Thali was suddenly glad her mother had convinced her to wear a nicer dress.

Hammy walked in and smiled widely. "Thank you so much for coming to call on us."

"And Lady Dougal," the footman announced this time.

An older woman, older than Thali's parents by perhaps a decade, walked in, chin high and back straight. She seemed to suck the heat right out of the room, but Thali's family repeated their greetings.

The older woman sat across from them then, and Thali let her mother and father do the talking. Thali was now very glad Hammy hadn't brought her here.

Hammy slid over and leaned close. "Lady Routhalia, could I show you my favorite tapestry?"

Thali stood up and took his arm more quickly than she probably should have, and he led her away.

Before she had a chance to open her mouth, Hammy spoke. "I'm sorry I never told you who I was. But this is why. When you met me and didn't already know, it was a welcome relief. I could just be me. It was a little selfish of me," Hammy said.

"I think I can understand what it's like to want that," Thali said. She thought of how she and Rommy had just been arguing about how everyone knew who she was because she looked different from everyone. She wasn't sure she'd ever met anyone like her.

"You'll forgive me?" Hammy asked.

"Yes, absolutely," Thali said.

"Does that mean I don't even have to bribe you for your forgiveness?" Hammy asked. He quirked an eyebrow.

Thali recognized the same old Hammy in his expression. "What did you have in mind? I'll have to check if we have space for cows on-board." She doubted he would gift her cows, though a small part of her wanted him to.

He laughed but covered it with a cough so as not to draw attention to them. Her family and his mother were still on the other side of the room. "You have a pocket in that voluminous skirt?"

"Always."

He turned to the tapestry beside them and made her turn too so no one would see their hands. Then he handed her a cuff bracelet. Made of silver, it looked like the stalks of a plant with little purple thistles throughout. The thistles were made of tiny amethysts. It reminded her very much of the bushes they'd had to wade through whenever they'd hidden from cows or the other children.

"It's beautiful," Thali said. She tilted her chin back up as she stared down at it.

"It's a family heirloom, so don't lose it." Hammy grinned as he turned to look at her.

"Thank you," she said as she tucked it into her dress pocket. "You didn't have to bribe my forgiveness though." She turned again to look at the tapestry as they spoke.

"I wanted you to have a piece of me, before ..." Hammy took a deep breath in and then out, rushing through the rest of it. "Before I get married and take over the noble duties."

"You're getting married?" Thali asked. She was fourteen, so Hammy couldn't be more than sixteen.

"First duty of a lord is to have an heir. The heir is preceded by marriage."

"Do you know your bride?"

"I've met her once," Hammy said.

Thali's brow furrowed. She didn't like that Hammy was being forced into a marriage.

"The next time we see each other, it'll have to be in rooms like these, maybe with my children running around if you're lucky," Hammy said, a touch of sadness behind the words.

His jaw was tense, and Thali was worried for her friend. "Is that what you want?"

"It doesn't matter what I want. It's my familial obligation. My future bride seems lovely. I hear she's quiet and shy." He nodded as if to convince himself. "Don't look at me like that, Scratchy. I'll try to get away the next time you visit, maybe with a husband. A married man and a married woman can go off riding together at least."

"Wait, you can ride now?"

"I had a good teacher. Of course I can ride now." Hammy looked offended, so Thali didn't know what to say. Hammy was quiet for a minute before he continued. "My family holds the lives of many people in our hands, including your family. I don't mean that as a threat, it's just a lot of responsibility. The sooner I have a wife, and sons, the sooner everyone's futures are secure. Many lords might squander their resources, impoverishing their people and communities, but I can make sure that doesn't happen here."

Thali held her tongue. She knew well enough when to stop pushing. Her family lived a very different life even from most nobles in the Kingdom of Adanek. She was never at court long; in fact, she had never really spent time there and certainly not enough to even make friends or even acquaintances. And Thali's father's family was a low-level noble family only because Hammy's family, she supposed, had made it so. Instead, Thali patted the silver filigree cuff in her skirt pocket. "Thank you for my gift."

"When you get back, look at the point where the two ends join." Hammy glanced over at it, and she saw the sparkle in his eye.

"Hamish, I'm starting to tire. Would you mind escorting me back to my rooms?" The older woman's voice floated over.

"Duty calls," Hamish said.

At Thali's nod, he walked her back to her family at the other end of the room. Thali glanced around and noticed her brother's annoyance. His lips were pressed tightly together, and his eyes had narrowed. And the way his shoulders rolled forward just a little told Thali he was upset.

"If you ever have need of me, please let me know," Hammy said as he made a show of bowing over her hand, then smiling and nodding to her family. He escorted his mother away, and her family was left alone again.

"Well, shall we?" Thali's mother asked. She stood as Thali's father took her arm, and they all headed back to their carriage.

Thali took Rommy's arm and wondered if she should ask him what was upsetting him. Deciding she had to know, she used a finger to trace letters on the back of his hand when she took his arm on the way out.

His tight nod told her he couldn't talk about it right then. Thali could guess what was bothering him. Intuitively, she knew Hamish's mother didn't like low-born nobles or nongenerational nobles, and Thali guessed that Hamish's mother thought they were too low to associate with. Thali supposed if her father's family worked for them, she could see that. But those kinds of people always rubbed Rommy the wrong way. He always got worked up about being underestimated.

Thali was glad Hamish wasn't like that. But she did wonder if she would ever have fun with him again. He wasn't the first of those she knew to get married, but she certainly hadn't expected to hear he would be married within the year. Part of her was surprised she hadn't been invited to the wedding, but then another part of Thali knew that if his mother thought her standing in society was too low, it made sense she hadn't been invited. Hamish must not have had much say in his own wedding, or she would have been.

Rommy jerked her arm almost out of her shoulder socket as they stepped up into the carriage then, and Thali scowled. She hated that her brother's mood affected hers so much.

A TALE OF MAGIC

THALI RAN HER THUMBS over the silver vines of the cuff bracelet. Her callouses caught on the tiny amethyst gems, and she smiled at the inscription inside. She was probably overdue to write to Hammy. His wife seemed nice too. Thali had only met her briefly at her own wedding to Elric, but she seemed to make Hammy happy. Thali had even exchanged a few letters with her directly but didn't think she could carry on a lengthy conversation with her easily.

A knock on their door startled Thali back to the present. She turned as the conversation paused and glanced at the door with everyone else.

Isaia poked his head in and looked around. "Just wanted to check all was good in here."

"Would you like to join us?" Thali asked. Isaia was as much her friend as her guard.

"I shouldn't. I'm on duty."

"I think you can guard as well in here as you can out there," Daylor pointed out.

Mia muffled a yelp and bumped into the armoire. When everyone looked at her, she looked grumpily down at her thumb. "I stabbed myself." She put her thumb to her lips and sucked it.

Thali had seen something roll out but could only see a cream-colored ribbon on the floor.

"I know value is found in all kinds of things, but a ribbon?" Elric pointed to the ribbon.

It was only an inch wide and maybe a foot long, but Thali swallowed and spun around, looking for the bracelet that was supposed to be attached to it. Her gaze moved here and there as she continued to spin around.

"What's the matter?" Elric asked as he shuffled some of his papers aside. Her friends looked curious too.

"Do you see a bracelet of orange leaves?" Thali asked. She shuffled to the armoire and looked inside. Squinting, she started pulling drawers out and moving things around.

"Do you mean this?" Isaia stood at the door, an orange-leafed bracelet on the end of his finger.

"Yes!" Thali said and she exhaled, her shoulders dropping.

"What is it?" Tilton asked. "You don't panic like that unless it's important," he added.

Isaia walked the bracelet over to Thali, and she gently tied the ribbon around the bracelet as Isaia held it out. Then she opened an armoire drawer and moved a few things around to make sure the bracelet would fit securely when she put it down.

"Sorry again to intrude," Isaia said.

"It's no bother. You're welcome to stay," Elric replied.

"I've got snacks!" Daylor offered him the tray. Alexius had apparently refilled it magically.

"Sorry," Tilton said, leaning closer to Thali and whispering, "Do you want us to go? We can go."

"No, no, it's all right." Thali laughed. She really loved that her friends were all here.

"Thali, why are you holding that thing like it's going to explode?" Daylor asked as he swung his legs over the arm of the chair and grabbed a handful of food.

Alexius stood and approached Thali as she held the bracelet by the ribbon. He didn't touch it but brought his face very close to it. "This has ancient magic woven right into it."

"It's a magic inhibitor," Thali explained as she gently placed it back in the space she'd made for it. The leaves had never dried, and she understood better now than she had before that this was powerful magic.

"Where did you get it?" Alexius asked.

"Down in front, Alexius!" Daylor said. "Or at least let Thali tell everyone the story!"

Alexius shot him a look that made Daylor close his mouth, but he stepped back and sat down again. Ana groaned loudly, shifting to drape over Daylor's side and drip into Isaia's lap.

ZANA

T HALI BLINKED HER EYES open and saw fur. Brown fur, with black mixed in. She breathed in the salty, earthy smell that always stirred a warm fuzzy feeling within her. She loved waking up like this. Reaching out, she scooped up the dog that had found her yesterday, following her and Rommy as they'd walked through the mountains. He had growled and pointed his nose whenever a snake was too close to the path. Thali's parents hadn't let her bring him into the low cabin she and her brother slept in, but the dog must have found a way in. Either that or Rommy had taken pity on him and let him in. She slid the brown dog closer, nuzzling the warm fur of his neck. He turned his head and licked her cheek, and she gave him a kiss on the snout.

Thali looked past him then and saw her brother sleeping behind the door on a thin mat. No one would be able to open the door without waking him; then again, no one would be able to open the door at all really. His body was blocking the inward swing of it.

She shook her head, wondering if her brother would ever relax. Thali could handle herself; she'd been taught vigilance as consistently as he had. She'd had to master the skills to her mother and Crab's satisfaction just as Rommy had. Thali looked around and noticed the two windows were shut, and Rommy had even tied bells to them. He must have let their new friend in, she decided. The brown dog turned around and licked Thali under her chin, along the jawline, his nose right below her earlobe. His soft breath tickled.

She looked at the dog's paws, automatically checking him over as she did all her new animal friends. He was in good health but younger than she had thought. He was so relaxed, he even let her look under his lips to see the young adult teeth freshly pushed through his gums. As he rolled over to ask for belly rubs, she realized he was a she.

A drum started to beat outside. Thali's head shot up just as her brother shot up from where he slept. The dog lazily rose to all fours.

Thali leapt up to peek out the window as the brown dog followed. She peeked outside, and before she could even call her brother over, he was there. "Where... I thought..." she began.

"I'm not sure," he replied.

Out the window, they should have seen a clearing with low cabins like theirs around a fire pit where the villagers gathered. There should have been a fire burning, tended to all day and all night to warn away animals and other dangerous creatures. That's not what she saw now.

Thali rubbed her eyes. Through the window was a lush green meadow. Leafy trees surrounded it, their leaves orange and yellow. It was supposed to be summer, not fall. Thali turned around, reacting to the brown dog's whine as it padded across the cabin. With its last two steps, the dog leapt up into a standing position and transformed into a human girl, covered from shoulder to thigh in furs.

Thali's eyes went wide. Rommy reached behind him for the staff leaning against the window, then stepped partly in front of Thali, shielding her.

"My name is Zana. I'm sorry if I've frightened you, but my people need your help." The girl, hands raised, looked at Thali. Zana flicked her gaze to Rommy momentarily, then fastened it on Thali.

"Why didn't you just approach us?" Rommy said.

"We are not friendly with the people you're visiting," Zana said.

"And why would my sister be able to help you, rather than me or our parents or anyone else?" Rommy asked.

"Because of her skills with animals. We sensed it, the last time you were here. But we had no way to contact you," Zana explained.

"Then why now?" Rommy continued pressing her.

"Our situation is more dire now. We've been planning how best to contact you since you left last time," Zana said. She continued to keep her hands up.

The last time Thali and her family had visited here was a year ago. "How did our surroundings change so much since last night?" she asked.

"We moved the insides of the cabin here in the middle of the night."

Thali didn't know how they had managed that without waking anyone in the village, but then there was much she didn't know of magic. But her parents would have a fit once they saw.

"That seems like an awfully complicated plan just to bring two children to your people." Rommy must have been thinking along the same lines as Thali.

"Once we explain our plight, you are welcome to return. We will even show you how."

"Why should we trust you?" Rommy insisted.

"Please. Just let us show you and then you can decide for yourselves," Zana said.

"All right," Thali said. She nodded and stepped in front of her brother. If Zana had really wanted to hurt them, she'd had all night to do so. But she hadn't. "Your people, can they all change into dogs?"

"No. The type of animal runs in families. My family can shift into dogs if they so choose. Other families can change into foxes, bears, or other animals." Zana nodded, smiling, and went to the door. Thali noticed a cream-colored ribbon in her hair, the only adornment on her fur. She turned to look at Thali and Rommy again as if asking if it was all right to proceed.

Rommy, who had muscled his way in front of Thali again, nodded.

Zana opened the door, and they stepped out into the meadow. Rommy scanned their surroundings as soon as he stepped out before he moved aside to let Thali exit behind him. She rolled her eyes. She really didn't think they were in any danger. To illustrate that, Thali took a few bigger steps in front of her brother and stood next to Zana.

"It's this way," Zana said. She turned her back on them and started walking through the trees.

Thali followed right behind her before Rommy could block her again. It was childish, but she didn't care. She was tired of Rommy's overprotectiveness. She could take care of herself. Her mother had ensured that long before she'd ever been allowed to go ashore.

They followed Zana, Rommy finally giving up on trying to get ahead of Thali. She felt him roll his eyes at her and knew he would have strong words for her when they were alone again.

Zana stopped suddenly in the middle of the forest, or so Thali thought. She looked around at the unfamiliar surroundings, then up to the treetops. the canopy of leaves started many feet above their heads. If Thali squinted, she could see a few round nests tucked into the branches high, high up.

"They're over here." Zana turned left and ducked around a particularly thick grouping of trees. There, in front of the trees, was a fence made of five thick logs stacked atop each other to create a kind of pen. Beyond the man-made pen were a few elders sitting on rocks and patches of moss, using a tree as a back rest. Some were cleaning tools, and some were weaving orange, brown, and red leaves.

Thali brought her gaze back to the pen that stood up to her hip, a little wary of what might be inside. Rommy, who was taller, peeked in, then looked at Zana with confusion.

Thali peeked in too, and her heart melted. Five fuzzy little puppies slept in a pile in a corner. As if sensing they had visitors, the puppies sniffed and then woke, one by one, and started to cry as they tried to climb out. But they were only one log tall at most, so the five-log wall was too formidable an obstacle.

Rommy turned his attention back to the puppies. "I don't understand. They seem perfectly healthy."

"They are," Zana said. She looked back at the elders, busy with their tasks as they pointedly ignored Zana, Thali, and Rommy.

"Are they in danger? Or dangerous?" Thali asked as she nudged her chin in the puppies' direction. They looked like innocent puppies, but perhaps she was missing something.

Zana shook her head, and Thali looked at Rommy. He was gazing at the elders. It was strange not to see homes anywhere. The people were just leaning up against random trees as if the trees were their front doorsteps.

"We normally cannot start transforming until we become adults: the first bleed for women and the drop in voice and organs in men. But these children changed as three- to five-year-olds," Zana explained, "And they haven't changed back. We go through extensive training to learn to change back and forth. But they haven't even started theirs yet." Zana stopped. She watched Thali carefully as if trying to judge whether Thali would help.

"I still don't understand how you think we can help you," Rommy said.

Zana furrowed her brows and wrinkled her forehead, making Thali wonder for a moment if Zana was older than she looked. "I thought you could communicate with animals. We hoped you would be able to show them how to transform back into humans."

"How long have they been in this form?" Rommy asked, not admitting his little sister's skills.

"Two months," Zana said.

Thali's eyes widened. "That's a long time."

Zana nodded, looking even more sad now. "It's said that if we stay in animal form too long, especially when we can't control it, we won't ever be able to switch back."

Thali looked at her brother. Her parents had a strict no-magic rule. She'd been taught to keep a wall up in her mind to block that part of her, those magic threads that reached out to connect with animals. Rommy, however, had always tried to encourage her to try. He didn't think it was smart to not use a skill you already had.

"I think you should give it a try, Rou," Rommy said.

Thali looked around; she didn't see her parents. In fact, she hadn't even heard them. Surely, they would be searching for her by now, wherever they were.

"Please don't worry. Your family is near and being protected. They and the villagers are simply sleeping off the potion we gave them so they wouldn't notice your absence."

Thali nodded. "What exactly do you want me to show the children?"

"I was hoping you could connect with them first. If that's successful, then I'll show you how to teach them to transform back into their human form," Zana said.

Thali still didn't feel danger coming from Zana, only desperation and perhaps hope. Thali glanced at Rommy. He was staring at the puppies.

After they made eye contact, his lips tightened as he looked around. She knew he was suspicious that Zana wasn't telling the whole truth and was weighing whether they should leave or cooperate. But they were outnumbered and didn't even know how to get back to their family.

Rommy glanced at the puppies again, and his face softened. He placed his hands on the top log, then looked back at Thali, his lips curving up, looser now.

That told her he wanted her to try. He was always trying to find ways to help her practice without their parents knowing. And if their parents were truly asleep, then this would be a great opportunity for her to try. "All right, I'll do it," Thali said.

Rommy nodded. He stood a little taller, keeping watch.

Zana looked hopeful and stayed very still while she waited.

Thali looked at Zana and then Rommy. She felt guilty for going against her parents' wishes but was excited to try. And that added to her guilt too.

With a deep breath in then out, Thali closed her eyes and went to the door in her mind. She started to crack it open. The puppies were the nearest animals to her, so their threads were right there; she didn't have to look for their strands. The pups were even reaching for her already. "I have them," she said. She could see the memories of these puppies as babies: of being swaddled, of staring up at the trees, and of moving so differently than they did now. There was no doubt in Thali's mind these puppies had been humans before. She could even feel the sharp twigs and branches under her feet as the children ran around the forest.

Zana cleared her throat and brought Thali back to the present. Thali slid the door in her mind closed a bit so it was open just a crack and listened carefully to the present moment. It took a lot of concentration to do both. "I can't hold this very long," Thali warned.

"The easiest way for them to return to their form is to try and move as they would as humans. Ask them to stand on their back legs, to try and walk around as bipedal humans, to think of their human memories please. It's our best chance," Zana said quietly.

Thali nodded, then reopened the door in her mind and pushed through images of pups walking like humans—on their hind puppy legs. With those, she flashed their human memories, ones of them running in the forest and playing with sticks using their hands instead of their jaws.

"It's working," Zana said.

Thali's eyes popped open, and she saw the puppies using the sides of the wall to climb up to a vertical position, then trying to walk on their hind legs. They only took a few steps, but suddenly, the first pup fell back on all fours and in a blink, was human again. Zana scooped him up from the pen and spun him around, hugging him to her chest. Thali wondered for a moment if Zana, who was perhaps only as old as her brother, was a mother.

Two more puppies returned to human form then, leaving only two. They continued trying to walk on two legs, concentrating so hard their lips raised in a growl.

Thali closed her eyes again, connecting with their threads. She could no longer see the ones that were human but for a whiff of smoke, but the remaining two pup threads wavered as if they were trying to become human. But they were struggling. Their threads flashed brightly, then became smoky, then bright again. Thali wondered what she could do to help them as she connected with the threads.

She showed them images of human toddlers, running, walking, learning to grab a utensil for the first time. She thought of her smallest cousins the last time she had seen them.

One thread wavered once more and then disappeared into a wisp of smoke. Thali felt a breeze on her arm as Zana picked the toddler up. Then she focused on the last thread that felt like it was trying so hard to connect with her. She sent more images down the thread, this time more maternal ones. She'd watched some of her aunts carrying their babies, so she sent those images. Some aunts had even placed a baby in Thali's arms for a few minutes, so she tried sending that image too. The thread wavered again but stayed solid, and Thali worried that this toddler might stay a pup forever.

"Try showing her images from a human's point of view," Zana said softly.

"Think of your own childhood, Rou," Rommy added.

So that's what Thali did. She showed the pup a memory of holding herself up with the ring of a barrel and slowly taking her first few steps into her father's waiting arms as he sat on a barrel. She showed the pup how her father tossed her gleefully up into the air to celebrate, her brother ruffling her hair and patting her on the shoulder, and her mother setting her on the deck so she could toddle to Crab. He had seemed so gigantic to her then, but she remembered walking as fast as her legs would carry her to him. She remembered how he would envelop her body with his hands and bring her up to his height to see over the ship's rails.

The warmth of a hand on her forearm brought Thali back to the present, and her eyes fluttered open. Zana was lifting the last little girl up over the log fence. The little girl leaned over as she neared Thali, reaching for her with her stubby fingers before Zana placed her in the waiting arms of another elder now standing near.

"Thank you," Zana said.

Thali was still taking a moment to come back to herself. She blinked and felt something pulling her back into her mind. She didn't want to be rude though, so she smiled at Zana. "I'm glad to have helped." Thali looked around at the elders sitting against the trees. They each had a toddler in their lap and slipped tiny orange bracelets around the childrens' ankles. Thali recognized the jewelry of twisted, woven leaves they'd been making earlier.

"What are those?" Rommy asked.

"They'll block them from transitioning," Zana explained. "Usually, children start to wear them in their tenth year, a year before the earliest one has ever transitioned, but now we'll put them on the babies."

Thali nodded. She closed her eyes suddenly because it felt like some-one was pounding on her head. She squeezed her eyes shut as she focused on her mind and realized that she hadn't closed the door to the threads around her. So focused had she been on the threads right in front of her that she hadn't thought about the threads further away. They had started to reach out in curiosity, but now she felt them coming toward her, a half-dozen threads becoming more and more clear with every beating of her skull.

Shaking her head, she closed the door in her mind, sealing it shut with imaginary mud as she tried to keep those threads from getting into her mind. But the beating in her head didn't stop, and she heard Rommy gasp. Thali's eyes flew open. Five mountain lions stepped out of the forest.

Thali gasped too. Rommy tried to tuck her behind him, but as they turned, they realized they were surrounded.

Just then, five bears descended from the trees and faced the mountain lions. Thali and Rommy edged closer together, keeping Zana between them while the bears each stood before a mountain lion.

"I'm sorry. I think I called to them by mistake," Thali said. She was confused and scared.

"It's all right. We'll be fine. Just give them a minute," Zana said. She stepped closer to Thali and Rommy and took one of their hands in each of hers.

Rommy didn't let go of Thali's other hand though, so the three of them stood in a circle, hands chained together. As Thali blinked, she thought she saw the animals in front of her growing larger. But that wouldn't make any sense. Then the bears stood on their hind legs, looming over the mountain lions. The cats started to stalk the outer perimeter, then growled as their whiskers flared and their stares became more intense. What felt like hours later but was more likely moments, the mountain lions yowled their protest and melted back into the forest. Thali and Rommy still stood clinging to Zana as the bears followed the mountain lions.

When the animals had all disappeared, Zana let out a breath and turned to them. "Please, join us as we nourish ourselves." She led them to an elder with a few baskets. Other elders came to join them and brought more baskets.

Thali was still feeling a little shaken, but Rommy's stomach growled loudly, and he was quickly handed a bunch of berries. "Thank you." He popped them into his mouth as Zana handed Thali a few baskets so she could pick for herself.

"Zana, I hope this isn't rude, but where are the rest of the villagers?" Thali asked. She wouldn't have asked if her parents were around, but after what she'd just experienced with Zana, her curiosity won out.

"Oh, they're out gathering food," Zana said.

"Where do you sleep?" Rommy asked. He must have felt bolstered by Thali's question.

"Here," Zana said. She motioned around them and spread her hands out to indicate the whole clearing and the forest.

"Do you move around often? Does your community have boundaries? Do you visit our...friends often?" Rommy asked.

Thali was just as curious.

"We do have boundaries, and while we often cover much ground in our day-to-day lives and visit your friends from time to time, we usually return here. We prefer to keep to ourselves."

Rommy nodded, and Thali looked around. There were no buildings or places to store things like bowls and cookware. There wasn't even an obvious location to build a fire for cooking. Thali glanced at the berries in her hand. She supposed you didn't need a fire if all you ate was berries.

Thali looked again at Zana, wrapped in furs and held in place by a belt of woven leaves. She may have had a hidden weapon or two but wasn't even carrying a drinking vessel.

"Where do you get your water?" Rommy suddenly asked. He'd eaten all the berries given him, so he must be full. He leaned back as he looked around, likely thinking the same thoughts Thali was.

"We go down to the river," Zana said.

"What of your elderly or injured? How do they drink?" Rommy asked.

"We use those." Zana pointed up at the huge tree leaves, and Thali's forehead crinkled. The leaves were larger than most, but to carry water back and forth from a river one leaf at a time .... She couldn't imagine the effort. "Are you ready to return? I believe your family may be waking soon."

Thali and Rommy nodded. The elders gathered the baskets into a pile and placed it behind a tree trunk. Thali wondered if they stored more things behind the trees but she wasn't quite brave enough to look.

Brother and sister followed Zana through the woods and to their cabin—but it wasn't their cabin. It looked the same from a distance, but the wood was newer. Zana continued past it and through the forest as a fog appeared, then thickened. Thali wondered if she'd somehow been transported from her cabin to a lookalike cabin and how they would get home now. Would Zana put them to sleep? Was there a magic potion or an invisible force that would transport them home?

Thali didn't have time to think as she focused on keeping up. She and Rommy were struggling to keep pace with Zana as she wound around tree roots and uneven forest ground, not seeming hindered at all, even in the fog that kept getting thicker. They turned at invisible markers, and Thali knew she'd never be able to find her way back; she had to keep Zana not more than one step in front of her so she didn't lose her. Then Zana stopped suddenly.

Thali peered around her and saw they were at the edge of a forest, and the fog stopped at the treeline. Ahead, she recognized the buildings of the people her family was visiting. It was quiet.

"I leave you here," Zana said, her voice low as she turned to Thali. She took both of Thali's hands. "We are indebted to you. Thank you for bringing back our youngest ones."

"You're very welcome. I'm so glad to have helped. Thank you for keeping us safe," Thali whispered back.

Zana nodded.

Then Thali remembered something. "Zana, wait."

Zana turned around and raised an eyebrow.

Thali took the water flask off her hip, then reached over to her brother's hip and unhooked his too. She placed both in Zana's hands. "They hold water, much more than a leaf does."

Zana looked at her strangely but smiled. "Thank you." Then she turned away and was gone.

"I liked that water flask," Rommy said as they turned and emerged from the woods.

"You can get another," Thali said.

They walked between two buildings and found their parents in the middle of the square, looking around.

"There you are!" Jinhua said. "We've been looking for you. You weren't in the cabin."

"We went for a walk," Rommy said.

"And lost your water skins, I see," Ranulf pointed out.

Thali and Rommy shrugged.

"We have one more meeting after breakfast, but you two might as well pack up and get back to the ship," Ranulf suggested.

Thali nodded and followed Rommy back to their original cabin. Everything was back in place. She wondered again how Zana and her people had snuck them out without their parents and the whole community noticing, potion or no potion. She shook off the thought and packed up.

Thali and Rommy left the cabin, thanked their hosts over breakfast, and headed for the ship, carrying some of the goods their parents had purchased. There was no dock here as the island was too small, so they had to signal to the crew onboard to send a smaller boat to get them. They'd send the small boat and its crew member back for her parents afterward. The siblings waited on the beach as the boat rowed closer and closer.

"How do you think they did it? Transported us without anyone knowing?" Thali asked.

"I think they know more than they're telling us. Or maybe they don't understand as much as I suspect, only how to use what they have. I mean, we don't exactly know how your magic works either," Rommy replied. It didn't seem to bother him much.

"It doesn't seem to bother you that we were kidnapped."

Rommy shrugged. "I was with you, we weren't in any danger, and you got to practice your secret gift. It's a win all around."

"If you say so," Thali said. She changed topics as the boat pulled up. She peeled her boots off and rolled her pants up as much as she could, then waded out to the boat.

Thali handed her bundles to Mouse, and Rommy flung his own over the side of the boat. Then they climbed in. Mouse secured the packages as Rommy and Thali grabbed the oars and started to row.

When they reached their ship, Thali carried her boots on board with the bundles. Her parents disapproved of her going barefoot on deck, but they weren't back yet, so she happily kept her feet bare as she helped put the products away before returning to their family quarters.

After putting her big shore boots away, she opened a small cage and let her rat climb out and up her arm to sit in her vest pocket. As she reached for the softer leather boots she wore onboard, something orange caught her eye.

There atop her soft boots was a large yellow leaf, on which was written, "Thank you." When Thali looked closer, she spotted something underneath the leaf, so she gently pulled the leaf up. Underneath was a bracelet woven of orange leaves, just like the ones the children wore to keep them in human form. A cream-colored ribbon was tied to it. Thali was curious if the leaves would take her magic away, so she hesitantly touched it.

The feeling wasn't the most unpleasant thing she'd experienced. It was like she had drunk something cold, and it leeched the warmth from her esophagus and stomach as it descended. It started from the finger she touched the bracelet with and went to her middle, where it bloomed outwards, like a coolness that wasn't quite icy. Before it reached her other fingertips, she moved her finger so she wasn't touching the bracelet anymore, and the coolness receded.

She picked it up this time by the ribbon, a cream one like she'd seen in Zana's hair earlier that day. *How had Zana placed this here?* Thali wondered. *How had she gotten aboard their always-guarded ship and when?* It was Zana's, she knew, from the ribbon. Thali questioned why Zana would give her a bracelet that could remove someone's magical abilities.

Thali heard Rommy stomping in then, so she quickly grabbed the yellow leaf, wrapped the bracelet in it, and tucked it away in her box of treasures.

RECOLLECTIONS OF A PAST BETROTHAL

THE DRAWER CONTAINING THE orange-leafed bracelet was still open, so Thali touched a finger to one of its leaves. She closed her eyes as she felt the magic drain out of her like peppermint pulling heat away from her. A moment later, she pulled her finger away and took a deep breath. Her body warmed again, and she felt her magic return as she took another deep breath. The sensation was more unpleasant now that she had more magical ability.

"Cookie?" Daylor asked as he tossed one at her.

Thali caught it before shoving it in her mouth.

You all right? Alexius asked in her mind.

Thali nodded subtly. *Did you feel it drain my magic?*

I did. It's unnerving. I didn't think I'd find anything in this world that would do that.

Thali nodded. She closed the drawer with the orange-leafed bracelet. She didn't want to have to touch that thing ever again. Then she glanced at Mia because her best friend had caught her attention when she put her sewing down. That was rare.

"There's definitely one story you haven't told yet," Mia said. She wiggled her eyebrows, making everyone else lean forward.

"I don't know what you're talking about," Thali said. She suspected she knew exactly who Mia was alluding to, but it had been a long time since she'd thought of him. He wasn't much of a letter writer, though he made the effort a few times a year for her.

Bardo slithered down the armoire and onto Mia's shoulder. "Tell it," Mia warned, "or I'll sic Bardo on you." Mia reached toward Thali, Bardo wrapped around her wrist.

He obligingly stuck his tongue out at Thali a few times, and she laughed. Mia wouldn't have been that comfortable with her snake a few years ago. So much had changed in those four years.

Thali took a deep breath, turned back to the armoire, and took out a small black ring. "This is from the time I almost got married."

Mia reached for it first, took a closer look, then as if they were doing show-and-tell, passed it to Daylor.

"Sorry, did you say you almost got married before me?" Elric asked.

Daylor handed the ring to Tilton.

Thali nodded. The others started to giggle. They were all overtired. It was late now, and they should really all be going to bed soon. "He never actually asked me, if that makes you feel better," she said. She liked riling Elric up.

"It's beautiful," Tilton said before handing the ring to Alexius.

"And ..." Elric waved his hand, his gaze never leaving Thali's.

Thali shrugged. "He's a childhood friend. He was going to ask me but then realized he couldn't pull me away from my life at sea," she finished quietly as she realized that was exactly her life now: landlocked, no ship, not a leader. That's exactly what Elric had turned her life into.

"He was an idiot then," Elric said as he fluffed his pillows and sat back in bed.

Alexius handed the ring to Isaia, whose brow scrunched as he looked at it. "Is this made of wood?"

"Horn and rock," Thali said.

Isaia returned the ring to Thali, but not before Elric snatched it and took a good, careful look. "It's very intricately carved," he said.

Indi's tail swished in annoyance when Elric leaned over her to take the ring, then again as he leaned over her yet again to hand the ring back.

"Sorry, Indi," Elric said with a grimace.

Thali examined the black ring with the red interior. The red rock was unique to her friend, Jaon's, corner of the world, as was the black horn overlay.

JAON

THALI HOPPED OFF THE gangplank onto the dock with a light skip and jump. As a fifteen-year-old girl, she was excited to be off a ship filled with old men who hadn't seen a bath for weeks. Coins jingled in her pocket as she went to find the dockmaster to pay their fees. She stood waiting at the dock's entrance for the dockmaster to give her their seal, while her family's crew went about their business, getting all the goods they had brought to trade ready for their meeting the next day. Her mother was on board supervising and shouting orders, and her father was examining the ship.

Thali narrowed her eyes when she started to hear a deep, rhythmic thumping. The dockmaster was taking his time with the seal, and she tapped her finger on the stack of crates he used as a desk. The thumping got louder and louder; the sound was approaching them. Her father popped up on the ship's deck, and her mother stopped to turn and squint in their direction. Her brother strode toward her, armed to the teeth as always. His staff was already in hand when he caught up to Thali and strapped an extra knife around her middle. Suddenly, the source of the thumping appeared around a corner. The entire Moas tribe marched toward them.

The Moas were a warrior tribe and had become quite close to her family. After meeting with them the first time, her father had taught them to mine a valuable rock on their land to trade for other resources. In thanks, the Moas traded exclusively with her family. Thali and her family often stayed with the tribe for days when they came to visit this port, even though it was a full day's ride inland. The Moas rarely met them at their ship.

The rhythmic marching looked more like an honor guard than a threatening advance. Thali glanced at her brother. His eyes were narrowed. Though obviously imposing, the warriors were clean and their daggers were decorative. "They're smiling," she said.

"That doesn't mean anything." Rommy said.

"I don't think they're here to threaten us."

Rommy was trying to edge her behind him, but she stood her ground. The ship's crew, her family, and her brother were all constantly pushing her behind them or protecting her, and she was tired of not being able to use her training.

The dockmaster quickly disappeared with his paperwork.

"Get behind me, Rou," Rommy hissed. The warriors of Moa marched closer and lined the shore, creating a funnel toward the dock. They turned their backs to it, and Thali suddenly recognized a familiar face striding through them.

"Jaon!" Thali shouted, waving.

Jaon broke into the widest grin when his gaze found her.

Her brother had filled out in the last year and was broad-shouldered but slender in the waist. Jaon, however, was now a head taller than Rommy and at least a foot wider everywhere else. The Moas were large and muscular, and their ruling family was no exception. Jaon stood as wide as two skinny men, and the dockworkers stared. They made themselves scarce.

"Jaon. It's nice to see you." Rommy stepped between the Moa and his sister, putting his fist to his heart and nodding his head.

"It is good to see you, Romulus," Jaon replied.

Thali peeked her head around Rommy and noticed that Jaon's eyes hardened when he looked at her brother.

Jaon put his own fist to his heart and bowed low, lower than he should have.

"Jaon!" Thali shrieked and ducked around her brother to throw her arms around Jaon's neck.

Jaon stood, lifting Thali off her feet as he embraced her, and swung her around in a circle. "Little one," he said in Moan. His smile widened and he placed her gently back on the dock with a grin.

"Jaon, you're huge now! When did you grow so tall and strong?" Thali was excited to see her friend, for every time they visited the Moas, Thali played with Jaon, the younger son of the chief, running foot races in the fields nearby.

"And you, little one, you are more beautiful than I could ever remember." He quickly bent and kissed Thali's hand. It was an awkward movement, a custom of the city they were in but not of the Moas.

Thali felt heat rise to her cheeks. Jaon was acting strangely. He was four years her elder, closer to her brother's age, but since he was the younger son of the chief and a small, scrawny child, he'd been left to do what he liked. It had been two years since they'd last seen the Moas, but Thali suddenly felt very self-conscious. She looked into Jaon's eyes and only saw the same playful spark as always. It put her at ease, but this time, she let Rommy push her back.

"Jaon, while it is a pleasure to see you, we were not due to meet with you until five days from now." Rommy said as he angled himself between the large warrior and his sister again.

"Romulus, you are correct. But I have been so excited to see the little one. I was impatient." Jaon again turned to offer Thali a grin.

Thali couldn't help but grin back. Jaon had always called her "little one" sarcastically because she'd been thicker and taller than Jaon when they'd met. But now, she was definitely smaller in every way.

The dockmaster finally returned with the paperwork, and Rommy said, "Thali, run the seal back to the ship. Pa will want to put it away."

Thali narrowed her eyes but turned obediently. She knew that when her brother used her common nickname "Thali" and not "Rou," his own nickname, it was a strong request. She couldn't imagine why since Jaon was a good friend. Though as she looked over her shoulder at Jaon and Rommy speaking in low voices, she thought Jaon didn't look much like the scrawny teen she'd waved goodbye to as their ship had sailed off two years ago.

"Jaon has grown," Thali's mother said as she took the seal from Thali and handed it to her husband.

"He certainly has. I thought we were supposed to meet with the Moas after our business with the duke." Lord Ranulf scratched his head as he stood with his wife watching his son.

"We were," Lady Jinhua said.

Rommy and Jaon left the other Moan warriors then and walked together to the ship. Jaon's relaxed stride contrasted Rommy's tense jaw.

Thali ran back down the gangplank, giving her brother a wide berth before tucking herself under Jaon's arm. She noticed her brother's sharp look and wondered what his problem was.

Looking up into Jaon's grinning face, she thought back to the first time they'd met. She was six and thickly built. At the time, she'd been innocent to its meaning, but most other girls avoided her or snickered behind her back. So back then, Thali usually stayed with her parents and Rommy through all the boring meetings.

One day, they were all in the chief's tent with his family when the chief said, "Jaon, come." Thali's gaze was drawn to the movement of a small, scrawny boy who looked about her age, maybe even a year younger. He strode reluctantly to his father as if his feet were stuck in mud. His older brother, Tihon, was Jaon's total opposite. Tihon sat confidently and proudly at his father's side, chin up and smiling brightly at the newly arrived guests. Jaon looked like he wanted to melt back into the shadows.

When his father saw him, he spoke quietly and then repeated himself for his guests' sake. "Jaon, come, come. You will be host to Miss Routhalia here. Go and have fun while we talk business, but her safety is your responsibility, understand?"

Jaon nodded mutely. He went over to Thali and held out his hand. Thali jumped up and took his hand, and they strolled out of the tent. Jaon startled almost imperceptibly when she took his hand, so when they left the tent, he guided her to where the other children were playing and let go immediately.

He didn't speak the same language as she did, so he just looked at her, then to the other children, then down sadly. Thali decided in that second she'd rather make a friend than run around with the other kids. So she gently took his hand again and stood silently with him. He stared at their combined hands, and they stood quietly together watching the other children play. Just when Thali thought she might sit down, Jaon turned away from the children and pointed in the opposite direction, but he didn't pull at her hand.

She nodded and followed him as he led her to a big tree, still not releasing her hand. He pointed to a wide, solid branch. Thali was not good at climbing trees yet, so she just looked up at the tree and shrugged. He nodded, then gently took their joined hands and maneuvered her behind him. He took her other hand, wrapped her arms over his shoulders, and joined her hands over his chest. She was a half a head taller than him at the age of six and wondered whether he realized she probably weighed more than him. He squeezed her hands together, then started to climb the tree. She scrambled to hang on to him as he scaled the tree with ease. She held her breath and squeezed her eyes shut as she felt the rough bark brush her hands, then clasped him tighter with all her limbs. Even when she felt him straddling the big branch he had pointed at, she still didn't open her eyes.

Once he was settled, he moved her legs so she too straddled the thick branch, then slowly took her hands from around his shoulders. But he didn't let go. Only when she slowly opened her eyes did he let go, then shift to face her. He reached up and pulled some leaves off the branch above by their stems and formed her hands into a bowl.

He continued picking leaves and placing them in her cupped hands until there was a small mound. Thali quirked an eyebrow, but Jaon just started to twist and bend the leaves together, focusing intently on them as she watched.

She didn't know how old Jaon was, but she sensed he was a sweet, calm soul. As she watched him twist the leaves together, they suddenly took the shape of a horse. Her eyes bugged out of her head, and he offered her the leafy horse. Thali took the horse gently between two fingers and examined it carefully. Then she set it down between them, reached up, and grabbed some leaves, carefully plucking them by the stems as he had done. They spent that whole afternoon making an army of little leaf horses.

The next day, he came to her family's tent after breakfast, took her hand, and led her to the same tree. But instead of letting him carry her up on his back, Thali made him teach her how to climb the tree. They spent the day practicing on any tree they could find. Since they didn't have a shared language, he moved her limbs in different places to teach her. By the next time her family had visited the Moas, Jaon had taught himself the common language, though they often went hours without speaking to each other anyway, comfortable just spending time together.

And ever since their first afternoon together, Thali and Jaon had been inseparable.

"Jaon has rearranged our days at the behest of the duke. If it pleases us, we are to ride to the Moas' village first, then return to the duke afterward," Rommy said between clenched teeth as he stared pointedly at their father, shattering Thali's reminiscing.

"That's fine with me," Lord Ranulf said as he turned to his wife. Lady Jinhua cocked her head to the side but nodded in response.

"Crab, you take care of the market goods, and send Lobb with the goods for the Moas. I don't want to keep our hosts waiting," Lord Ranulf said.

Crab nodded, and Lobb nodded behind him. They continued their work as Thali and her family started back up the dock. When Thali reached Jaon, he gently took her hand and led her up the dock toward the other Moan warriors, leaving Rommy to speak with her parents behind her.

"Jaon, I can't believe how much you've grown since last I saw you," Thali said, squeezing his hand.

He only grinned in response as they walked among the Moan warriors. The honor guard escorted her family to the edge of the city, where they found a pack of horses waiting for them. As they mounted their horses, Thali was excited that Jaon was letting her ride his favorite mare. Just like many times before, Thali and Jaon raced each other when the path allowed and led the pack of horses as they traveled toward his home.

When they stopped to set up camp for the night, the guard caught their dinner and roasted it as they settled around the fire. The warriors moved effortlessly, setting up a perimeter and taking shifts for watch as they'd done many times before.

Her family was often escorted to their community, but it wasn't often a member of the chief's family accompanied them, so Thali wondered what had changed. But she shook off the thought, and after dinner, she set up her bedroll a little ways away from the others so she could stare up at the stars. Whenever her family stayed with the Moas, she and Jaon often snuck their bedrolls outside to watch the night sky. They'd exchange stories about the constellations, and Thali had loved every minute of it. Tonight, Jaon set up his bedroll near hers as he always did, but before she could ask him to tell her the story of the great badger again—one of her favorites—her brother strode over with his own bedroll and wedged himself between them. After wiggling into his bedroll, he crossed his arms and stared at the sky.

"Rommy, what is your problem?" Thali asked. She had been looking forward to catching up with her friend in private, and Rommy had been acting strange ever since he'd seen Jaon.

"I don't have a problem. I just want to sleep over here tonight," he said to the sky.

"Then I'll sleep over here. Come on, Jaon." Thali pulled her bedroll twenty feet away from her brother's and set it down. Jaon didn't move, so she stomped back to Jaon's bedroll and moved it next to hers. Jaon didn't move. He only looked at Thali, so she went over to him, stuck her tongue out at Rommy, then took Jaon's hand and guided him over to where she had moved her bedroll.

They were just starting to wiggle into their bedrolls when Rommy swam into her view and planted his bedroll next to hers. He sat on top of it, crossed his arms, and stared out into the desert.

Thali rolled her eyes, but she turned away from him and toward Jaon instead. "Will you tell me how you've been, Jaon? Besides growing like a weed!" she whispered to her friend.

"I've been well, Little One. My family has slowed our mining compared to past years, but our community is doing so well that we do not need as much anymore," Jaon said.

"My heart is glad then." And in the waning light, she reached her hand out to hold his. She found comfort in her dear friend's touch, and he took her hand and started to draw animals in her palm. Thali fell asleep before she could say "deer."

The next morning, they packed up and continued riding, her brother riding behind her as she and Jaon raced. As soon as the village came into view, Thali appreciated how well-built each hut was and how well the tribe had improved them since her last visit. Gone were all the holes and patches she remembered from times past. They all slid off their horses, and Thali's family bowed to Jaon's in greeting.

Thali was surprised to see that Jaon had caught up to Tihon in size and width as the brothers embraced each other with wide smiles. She was glad to see that Jaon had come into his own and was happy for her friend's newfound confidence.

The chief himself escorted Lady Jinhua, and Lord Ranulf offered his arm to the chief's wife in turn. Thali couldn't help but glance at Jaon, excited to depart on their own adventure while the adults met. Tihon motioned for Rommy to join him, though Rommy's gaze lingered on Jaon.

"Don't go far," Rommy told Jaon before turning on his heel and nodding at Tihon.

"I'm sorry about my brother. I don't know what's gotten into him." Thali rolled her eyes at her brother's back and took Jaon's hand. "Where are we going today?"

As was their way, Jaon squeezed her hand and silently led her through the huts to their tree. She climbed up easily, swinging from one trusted branch to the next. She moved further away from the trunk on her chosen branch, thinking Jaon's new bulk would need the trunk's support.

There they sat, silently listening to the wind.

"Thank you for teaching me how to climb trees," Thali said softly.

"Thank you for not leaving me for those other kids," Jaon replied.

"So what did you do? To get all that, I mean." Thali motioned at his arms and chest.

Jaon grinned. "Late bloomer I suppose. Shot up a foot and a half in six months and then I was suddenly starving all the time. I could have eaten a whole buffalo in a single meal."

Thali made a face as she imagined what that would look like. "Oh Jaon, I can't even wait to tell you." She grabbed both his hands and held onto the delicious moment a bit longer. Jaon waited patiently. "Papa finally said I could take my own ship out! It's not very big, and I'm not allowed to go very far, *and* I'm not allowed to until next year, but Rommy did a small route a few times a year when he was my age. He's going on a longer route next year, but I'm so excited to run my own trade route!"

Jaon's face did not reflect the same happiness or excitement Thali felt. "Come on, Jaon. I've been waiting for this my whole life! I bet in five years, I'll have my own fleet! I've already convinced Lobb to be my second. And then I could even come visit you anytime I pass by! Instead of only seeing you every two years, I could come every year, or even twice a year!"

Jaon smiled a false smile. "I'm very happy for you, Little One."

Thali noticed Jaon still wasn't as excited as she would have thought. Her own excitement deflated. "What's the matter?" she asked quietly, searching her friend's face.

Jaon swallowed. "Nothing is the matter. I'm very excited for you. I've just ... I've just realized I need to tell my father something." He swallowed again, then looked at her. "Want to go for a ride?"

Thali always loved riding but wondered if Jaon was using it as an escape. They scrambled back down the tree, and Jaon held her hand as they walked back to the gathering of huts.

"I'll be just a minute, promise," Jaon said. He let go of her hand, and Thali went to get the horses. He looked back at her once before entering the hut, and she motioned for him to hurry up.

Animals always cooperated with her, even sought her out. The Moas rode with minimal equipment, so Thali had the two horses ready in minutes. Thali and Jaon could ride as well bareback as with a saddle.

Thali was back at their meeting spot with both horses before Jaon appeared, but she didn't wait long. The third time she looked at his hut, Jaon was running out, grinning.

They leapt onto their horses and raced to the field, following the deer path. They rode all the way to the waterfall nearby, leaving the horses to swim in the stream in the afternoon before starting to head back. It was dusk as they rode back into the village, and they took the long way around to return the horses to the herd before the friends made their way to the celebratory bonfire. Impossible to miss, the fire was ten feet high. The moment Thali and Jaon stepped into the light, Rommy's gaze was on them.

"I'll find you in a bit. I need to converse with my father," Jaon said.

Thali squeezed their joined hands, nodded and let go. Her hand felt cold.

"What did you and Jaon talk about this afternoon?" Rommy asked as he brought Thali a leg of roasted rabbit.

"Why does it suddenly matter to you?" Thali said. Her brother had been nothing but rude and defensive these past few days.

"Rou. I'm sorry for the last few days. Jaon... he ... well, whatever it was, you're my little sister, my little Rou Rou. It's my job to keep you safe."

Thali snorted. "You think Jaon would hurt me?"

Rommy looked at his little sister, scanning her face and narrowing his eyes, but before Thali could ask what he wasn't telling her, Jaon strode over with her favorite drink. He leaned close to whisper in her ear. "From my mother's private stash."

Rommy nodded at him and left. Thali carefully took the drink with both hands and sipped it. It was still warm, and she sighed into the bowl. She faced the fire, warming her front side and enjoying the warmed honey milk Jaon's mother was famous for.

A chill ran up her spine, and she turned around so she could warm her backside. Jaon stared at her and lifted an eyebrow. She turned back around and used Jaon like a cloak, draping his arms over her shoulders to keep her back warm. This was how every celebratory fire ended. Jaon always exuded heat, no matter how small he was, and Thali always took advantage of it. No one in the village had ever paid it any attention until tonight. They had always been very physical as friends, and Thali still thought of them as childhood friends, so she didn't understand the sly glances of the other village men or the knowing smiles of the village women as the friends stood together, Jaon resting his chin on top of her head.

"No matter what, little one, you will always be able to count on me," Jaon said quietly.

"And you me," Thali said.

A thought entered her mind then. If Jaon was willing to travel, if he was willing to live the life she did, they could be married. She always felt safe in his arms, now more than ever, but she knew he would soon face the pressure of finding a wife. He would not be able to show such physical affection with another woman soon. But Jaon had always been clear about his community; they were his first duty, and he wouldn't be willing to leave. Despite how poorly they had treated him as a child, they were his family. Thali pushed away her brief flight of fancy and enjoyed the moment she had.

Thali ran through her drills with her mother and brother, as was required of her every morning. Then she went to bathe in their tent, and by the time she was back outside, Rommy and Tihon were standing in the front of the tent with Jaon.

"Don't be too late getting back tonight," Rommy warned Thali. "Tihon is getting married."

Thali blinked to make sure she'd heard her brother correctly.

"What, didn't think I'd get married, little one?" Tihon said, turning his full attention on her.

Thali shook her head. "Aren't we a little young to get married?"

"No," Tihon said. He opened his mouth, but Jaon shoved him, and Rommy narrowed his eyes.

Jaon pushed through them and continued walking past Thali. He didn't reach for her hand like he usually did, and she felt strangely reluctant to reach for his too. They'd always been so comfortable around each other, but now, it felt strange.

Thali walked a couple of steps behind Jaon, noticing the stares of young women on him as they continued. Some were older than him, but still, they eyed him and stopped what they were doing as he walked by. Thali pressed her lips together so she wouldn't laugh out loud.

Only when they were finally past all the homes and walking in the tall grasses did Jaon slow and take her hand. When he did, all was right with the world. It was simply nice to hold his warm, dry hand and follow, not worrying about the uneven ground or focusing on their direction. They walked all the way to where a herd of buffalo was roaming, and they stood to watch. The buffalo were calm and avoided them. Thali and Jaon climbed onto a wide, flat rock and sat, back to back, holding each other up as they watched the buffalo grazing and the sun rising to its midday point.

Thali laughed. "Guess it was just a matter of time."

"What do you mean?" Jaon asked.

Thali didn't reply. She felt the shift in their relationship; they were growing up. No longer could they be carefree children; they now had to face being adults.

Jaon reached again for her hand again. "Tell me, Little One."

"We used to scamper around the community without anyone taking note. It was like we could live in our own made-up world, and no one even blinked an eye. But now ... now you're not a boy anymore, Jaon. I'm only fifteen, but I know what happens when boys become men."

Jaon blushed, and though Thali was surprised, she continued. "You'll find a wife, one of the dozen girls that couldn't stop staring at you as we walked through the village. You'll have children. You'll join the hunt and eventually lead the hunt."

"Why do you think I'll lead the hunt?" Jaon asked quietly. Leading the hunt was the highest honor aside from being the chief.

"I taught you how to use a dagger, how to throw one. And I've seen you use a bow. Trust me, you'll lead the hunt," Thali said. She sighed. "This will probably be the last time we'll get to be carefree kids, the last time we won't be expected in the meetings with the adults."

Jaon was quiet for a few minutes, but it was a comfortable silence. Then he reached back and turned her around so they were facing each other. He placed something in her hand. He covered her hand with his and didn't let go.

Thali could feel it without looking. It was a ring—a cool stone ring. The memory of the ring on Tihon's hand flashed in her mind. "Jaon." Thali's heart started to race in panic.

"It's all right. I'm not asking for your hand, for you to join with me," Jaon said.

Thali's heart slowed, but not enough.

"Will you listen to my whole explanation?" Jaon asked.

Thali nodded. He seemed nervous and she didn't understand why.

Jaon took a deep breath, then began. "My brother and I are expected to take wives soon, to start the next generation. To help us choose a wife, our father asked us who we loved to speak to most, who we thought was wise and could seek council from. I could think of no wiser woman than you."

Thali opened her mouth, but Jaon squeezed the hand with the ring in it with both of his and continued. "I rearranged your timings with the duke so your family could come here first in hopes of proposing a joining with you because I was so excited to be united. But yesterday, as you spoke of your excitement to get a trade route, your own ship, I realized I hadn't considered what you might want in life."

Jaon took the ring from her hand and slipped it onto her middle finger. "It is a shame that I must stay with my community, and you wish to sail the world, for I think we could have made each other happy in this life.

But I could not live with myself if I took you away from something that brings you such great joy."

Thali brought her hand up and looked at the black-and-red ring around her finger. The black exterior was buffalo horn and had a delicate carving of their tree. Within, the red rock the Moas were famous for hugged the black buffalo horn. The ring fit her middle finger perfectly.

The blood roared in Thali's ears as she tried to sort and calm her emotions, trying to process what Jaon had said. She could have been getting married.

The buffalo around them all threw their heads up into the air, their gentle meandering suddenly taking on a more frantic pace as they started to pick up speed as a group. They started to circle her large boulder. Then their walking became running.

The boulder Thali and Jaon sat on started to shake with the thunder of hooves mere inches away from them. Jaon crouched in the middle of the boulder, wrapping his arms around Thali as she crouched too. The panic in Thali's heart started to intensify, and Jaon pushed them to lay on their sides so they were more stable. Then he folded her body into his. She could feel his warmth, and it eased some of her panic as the buffalo ran circles around them, pressing closer and closer to the boulder.

"Focus on my breathing, little one," Jaon said. "You are safe."

Thali thought of the chest pressed against her back. She started to match his breathing as his chest expanded and then slowly deflated. She closed her eyes, focusing only on breathing with Jaon. The buffalos' pace started to slow.

Thali only focused on inhaling and exhaling with Jaon.

Finally, Jaon said softly, "We can get up now. It's safe."

Thali's eyes fluttered open. She must have fallen asleep given how calm she was feeling and how low the sun was in the sky now. The buffalo had returned to their meandering grazing, and Jaon pulled Thali up to stand on the boulder. He didn't ask about why the buffalo had changed their behavior so suddenly. He didn't ask if she had anything to do with it, though Thali knew it must have been her. Her emotional state had affected the buffalo, and it had almost gotten them both killed. Jaon could have been angry with her—her parents would have been. Her brother would have looked at her in wonder and asked how she felt. She was surprised that Jaon didn't ask her anything, didn't even address it.

He helped her climb off the boulder and took her hand, his thumb touching the ring on her finger as they walked back to the village. When they emerged from the forest, Jaon didn't let her hand go. Thali was glad. She didn't care about the adults' gazes on them. She was spent and unfocused, tired from connecting with the buffalo by accident. Adrenaline from almost being trampled to death had drained her. She just wanted to let Jaon lead her.

Everyone was gathered around the bonfire. White flower petals—very expensive in these parts of the world—were sprinkled in a circle in the front of it. Jaon guided Thali to her family, and Rommy put a hand on her shoulder as they stood, waiting for the ceremony to begin. Jaon disappeared into the crowd as they all waited, staring at the bonfire and the circle of petals.

Those in the back of the crowd began to stomp their feet, and as the sound moved closer to the bonfire and the circle of flower petals, a chain of women with gauzy, creamy fabric wrapped around them started to weave between the people gathered, and Thali was remind-ed of waves breaking on the ocean. The women held hands, and as the end of the procession neared, Thali saw a bright orange swathe of fabric. As the swathe got closer, Thali recognized Jaon and Tihon under it. They stopped just outside the circle of petals. Tihon hugged his brother tightly before Jaon stepped back, joining the line of women as Tihon stepped into the circle of petals.

The line of cream-colored dancers started weaving again, and this time, they brought forth two figures in yellow. The yellow was so deep, it almost looked gold in the light of the fire. As the two figures were guided to the circle of petals, Thali saw that they were Jaon's father and mother. They approached, and the father's gaze flicked to Thali for a moment, then to Jaon, then back to Tihon. But then he smiled and hugged his oldest son. The dancers made a third round, and this time, brought a dancer in light blue. Thali assumed this must be Tihon's bride. The dancers swayed around the chief's family, and the woman in blue stopped just outside the circle. Thali had a hard time seeing her but thought the bride must be a few years older than her.

Thali clasped her hands, her fingers covering the new ring. She swallowed as she wondered if this was supposed to have been both Tihon and Jaon's joining ceremony. Had Jaon asked and she accepted, would they have had the ceremony today? Thali swallowed. She looked at the hands of the woman in blue. On her finger was a black ring. She wondered if Tihon had carved something significant on it. Jaon had carved their special tree on hers, the tree they climbed all the time, every time she was here. Did Tihon and this woman have something similar they shared?

"You are the light of my life."

Thali briefly tuned into the words being spoken.

"I will lead the hunt for you, bring you home the biggest buffalo, make the strongest home for you," Tihon was saying.

Thali felt her brother draw something on her shoulder blade. He could always sense when she was upset, and he was checking in to make sure she was all right. Thali blinked so she could focus on the ceremony. She could only pick up a few words here and there, but Tihon and his bride smiled at each other. Then the chief put their hands together and slowly raised them, as if to show everyone that they were joined. Thali swallowed, realizing she and Jaon really shouldn't be holding hands anymore. It saddened her to think of how much comfort they gave each other, even though it was platonic, and how society wouldn't allow it.

"You all right, Rou?" Rommy leaned in close behind her.

Thali nodded and swallowed again. She supposed as she grew up, changes would happen. It was an inevitable part of life.

The ceremony finished and everyone cheered and joined the dancers in their creamy clothes and floating scarves. Thali wanted to go find Jaon but resisted when she saw him join his father and mother.

Rommy pulled on her shoulder and steered her away from the group. "What's the matter?"

"Nothing," Thali said.

"Don't lie to me. I know something's wrong. You'll feel better once you tell me."

Thali could feel her mother's eyes on them and knew that if she didn't say something quickly, her mother would get involved, and her father, and that felt silly. "I can't hold Jaon's hand anymore."

"What do you mean?" Rommy asked.

"People look at us now, and soon he'll have to find a wife. It won't be appropriate for me to hold a married man's hand," Thali said.

"And why does that make you sad? Do you want to be his wife?" Rommy asked.

She looked up and into his eyes suddenly, but he had his mask of indifference on as he examined her face closely. "No. I don't want to be anyone's wife. I'm too young for that. Jaon and I, we're just friends. But when we hold each other's hand, it gives us both so much comfort." It sounded silly to her ears, and she felt her cheeks flush with heat as she spoke the words. But she did feel like a weight had lifted. Rommy was her confidant and best friend.

He took a deep breath and pulled Thali into a hug. "It's difficult sometimes for us to navigate so many different cultures. There are so many norms and nuances, and we're expected to know them all and abide by them. You're right, growing up, it presents its challenges. In a different world, I think you and Jaon would have been a good match.

Or maybe had you two grown up in the same community, you'd be hunting friends and nothing more. I'm sorry for the loss that growing up brings, for the loss of the innocence of finding comfort in touch. You'll always have me though, I promise."

Thali swallowed. He was right. And she knew with every fiber of her being that she really would always have Rommy. He would stand with her against the whole world if that's what it took.

"You'll always have your friendship with Jaon. And you'll always have this." Rommy raised her hand and touched the ring Jaon had given her.

ALL IS WELL

LOOKING AT HER ALMOST-ENGAGEMENT ring again, Thali slipped it onto her pinky. She missed her old friends. All of them. It had been so long since she'd seen them in person. A few had come to her wedding, but they hadn't all been able to make it, and it had been such a chaotic time, she'd barely had time to visit with anyone.

"I have a question," Daylor asked, bringing Thali back to her roomful of friends.

She chastised herself for not being grateful for them. She got to see them almost every day, and she loved them dearly.

Mia piped up. "When have you ever waited for permission to ask a question?"

Thali had been thinking the same thing.

"Prince Tariq is a close friend," Daylor began. His glance slid to Nasir, one of Tariq's guards once, but he bravely continued. "Surely he's given you something?"

Thali laughed so hard she doubled over. Mia stood and disappeared with her voluminous pile of fabric. Soon, they all heard a heavy trunk scraping along the floor. Mia appeared then, a huge trunk behind her. She didn't say anything as she popped the trunk open.

Even Elric's eyes bugged out of his head. "Shouldn't that be in the royal treasury?"

"Tariq's given you an entire trunk of gems?" Tilton said. It wasn't often that he spoke without a filter, but Thali knew he was flabbergasted because she and Mia had kept it hidden.

"This is just what she got for their wedding. There's three more, plus small boxes full in her armoire," Mia said.

"You have four trunks of gems sitting in the closet?" Elric asked.

Thali nodded. "We weren't sure what to do with them."

"We have a room for that, a secure, triple-locked, automatically shut-in-case-of-siege room," Elric said.

"I didn't know. We'll send them there then," Thali said, and Mia nodded.

"I think I regret asking my question," Daylor said. He was still staring at the mountain of gems in the trunk.

"I'd offer you all some, but Tariq has a weird way of knowing when something is missing, and he checks every time he's here. If I don't show him the jewelry I've turned his gifts into—or plan to—he sends more," Thali said.

"That's ..." Daylor started to say, but he was finally, for the first time, at a loss for words.

"That's the Prince of Bulstan for you," Nasir finished for him. He nodded his leave, as did Isaia, as they melted out of the room and back to their post at the door.

"I should get going too," Alexius said. He stood and gently placed a hand on the desk, where Bardo slid onto a thin cushion he often liked to sleep on. "Those were beautiful stories," Alexius said as he went to embrace Thali. She felt the cool gold band on his wrist through her thin shirt.

It was still awkward, but Thali knew Alexius was trying. He was learning there were customs that showed trust and a certain level of friendship between humans, and he tried his best to use them despite how new they were to him.

"Have a good night's rest, Alexius," Thali said, hugging him warmly back.

Daylor put Ana on the floor as he stood. He and Tilton moved the furniture back to where it had come from. When Mia started to drag the trunk back into the closet, Daylor spun around and said, "I'll help you with that, Mia."

"Thanks," Mia said.

"This gives me a lot more background for all those letters you're always sending," Tilton said. He finally handed her the papers he had originally come to give her. She glanced at them as he handed them to her and thanked him.

Daylor squashed Tilton, Thali, and Mia into a group hug. "Thanks for the entertainment," he said. Then he planted a kiss on the top of Thali's head before they all broke away. Daylor grabbed the now-empty snack trays and left with Tilton.

"Sleep well," Mia said. She gave Thali an extra-pointed look and then sent one to Indi and Ana. "You lot let her sleep. No kicking," she commanded before disappearing back into the closet. She had her own passageway from there to her rooms, but Thali knew Mia tended to lose herself in her projects before bed.

"And then it was just you and me," Elric said. Ana groaned and the couple smiled. "I mean, kind of."

Ana shoved her face under a pillow, and Indi stretched out on their bed, leaving a sliver of space for Elric. If he hadn't currently been in the bed, he would have had a hard time getting in.

Thali put her papers away for tomorrow morning and reached out for Elric's stack. She thought about how different her life was compared to what she had imagined for herself as a child. She wasn't sailing at sea, her brother on a ship next to hers, but she was happy.

Elric handed his stack to her and then she climbed into bed, still having to shift a few paws around. Ana slept on top of their blankets, so Elric was able to slide an arm underneath her, ignoring her sounds of protest as he slid his arm around Thali and pulled their bodies close together. Ana was apparently happy to stay laying in the valley made by their bodies.

Under the blankets, Thali grasped Elric's hand, and atop the blankets, she patted around for a tiger head. After a few scratches, Indi tucked her head under Thali's knee, and Thali patted the curly dog partly on top of her. Knowing she'd get a cold nose to the armpit if she stopped, Thali fell asleep petting Ana, feeling fulfilled, happy, and safe.

If you enjoyed this story, considering joining my newsletter to keep up with all my latest releases!

Note from the Author

This book started as a bunch of short stories about Thali before her time in Lanchor and before she arrived at the school that would change her life. I wasn't sure how to sew them together, until a dear friend told me they kind of missed Thali's current friends. I imagine this to happen sometime when Thali's at the palace with Elric, but it will fit nicely in between books five and six as the friends we meet in this book will be returning in the final book.

Thank you for coming along this journey with me and if you want to find out more, come check out my website https://camillatracy.com

or scan this QR code:

Camilla Tracy
camillatracy.com

Continue exploring the world in...Merchants and Warriors

Experience the story of Thali's parents. When a young merchant makes it to the shores of Cerisa and falls in love with a young woman promised to a prince...

Available Winter 2025

Click here to buy now or scan this QR code:

Acknowledgements

S EVEN BOOKS WITHIN TWO years! I'm so grateful for the ability to publish.

The first thank you is always for you, dear reader. I appreciate you spending the time with my words and stories and I hope hold them with fondness.

A very special thank you to my dear friend Dana, who allowed me to use her name for one of the characters in the book.

Thank you to my communities that have rallied around me. For buying my book, for telling your friends and family about it, for taking the time to read it. I hope you get to see a piece of me in my work and that you are entertained!

Thank you to my writing group. My fellow grapes, you are so supportive and encouraging, it's a joy whenever we can meet up, chat, and work together.

Thank you to Char and Paul, my first readers. Your thoughts, observations, and feedback are essential in making this story be the best it can be.

Thank you to my editor – Bobbi Beatty of Silver Scroll Services. I'm so grateful to you for your careful attention to detail and for helping to make this story the best version it can be. A special thank you for naming all the present day chapters in this one.

Thank you to Lorna Stuber, author friend and marvellous proofreader! It's special to be on this journey with you and to have your skills comb through my manuscript!

I'm grateful to the very talented artists at MiblArt. Your group puts the most beautiful covers together for me and I appreciate working with you!

These books are possible because of the amazing support I have from my family. Thank you to my husband for his support and partnership. Special thanks to my mom for telling everyone she knows and selling my book to all her friends and acquaintances.

To my steadfast furry friends, Truffle & Udon, thanks for reminding me to get up every few hours and keeping my toes warm and keeping me company as I tip-tap away. To Kali, thank you for making sure I get outside for some fresh air and dirt under my nails.

About the Author

C AMILLA IS A LOVER of many mediums of storytelling. She loves to write strong heroines with animal sidekicks, who can triumph and find the love of their life. She always has projects on the go and loves to consume stories of all kinds—books, shows, movies, plays, amongst many others.

When she is not writing, Camilla is often found exploring animal behavior, crafting, drinking a hot beverage, and clicker training her animals.

Come visit her at CamillaTracy.com or on instagram @camilla_tracy. Sign up for her newsletter by visiting: https://geni.us/CamillaTracynewsletteror by scanning the QR code below:

Manufactured by Amazon.ca
Bolton, ON

45030562R00152